NOW WE CAN ALL GO HOME

Three novellas in homage to Chekhov

Also by Catherine Browder

Secret Lives: Stories
The Heart, a Feuillet
The Clay That Breathes: A Novella and Stories

Now We Can All Go Home

Three novellas in homage to Chekhov

Catherine Browder

BkMk Press
University of Missouri-Kansas City

Financial assistance for this project has been provided by the Catalyst Find of the Arts KC Regional Council and by the Missouri Arts Council, a state agency.

○═╍═○

Executive Editor: Robert Stewart
Managing Editor: Ben Furnish
Book Cover Design and Art: Zach Folken
Front Cover Photo: Rick Stare
Book Design: Susan L. Schurman
Author Photo: David Remley
Printing: BookMobile

○═╍═○

BkMk Press wishes to thank Elizabeth Beasley, Angela Elam, Megan Folken, Zach Folken, and Blaire Ginsburg, Courtney Lauderback, Timothy Leyrson, Marie Mayhugh Special thanks to Elizabeth Uppman.

Library of Congress Cataloging-in-Publication Data

Browder, Catherine.
[Novellas. Selections]
Now we can all go home : 3 novellas in homage to Chekhov /
by Catherine Browder.
pages cm
Summary: "An homage to Anton Chekhov, the novellas of Now We Can All Go Home envision a future for the principal characters in three of Chekhov's plays, The Seagull, Uncle Vanya, and Three Sisters, all set in Russia at the turn of the 19th and 20th centuries"-- Provided by publisher.
 ISBN 978-1-886157-93-4 (pbk. : alk. paper)
I. Chekhov, Anton Pavlovich, 1860-1904. II. Title.
PS3552.R6827A6 2014
813'.54--dc23
                    2014025376
This book is set in Cheltenham Colors of Autumn, and Christiana.

Now We Can All Go Home

Three Novellas in Homage to Chekhov

For Randall

PART ONE

A Visitor from Kharkov

(*Uncle Vanya*)

1. Yelena

Kharkov, Ukraine. Fall 1899.

She waited until after they were settled in the Kharkov apartment, her husband's books unpacked and attractively arranged, the domestics hired. The weather had been fair the day she finally made her request. She waited until after Alexander finished his second glass of wine and the maid served the fruit tart. When she finally spoke, Alexander lifted his face from the book he'd been reading throughout the meal. His expression didn't surprise her, for she had seen it many times: the pained frown of a husband burdened by an unreasonable request, a man placed in the unfair position of saying *no*. She did not like this face.

"Yelena, darling. Two insurmountable problems stand in the way: money and space. How could we possibly afford a piano? Even if we could, where would we put it?"

The second issue was the most hurtful since it implied something she'd learned only after they'd married: music distracted him, especially when he felt ill, which was increasingly often. The irony of this reached out like a thief grabbing a necklace from her throat. A graduate of the Conservatory of Music in St. Petersburg had married a man who disliked music.

She folded her napkin and put it on the table. "Perhaps we can engage a teacher who has his own studio."

"I doubt we could afford it from the miserly income Voinitsky sends us."

He returned to his book, and Yelena leaned back in her chair. Her stomach tightened whenever he mentioned the farm. She could only think of her husband's daughter, Sonya, and the despised Voinitsky—Sonya's beloved Uncle Vanya— laboring over the crops and the orchard, stooped over the accounts in Vanya's study, arranging the mowing and planting and the oil press. The farm was not Alexander's only income, and he had not a single notion of what took place there, as if keeping his scholarly hands clean allowed him to dismiss the labors of those who managed a farm. *Dear Sonya*, she thought. *How hard you work.*

"Alexander," she said after a long silence. "I would like to say one more thing."

He closed his book and gave her his weary attention.

"All day you work, often with my assistance. I am a trained musician who isn't allowed to practice."

His eyes widened. "You haven't said anything before."

"I'm saying it now. It was a pleasure to play Sonya's piano."

"Oh? I don't remember hearing you." His nostrils flared slightly, his lips sliding into a frown. "I've become an old man, Lena. And after four months with Voinitsky and his tiresome mother—God save us! Need I remind you he tried to shoot me?"

"And failed. Deliberately."

"I didn't enjoy being a target."

"Of course not. But he was distraught, if I remember."

"I prefer not to remember."

"Then let's not discuss the farm anymore." She rose from the table, informing the maid she would take her tea in the living room.

For reasons that even now sounded absurd, her husband had made the cavalier suggestion to the entire Voinitsky household, including Sonya—people whose life and livelihood depended on the estate—that they should sell it, invest the sales and live on the interest. Alexander had not given a single thought to what the Voinitskys might want or need, or even where they would live. All he could focus on was his own retirement. Vanya became hysterical and in a fit of theatrical madness brandished a gun. Had Alexander mentioned his idea to her first, she might have been able to dissuade him before he made a fool of himself. But he had not, nor was the farm even his to sell, but his daughter Sonya's property. Even now Alexander's lame defense embarrassed her: *I am not a practical man.* She overheard her husband tell Masha that he would take his tea with his wife. He entered with painstaking steps and slowly eased himself into his armchair. The stress of setting up a new home had aggravated his gout and triggered insomnia. They'd come to Kharkov for several reasons, including its modest cost of living. Yet Alexander couldn't resist ridiculing its limitations, its location in the Ukraine, "that Cossack outpost." There was, in fact, a more hopeful reason: an old university colleague had urged him to come.

"I suppose, my dear," he began, "if you could find a tutor with his own piano...."

She had already thought of this and written the Music School, located nearby on Kharkov's main street. She would use her own money, if need be, but chose not to say so for fear of souring Alexander's small concession.

Masha brought in the tea tray and set it on the table between them.

"Do you realize," he said, leaning forward in his chair, "breweries were among the first enterprises in this city?" He snorted and fell back dramatically into the chair. She sipped her tea, afraid of the unhappy route such a conversation might take. "I didn't expect so much pollution either. And Masha tells me, by the way, there are only six hospitals."

"Didn't Astrov give you a reference?"

"Who would he know that I would care to consult?"

"You're against him because he's a friend of Vanya's. Astrov is as intelligent and capable a doctor as any you'll find."

"And a drunk."

She stared at him, helpless, as if he'd stolen her breath and her wits in one stroke. How unfair he was!

"When we are better settled," she said, composing herself as she spoke, "you will feel more kindly toward Kharkov." She would ask Masha to find the doctor Astrov had recommended, and not tell Alexander.

Her husband was in his study when Yelena left the building. Cook had recommended a milliner, and she was eager to get away from the apartment. As she put on her hat and gloves, Masha announced with pride, "We're not as cold here as in Moscow. We're more TEM-per-ate." She gave the word a self-conscious nudge as if she'd recently learned the meaning and was showing it off, like a new bonnet. Yelena smiled. It was true; she only needed a light wrap. The October air felt mild, as if the climate here were a month behind Moscow, a month warmer.

When they first arrived and engaged the sturdy young maid and middle-aged cook, the girl escorted her everywhere, even came with her on the horse-drawn trolley down Sumskaya Street, on what amounted to a guided tour of shops and architectural highlights: the Drama Theater and Opera House, past the Music School, on to Kharkov University and the University Garden, even a side trip to the Cathedral of the Annunciation. So many glorious Byzantine and Ukrainian churches, but Alexander chose not to come, saying he'd seen it all in his youth. He didn't approve of the trolley, either. "Too public," he said. "Hire a carriage next time." Yelena, on other hand, had enjoyed herself for the first time since their arrival.

It would have done him good to get out. He needed exercise, fresh air. Instead Alexander had become a stay-at-home and quarrelsome as a result. They'd had four good years before he was struck by gout and headaches and then insomnia. She felt doubly distressed when she realized he intended her to be his nurse. She had been so young when they met, and now she felt faded and discouraged and bored with her life. She forced herself to pause in the course of each day and reconstruct in her mind the time they had met, his delicate wooing and her delighted response, reminding herself of the feelings they'd once shared. He had not been so possessive when they were first married. Retirement, then ill health, had changed him. As his circle of admirers shrank, the querulous behavior set in. And during her increasingly frequent pauses-in-the-day, she remembered how safe Alexander had once made her feel. Here was a man of stature, his reputation secure. A refuge.

Young men had pestered her throughout her training at the Conservatory and then again in Moscow, where she moved afterward to live with her aunt. Eventually she understood why she was so bothered by men, astounded that something over which she'd had no control, her physical appearance, could have such an effect. Aunt Katya took it upon herself to introduce Yelena into society, something her widowed father seemed unable to do, and Yelena met young men everywhere: at recitals and concerts and the opera, at parties and balls given by her aunt's friends. Yet every young prospect behaved as though he'd lost his wits the moment he came to call. When this first happened, she looked at herself in a mirror afterward and wondered, what exactly is wrong? Her hair was a burnished blonde and plentiful, her eyes large and well shaped, as were all the bones of her face. She had enviable skin, a naturally pink mouth that was neither too large nor too small, and a figure her conservatory women friends told her was "perfect."

Even as a child, Yelena had trusted her mother's younger sister, visiting her often. She was intelligent in ways her mother was not, for this younger aunt had married well and been widowed—a situation her aunt had indicated was not at all unpleasant. "A woman can manage quite well on her own," she'd said, "as long as she has money." Yelena's mother seemed drawn to some ethereal world, distracted by good works and sorrow. Aunt Katya focused on the world at hand, and Yelena knew it had been her good fortune to live with her.

As young men came to call, her aunt chaperoned, hoping

to train Yelena to sort through the various fledgling scholars and army officers, young lawyers and bureaucrats, but the older woman soon grew as weary of Yelena's callers as Yelena did. The exercise of "sorting through prospects" took on such a hopeless aspect that the women often took the carriage and went for rides or attended matinees rather than endure another call from another giddy young man. Were it not for her aunt, she might have thought her God-given appearance a curse.

One evening before bed, as Yelena was undressing her hair, her aunt came in with a cup of warm milk and honey, to help her sleep. The older woman offered to brush her hair, took the implement from Yelena's hand and, standing behind her, gently pulled the brush through Yelena's abundant hair. It was such a golden blonde that people had an unfortunate habit of stepping too close to see if it was real.

"My dear...." Yelena closed her eyes and submerged herself in her aunt's consoling alto, for her aunt had taken pains to remove her parochial accent. What Yelena heard was richer and more precise than her mother's voice, and far more confident. She felt instantly reassured whenever she heard Aunt Katya's voice in the house. As the older woman pulled the brush through her hair, Yelena felt lulled and sleepy as a child.

"Yelena, dear," her aunt said, "there are many kinds of beauty. Beautiful deeds and words. A beautiful soul. And of course physical beauty, which you are blessed with. Your mother—may she rest in peace—was a woman of great interior beauty. All beauty is a gift, Yelena darling, but a beautiful face and body are the most vexing of all. It doesn't so much refresh the viewer as blind him... I feel obliged to counsel you to find a mature man who can appreciate all your assets."

Before the end of the year, Alexander Vladimirovich Serebryakov, distinguished professor of art history and a widower, entered her life. He never insulted her with gushing or speechless infatuation but steadily set his mark and lured her like bream from a river. She was drawn to him because he was patient and famous and safe. A fascinating life swirled around him, with students and colleagues, dinner parties and lectures and salons, and these attracted her as well. Because of Alexander, her narrow life opened up. Then one day she took her aunt aside and said, "I believe I'm in love."

If Aunt Katya had not died two years ago, she and Alexander might have found a welcoming home with her in Moscow. What a balm that would have been!

Alexander was having his tea when she returned from the milliner's. She gave Masha her coat and hat, keeping the small packet of sweets with her. She passed through the living room, picking up the silver candy dish, and brought it with her into his study.

"And did you find your gloves?" he asked.

She ignored the peevish tone. "I passed a confectioner." Alexander was in his armchair, a lap rug over his knees. "For you."

She gently emptied two small paper cones filled with peppermint drops and licorice logs, then placed the dish on the small table beside him. She studied his face.

"Ah, thank you... I suppose I should be watching my sugar."

"A small sweet won't hurt you."

"I remember when I first discovered licorice," he said. "A boy alone, studying in his room. Mother took pity on me and smuggled in the licorice with my tea. My father, you see, was bent on not spoiling the children."

He picked up the small log of candy and put it in his mouth, savoring it. When he smiled, she thought she might cry.

"Tell me. How did you find our provincial city?"

"Not so provincial, Alexander. It's now a railway hub."

"Not a Cossack in sight?"

"Everyone speaks Russian. You should know that."

"Ah, from border town to railway hub."

"Why are you so scornful? You suggested Kharkov."

"I assume it will be temporary."

Her heart raced at the thought of another move. They were scarcely settled, and any talk of relocation revealed how unsettled her husband remained in his mind. They might have thought better of the move had they not felt a need to flee the farm. Vanya had upset them both—that restless, garrulous, unhappy man, with his expensive ties and intemperate tongue, pursuing them, annoying them. Yelena pinched her eyes shut. Why couldn't Vanya have remained a friend? As their stay lengthened, Vanya changed somehow and not for the better. Then that horrid incident with the gun. Yelena pulled her mind away and sat straighter, inquiring when Alexander would be calling at the University.

"I've already sent Andreyevsky a letter. When I hear back, I'll arrange a visit."

Masha appeared with the tea and Alexander sighed, sucking on the licorice.

"Tell me, my dear. Are my teeth black?" He grinned at her like a dog baring its fangs, and Yelena broke into a laugh. He joked so seldom it took her by surprise.

The secretary of the Music School was expecting her. Yelena took the offered seat, deciding she would not be staying long enough to remove her gloves. She gazed at the plump, middle-aged man, giving him her full attention. Aunt Katya had taught her that some secretaries wielded considerable power.

"I read your note with interest, Mme. Serebryakovna. Your husband is the distinguished art historian, is he not?"

Yelena leaned forward, startled slightly that this short, unprepossessing man with the furry beard and pince-nez would know of Alexander. Alexander's reputation always surprised her and then left her feeling ashamed that she had been surprised.

"Yes," she said. In her shyness her voice had dropped out of listening range, and she cleared her throat. "Yes," she repeated and smiled. He flashed a quick, broad smile. "And you are a graduate of St. Petersburg?"

"The Conservatory, yes."

He continued to probe, and she explained her situation—they were newly settled and without a piano. She had written with her request: a teacher and access to an instrument.

"I am wondering if you need any instruction?" the secretary said and smiled again, and Yelena was struck by the size of his teeth.

She felt herself growing restless. Every question he put to her had an answer in her note, which he'd clearly read.

"Can you recommend a person?" she said finally. "I'm of course prepared to compensate any music instructor for his time and the use of his instrument."

His gaze was too attentive, and she felt as if her clothes were falling away under his scrutiny. He was talking too much, stalling the interview in what should have been a simple business transaction. Just when her annoyance had reached a point where she would need to excuse herself, he stood and apologized.

"Levchenko should be here any moment. I've already taken the liberty of speaking with him."

He excused himself and left the small reception room and stepped into the hall. She looked up at the framed photograph that hung on the wall behind his desk. She hadn't noticed it while the secretary stood examining her. She rose to take a closer look just as the secretary came back into the room.

"Can you make out Tchaikovsky?" he asked. She wished he would stop smiling. It didn't suit him. "The first row, the tall gentleman with the white hair. Those are our teachers. The picture was taken in January of 1893. We're very proud of Tchaikovsky's visit. Sad to say, he died that very year." The secretary clucked his tongue.

He returned to his position behind the desk again but stood to one side, pointing out the men in the photograph, introducing each teacher, one by one, until someone knocked on the door and the secretary barked, "Enter!"

Yelena turned. In the doorway stood a tall, willowy young man with remarkably pink cheeks, pale blond hair and muttonchops. With a bow, he took Yelena's hand and kissed it formally. "Valentin Viktorovich Levchenko. At your service." His face had the gentleness of a hare, and she gazed at him. He was certainly not one of the men in the photograph with Tchaikovsky. He was too young.

"Levchenko joined us only last year," said the secretary. "A most promising music theorist and pianist."

The younger man bowed toward the middle-aged secretary and mumbled his thanks, "Too kind, sir, really."

"Mme. Serebryakovna and her husband are newly settled in our city."

Levchenko offered an effusive welcome while the secretary glanced at her secretively, fiddled with the chain of his pocket watch and said, "Our Levchenko is famous for his charm."

"Forgive me," the young man said and cast his gaze to the floor.

"Come," said the secretary. The three of them left the office and walked through the chilly halls of the Music School while the secretary pointed out the features of the institution: the acoustically improved performance hall, the smaller recital rooms and rehearsal spaces, the number of pianos, the number of students. On the second floor, they came at last to a cubby of a studio with a small writing table, an upright piano and two stools, with scarcely room to turn around. Above the piano one round window let in a feeble ray of light. She wondered if this window opened in summer. The secretary excused himself after a flurry of goodbyes and left her with Levchenko, who seemed too tall for the space.

When she brought up the subject of remuneration, he turned his head, his eyelids fluttering. "Perhaps, Madame, we could discuss it next time, please."

He pointed toward the piano. Yelena laughed nervously and sat down on the stool, removed her gloves, and placed these across her lap. She ran her fingers up the keys in a simple C major scale, then another in C minor.

"Our instruments are tuned regularly," he said as if this information were expected. "Perhaps an étude? Something by Bach?"

She didn't know if she could pull anything from memory so suddenly. There was a time when she'd memorized a considerable amount of piano literature. She began a simple Clementi sonatina, hoping her fingers would remember. After the first section, she stopped.

"It's been so long since I've practiced."

"Not at all... you're doing splendidly."

She continued with the piece, and when she'd finished, she caught him staring at her hair. At least that seemed to be where his eyes were pinioned. He pulled his gaze away.

"Well done."

It was not well done but a lifeless test of memory. From the stack of music on the small table, he pulled out a Mozart sonata and placed it on the music stand. "Can you sight-read?" She could but again performed like the good schoolgirl she had once been. It was such a bland performance she was overcome with embarrassment and didn't wish to play anymore. She didn't realize she'd be asked to play and had not worked herself into the proper frame of mind. In a great rush she told him so, and he nodded. "Of course. I understand completely. Tell me about your studies."

Her relief was so large that she heard herself rattling on as if she were asked to recite her life's history. He listened, nodding from time to time, inserting a question now and again. She stopped abruptly and laughed.

"Would it surprise you to know that I'm not usually such a chatterbox? I would very much like you to have tea with my husband and me. Perhaps we can arrange our terms then..."

When Levchenko arrived on Thursday, all visible implements of Alexander's infirmities had vanished—cane, lap rug, even the wheelchair he used on especially bad days. Without grimacing, Alexander rose to greet the younger man, escorting him with an unnatural spring into the living room. His voice was hearty, his questions sharp, and within moments he had taken over the interview, as Yelena expected.

Did Levchenko know his wife was a graduate of the Conservatory in St. Petersburg?

She leaned over and touched his arm. "Our guest knows my background."

"Indeed, I do know," Levchenko said. "That's why I agreed."

Alexander nodded and moved on to the subject of his own credentials. Yelena was relieved that she was no longer the topic of discussion, but Alexander puffed himself up so strenuously, she fidgeted in her chair. Levchenko heard about Alexander's professorship, his articles and books and colleagues, the monologue relayed in a confident, jaunty tone, as if the older man were only on extended holiday in Kharkov, which the younger man kept pronouncing *Kharkiv*. She'd assumed he was a Ukrainian, but his Russian was as natural as hers. All of which flew past Alexander, who only seemed interested in relaying his steadily enlarging résumé. She would have to caution Alexander in private before he made some tasteless joke about Cossacks.

She rang the bell, and Masha appeared so quickly with the samovar that Yelena imagined the girl waiting on tiptoe behind the door. When the maid returned with the tea things, the conversation lulled, and Yelena asked when she might use the piano at the Music School.

"I propose three afternoons a week," he said.

Alexander gave his basso laugh, the one that made her flinch. "My dear, you can't be running off three afternoons a week. Here is a busy young music professor. I know what his responsibilities must be."

"Not at all!" Levchenko interjected. "You are so close to the Music School. The piano will simply stand idle. It's no imposition on me, Your Excellency."

Alexander seemed to grow taller. For an instant the Voinitskys' friend Telegin came into her mind—an odd little fellow, with smallpox-scarred face, who played the guitar and coddled Sonya and flattered Alexander: Your Excellency this and Your Excellency that. It was not lost on her that Telegin was one of the few people on the estate her husband never criticized.

"Mme. Serebryakovna could come any time after three."

When Alexander asked for the young man's credentials, his teachers and recital venues, and future projects such as they were, Yelena held her breath. Levchenko's curriculum vitae would need to strike a proper balance, something he could not possibly know. He would require sufficiently impressive training with, as yet, limited accomplishments—a dazzling future held at bay by a small and mundane present—so as not to put her husband at a disadvantage. Yelena leaned toward the tea table.

"I want you both to try this extraordinary lemon cake." She served each a piece on a plate. "It's become my favorite since we moved here. Tell me, Valentin Viktorovich. Is this lemon and-poppy-seed cake a Kharkov specialty?"

He leaned toward her, visibly pleased, his cake plate balanced on his knees.

"I must confess," Alexander interrupted. "I miss the bakeries in Moscow."

"We're such a small city," Levchenko said. "We certainly cannot compete, but I'm delighted, Madam, that you've found one local delicacy that pleases you."

"It's a bit dry, my dear. Don't you think?"

The cake held a perfect balance of moisture. What could Alexander be thinking? She gave a small laugh. "Well, all palates are individual, don't you think? I confess, I don't find it dry at all."

"*Chacun à son goût*," her husband replied with a small dismissive flourish of his hand.

"Concerning the practice room, Madame. I have taken the liberty of procuring you a key."

Levchenko rose and leaned toward her and handed her the key. For one sickening instant, she thought Alexander was going to lurch forward and snatch it out of the young man's hand. But he remained seated, seemingly disinterested, and sipped his tea. She'd become as unsettled by the move as Alexander. When his gout flared and insomnia set in, her imagined fears reared up in alarming readiness, exasperating her at every turn. Now here came this polite Ukrainian, whose very youth might become a chronic thorn.

"The piano room is not usually locked," he said. "But just in case. Our building warden is vigilant."

Alexander was restless after dinner, and irritable. Yelena suggested she read to him—some Pushkin perhaps? Or Lermontov? He chafed and announced that since he had his own eyes, he would use them.

"I was only suggesting something we might do together," she answered. "Or something I might do for you so that you might rest your eyes."

He gave her a baleful look. "I'm not in my grave yet, you know."

"Who said you were? I don't understand why you want to put me in such a false position."

He averted his gaze, and when he looked back his eyes reflected the light in an unnaturally glittery way. Tears, she realized.

"Why did you marry me, my dear?"

Yelena couldn't look at him. She rose and crossed the room to a bookcase and removed a narrow red volume.

"You're not feeling yourself. Otherwise you would never have asked such a question."

Serebryakov arched a hand over his eyes. "You're right. Forgive me. I've slept poorly since we moved."

"I know. That's why I suggested the poetry. May I suggest something else as well?"

He nodded, and the look in his eyes was pleading.

"Visit your colleague at the University immediately. You need company, Alexsya. You need your academic comrades."

Yelena instructed the maid to be especially attentive to her husband on the first afternoon she went to the Music School. Sometimes he napped in the afternoons. Otherwise he worked, poring through his books as he prepared a new article. She'd told him before she left to ask Masha for whatever help he needed. Masha was a clever girl, and she could read, a comment that caused Alexander to raise an eyebrow.

When she reached the Music School, Levchenko was waiting for her in the foyer.

"I was concerned you might not remember how to reach the room."

She followed him up the flight of marble stairs, and along the dim hallway to his small piano studio at the rear of the building.

"Here we are." He opened the door.

The room was as small as she remembered and as dim, even though all the lamps were lit. He'd placed several pieces of music on the stand. A coal grate threw out a weak puff of heat.

"You didn't mention whether you had your own music. So...."

"I have music somewhere. Stored in a box."

"Please use mine, or not. As you like."

He appeared to be wearing the same brown suit with a cravat so old and dark that it seemed colorless. When he reached up to remove a sheet of music, she saw the frayed jacket cuffs and the slightly gray edge of a shirt peeking out. Even in the dim light there was something hollow about his physique, and she wondered if he ate enough.

She was familiar with the Mozart but not the Bach, sight-reading it awkwardly. As she played it again, he suggested some fingering changes. Occasionally he hummed along or lifted an arm and gently conducted, his body swaying, his arm articulating the musical line—the sweep or staccato or closure. She was distracted at first, seeing the arm move out of the corner of her eye. Finally, she asked if he might listen to the Chopin nocturne she'd committed to memory, the one secure piece in her fading repertoire. Perhaps he might advise her on her interpretation. She thought she might be rushing the tempo.

"So you like Chopin," he said with a smile.

"Very much. But my professors did not."

He threw back his head and laughed. "I don't share their bias. Please play your Chopin."

She composed herself, closed her eyes briefly, rubbed her hands to warm her fingers, positioned herself over the keyboard, and began. It was a clumsy performance, the musicality uneven. She'd last played it for Sonya at the farm. How quickly one lost the most basic skills! She supposed if she stopped walking for a month she would stumble as well.

"There is nothing wrong with your playing that regular practice won't cure." He said it kindly, in a reassuring voice. She hoped it was true. She wanted to believe he couldn't say something he didn't mean.

"I would love my own piano. Then I could play every day. But...."

"Perhaps it interferes with the professor's work."

She glanced up. How quick, and this from one short afternoon visit? "His health is delicate," Yelena said. "A piano doesn't console a man with insomnia and headaches."

Levchenko nodded and extended his arms to embrace the room. "Madame, feel free to come as often as you like. Every day if need be."

That would not be possible, but she thanked him, grateful for his offer. Perhaps as time went by she might use the piano more often. If she could establish some routine, in which Alexander was occupied, her absence might go by unremarked.

"If I may ask," she said, "how old are you?"

Levchenko laughed self-consciously. "Twenty-five. I know I look younger. Everyone tells me I have a boy's face."

Yelena's heart raced as she calculated the difference in their ages. In January she would celebrate her twenty-eighth birthday.

"And you are a native of Kharkov?"

"Kiev, actually. At least that's where most of my family lives. One uncle lives here, but I'm on my own."

"Tell me, are you the only musician in your family? I was the only musician in mine."

"My mother is musical, and my younger sister is far more talented than I am. She's a student in Kiev."

"Perhaps you'll return there one day."

"I'm content here, actually. It would be hard to leave a place that invited you to stay and become a member of their faculty."

His contentment was touching. How few contented people there were in her life. Only Alexander's daughter Sonya, and Sonya had chosen contentment in the face of grim odds. Or, perhaps, it was simply Sonya's enviable capacity for acceptance and her generous spirit.

"Come," he said. "Let me hear your nocturne again. Allow the music to breathe. Allow yourself to breathe. No need to rush."

She turned to the keyboard, stretched her back and then

her fingers and took a slow breath, listening to the narrative line of the music as she played. Her fingering felt more secure this time. Her interpretation was less dramatic but more satisfying. As she played, she intuited why her teachers had scorned Chopin. Students didn't perform Chopin with restraint' but forced the music into emotional peaks and valleys that were not intended. Chopin gave them the chance to thunder and weep. She let her fingers rest over the keys as the last notes resonated.

"Brava," Levchenko said quietly. "See how much easier it was with the new fingering? Yes, Chopin suits you. I have some music I'll leave on the piano."

She turned on the stool to face him. "Won't you be here?"

"Only when you want me here. I thought perhaps a lesson a week. Otherwise you should practice uninterrupted. I also tutor private students… at their homes."

Of course, she thought. How else would he supplement his income since she couldn't imagine a junior faculty member was well paid. She hadn't intended to blurt out her question. It was grasping on her part, with no company except Alexander and their employees. She blushed and turned away. He pretended not to have noticed and shuffled through the stack of music.

"Tell me, Valentin Viktorovich. Would you enjoy taking dinner with us at least one night a week? I'm thinking you might accept this as part of—forgive me. Your fee. Besides, we would enjoy your company."

He turned and bowed and her heart sank, afraid she'd insulted him. When he lifted his head, he was smiling.

"I would be honored."

When she shared her plans with Alexander, she was startled by his dismay.

"Please don't upset yourself," she said. "It's as easy for Cook to prepare a meal for three as for two."

"If he comes for supper, then you are involving me as well," he said pettishly.

"The company will do us good. Don't you recall how interested he was?"

"Many people are interested, my dear—."

"But few are worthy. Is that it, Alexsya? As yet we don't know a soul in Kharkov—"

"I know several."

"And you haven't called on a single one... Perhaps this young musician will be our tonic. Shall we give it a try? And if it doesn't work out, well... leave that to me."

He looked at her closely and, to her surprise, nodded.

When Levchenko made his first dinner appearance on Thursday, Alexander again hid all evidence of infirmity, reviving his role as convivial host. Alexander offered him a drink, but the young man demurred.

"I do not drink, Your Excellency."

"Indeed! You are the first young man I've met who abstains." Alexander glanced at his wife and raised his eyebrows.

"Neither should you drink, Alexander," she said with a smile.

"A little wine for my health, don't you think?"

Cook had prepared some sort of fowl—guinea hen, she assumed—but it was dry and flavorless. The beet soup was tolerable, but only the potatoes swimming in butter and gravy had any savor. The young man commented on every dish as if he'd had nothing to eat for days but oats.

"Once a month I treat myself to a meal out," he said. "I like mutton or fish."

"I'll remember," she said. "Alexander is fond of fish as well."

Had she ever met a man who did not drink? It was almost against nature, and she didn't know whether such self-denial made him appealing or suspect.

"Tell me, Valentin Viktorovich. Is there a special reason you abstain?"

Levchenko dropped his gaze and worried a small piece of potato around his plate.

"Ah, a boring story... I made the decision when I was still young and first decided to study music. I needed all my funds for lessons and sheet music. The Kharkov Music School had accepted me as a student, which meant leaving home. I would need money to return to Kiev from time to time, and that was another reason to be frugal. I knew my parents could only provide a small stipend for my expenses. I realized then I couldn't drink and pursue my art. Please don't think I disapprove of drinking because I don't. It seemed the best decision for me at the time, and so I never developed the habit."

He finally picked up the morsel and put it in his mouth, chewing thoughtfully.

"And didn't this decision put you at odds with your friends?" she asked.

"True friends don't care. They accept, and I have many friends. You can toast your friends with tea if need be and they'll still be your friends." He gave a small laugh.

Alexander stared at the young man and leaned back in his chair. "You're a man true to your convictions, aren't you? I believe I like you, Valentin Viktorovich."

She didn't realize she'd been holding her breath and suddenly felt dizzy and sighed.

"Few people earn my husband's respect so quickly." She placed her hand over Alexander's and left it there.

Even after Levchenko had left, the pleasant mood lingered like the perfume from a bouquet of roses. Alexander remained with her in the living room to talk over the evening, and for the first time in months she felt affection. When it was time for bed, Yelena rose and went to him and embraced him. With sudden ardor he held her and kissed her. Then they linked arms and walked slowly but confidently to the bedroom.

"Did you notice, my dear, that he was not only punctual but stayed exactly the right amount of time, neither too short nor too long. Quite amazing."

Slowly he sat in his chair, and Yelena perched on the stool and removed his shoes.

"I've always suspected that musicians had an uncanny sense of space," he went on as Yelena carefully removed the socks from his swollen feet. "Perhaps it's the innate sense of rhythm. It's not the same as yours or mine. They're in touch with the cadence of the spheres, and their sense of time has a different shape. They live on an entirely different level than the rest of us. Have you ever noticed, Yelena darling? Musicians are the least miserable of artists. They flourish on that elevated plane while the rest of us thrash around in the mud. Ah, my dear. I do believe I have the subject for my next article... When did you say he was coming back?"

Throughout what remained of October and into November, she traveled to the Music School twice a week, and sometimes three. On Thursdays, after she sat down at the piano, he would appear, as if some instinct told him when she'd arrived, or so she liked to think. More likely the secretary observed her arrival and sent him word. He didn't perform for her except to sit down at the keys and demonstrate a passage of Bach or Chopin or Beethoven, which he did with verve and confidence. He was far more gifted than she could ever hope to be. When she finally asked whether he would be giving a recital, he demurred. "I'll perform one day."

At first she practiced with the faint hope he might appear. After several weeks, she looked forward to being by herself in the small studio and took it as a sign she was reclaiming her musicianship. When an unexpected snowfall tangled the streets, she doubted she'd make it to the Music School. Alexander discouraged her from leaving the apartment. Never mind that they had endured far worse weather in Moscow and St. Petersburg.

"At least the capital knows how to deal with weather. It's moments like these that remind me I'm living in the back of beyond!"

"Stop it, Alexsya. It's as if you're holding Kharkov's history against it."

She paced and looked out the windows and made Alexander so fretful that he hid in his study, avoiding her. At four, Masha inquired whether she might go to the Music School on Mme. Serebryakovna's behalf and leave Levchenko a message.

"Yes!" she exclaimed. Forgetting herself, she embraced the maid. "I'll write out a note. Leave it with the school secretary if you can't find Levchenko."

She went to her writing desk and hurriedly penned the note and handed it to Masha. "I've explained my absence and invited him to dinner as usual, if he can make it. I'll tell Cook."

Masha took the note and disappeared into the rear of the apartment, leaving after a few moments down the back stairs. Yelena felt suddenly buoyant as though all the heaviness that had ruined her day had been replaced with warm air. She went to the front windows and watched for Masha to appear in the street below. When she emerged, she was wearing a formidable pair of boots that made Yelena laugh out loud. If she had such a stout pair, she wouldn't be afraid of snow or mud either. She went to her husband's door and tapped. "May I come in?"

She didn't wait for an answer but flew into the room. "Masha took Levchenko a note. Hopefully he'll come for dinner as usual."

His spectacles rested on his nose, his eyes peering at her over the rims. Yelena burst out laughing, giddy with relief. "How funny you look, Alexsya. Peering at me like that!"

He removed the reading glasses, and she sailed across the room and kissed his forehead, and then left as quickly as she'd come, calling out over her shoulder, "What a relief to have company. Don't you think?"

"If he comes," Alexander said gravely.

He arrived one hour later than usual. Masha opened the door, and a flushed Levchenko stepped into the foyer. Fresh snowflakes, like goose down, were sprinkled over his hat and coat.

"It's started up again," he exclaimed as if the weather were a pleasure and not an inconvenience. He stamped his feet in the entry as the Serebryakovs rushed to greet him, fussing over him, reminding him not to stand on ceremony. Yelena was surprised at how quickly Alexander reached the door.

"Come in, come in! If only you drank, I'd warm you with brandy."

Levchenko rubbed his fingers and laughed, following the couple into the living room.

"I have run an hour late all day. Have you ever noticed that whenever there is snow, someone always needs you urgently? The thought of being snowbound makes some older women desperate. So one of my students sent her carriage and insisted I come to the house immediately. More a visit than a lesson, mind you."

Alexander sat their guest in the living room and asked Masha for tea using such an imperious voice that Yelena recoiled. "I'll help you," she said to the girl, hoping to negate the sting of her husband's request. She followed the girl to fetch the samovar while Masha arranged the tea tray. The men were still discussing the weather. She liked the young man's tenor voice, the warm laugh and amusing turn of phrase. If his voice were a lamp, it would draw all the heat-seeking creatures of the night. Even Alexander seemed drawn to Levchenko when he spoke, for the tone announced he could listen as well as talk. Her husband rattled on, and she assumed this was because he hadn't flexed his own voice all day. Since Masha had not even noticed Alexander's bark and the men had not moved on without her, Yelena felt something close to merriment. As the women reentered the room, Levchenko rose.

"I bring good news," he said once everyone was seated and the tea served. His eyes seemed to send out darts of light. "This very matron—my student with the carriage—has decided to acquire a grand piano. She has offered to give me her spinet."

"What a wonderful gift!" Yelena exclaimed.

"Yes, Madame. A generous gift indeed! But what do I need with another piano? And where would I put it? There!" He looked at them expectantly, but the Serebryakovs stared at him through a long and awkward pause until he grasped their confusion.

"Therefore," he continued, "I offer you—Your Excellency, Madame Serebryakovna—this rather nice spinet. You would no longer need to travel to the music school. And I could come here for your lesson as usual. *Quelle chance!*"

Yelena held her breath, gazing hopefully at Alexander while everything inside churned. She looked forward to the nourishing solitude of her practice sessions, the privacy of their Thursday lesson, never worrying whether Alexander was annoyed, never fearful of what he might say if he were feeling poorly. As long as she returned promptly, he had come to accept the arrangement, especially when she reassured him that she only saw Levchenko briefly on Thursdays, the very day he joined them for dinner. She grappled with the offer, struggling to put her conflicted heart out of reach of her reason. Alexander spoke first.

"This is too generous. We cannot accept."

"Please do accept. We can't have this lovely little instrument go to waste. Why, it's not much larger than this little table." He pointed to Yelena's writing desk. "Please consider. Talk it over between you. I'll say no more right now."

He beamed at them, and Yelena turned to look at her husband. Before anything more could be said, Masha called them to the table.

They didn't discuss the spinet during the meal, and afterward Alexander invited the young man to his study. "I must tell you my new plan," Alexander said and placed a proprietary hand on Levchenko's shoulder. "You have inspired me, Valentin Viktorovich. You've given me an idea for a new and intriguing article that concerns musicians and the making of music." Alexander rattled off his plan and his hopes for Levchenko's help. When Levchenko moved to include her, Yelena declined and returned to the living room with her tea and a book, certain that the more opportunities her husband had to explore his new article with Levchenko, alone, the more accommodating he might be to the spinet.

The instrument arrived the following week with three workmen to haul it up the stairs. On Levchenko's suggestion, they placed it against the far wall of the dining room, an odd location but logistically favorable, for it was the farthest wall from Alexander's study. Yelena could not sleep the night it arrived. She hadn't lived under the same roof with a piano since their four-month residence at the farm. She could only hope it was the constant chafing hubbub of the Voinitsky household that had turned Alexander against it. Still she felt awkward that first week and scarcely played it, uncertain about when she might practice, devising schedules and opportunities until she felt exhausted.

The next week she suggested he listen while she practiced, during which time she could explain what problems she was encountering with the music at hand—the Mozart sonata or Clementi sonatina or Schubert étude—whether fingering or tempo or expression. Might this not prepare him for his article by offering a rough idea what the average pianist faced? Perhaps listening to her might suggest questions to ask Levchenko. Intrigued, he agreed to sit through one practice session, and she immediately regretted her offer. She sensed him sitting there in his dining chair, a dark woeful presence that lacked the tools to enjoy what he heard. While she was changing the music on the stand, she heard his fingers drumming on the tabletop, and her shoulders drooped. Her frame of mind became that of an entertainer and not a serious musician. She could not continue in this fashion and returned to her brief practice sessions while he bathed, or when he went to the University, then a brief performance for his amusement after dinner. He was restrained, applauded her evening recital, but saved all his questions for Levchenko. When she realized this, she was surprised how hurt she felt.

Levchenko arrived the following Thursday evening, and Alexander rose to greet him. For a moment she was afraid that Alexander would keep him standing in the entry all evening, discussing his plans.

"Please join me," she said finally when her husband paused for a breath. "I'm feeling lonely, sitting here."

The young man came into the living room and greeted her warmly. "Madame, how are you enjoying the spinet?"

She assured him she was enjoying it immensely, but Alexander's obvious impatience spoiled the telling. The men had scarcely sat when Alexander launched again into the subject of his article, throwing out an issue he had encountered that needed Levchenko's professional insight. The younger man sat perched on the edge of his chair, giving Alexander his full and polite attention. Finally he said, "I would be happy to help in any reasonable way. I do hope Your Excellency realizes that your wife is as good a source as I am."

Alexander's eyes rounded, and he straightened his back, unwilling to look at her, and gazed at the young man. "Yes, but you are a music theorist, and Yelena is... well, a performer?"

"But Your Excellency, as you outline your plan to me—to us—it seems that knowledge of theory is not what will assist your project. The execution and interpretation of the music, the recreation of music through performance: isn't that your subject?"

"Not at all, Valentin Viktorovich. It's the mind of the musician. How he thinks."

Yelena drew back. The very thing that had recently bloomed inside her now wilted. He had abandoned his own original impulse in order to return to what he knew best—the dry stick of analysis, of academic research, of life borrowed from ideas. She would have thought Alexander would want to listen to as much music as possible, attend concerts or opera events, but he did not. He was about to undertake another cerebral exercise that was in fact as far removed from the spiritual and physical world of music as she could imagine. How Valentin Viktorovich would deal with this or be a party to it, she couldn't guess.

"Perhaps we should have our lesson, Madame. You may find it beneficial to listen, Your Excellency. For a piano lesson is about both execution and musicality, about technique as well as interpretation. Think of it as a combination of fingers, head and soul. Shall we go to the piano?"

Together they rose and made their way to the dining room.

She missed her trips to the Music School, her hours in the grotto of Levchenko's piano studio. Now she was confined at home, where worry over the piano had caused her to lose her appetite. She still practiced when Alexander was out of earshot or out of the apartment, now that he was finally making visits to the University. But on more than one occasion he'd asked her to stop playing; he had a headache. She'd feared all along that as the weeks went by he would feel more and more emboldened to curtail her playing. Only on Thursdays, when he could share the young man, was he indulgent.

At first, she waited to serve dinner until Alexander was finished and the two men emerged from the study. When the consultation stretched beyond an hour, she finally acted. The next week she instructed Masha to lay the table thirty-five minutes into their conference. At forty-five minutes she asked Masha to tap on the door, wait, and announce dinner.

On this particular Thursday, Yelena opened the door herself and announced, "Gentlemen, Masha informs me that Cook is serving the soup. And Alexander, dear. You are forgetting yourself. Valentin Viktorovich is a teacher with a busy schedule."

The men brought the discussion to the table, where at least she could hear.

"Valentin Viktorovich," she said, waiting until her husband had had a second glass of wine. "I'm sure Alexander and I would love to hear you perform. Do the piano faculty give recitals? Or could we talk you into giving a recital for us and a few friends?"

She didn't know whom they might invite. Alexander's colleagues, perhaps, or the secretary at the Music School or friends of Levchenko's choosing? Then it occurred to her the spinet was an inferior instrument to the one in his studio or any piano at the Music School. She asked anyway, taking advantage of Alexander's expansive mood.

"Don't you think," she said to Alexander, "we might host a small event? We could turn the dining room into a recital space. We could invite your private students and Alexander's colleagues."

"And chairs?" Alexander asked in a bemused and ironic voice.

Levchenko laughed kindly and raised his hands in a gesture of surrender.

"Thank you, dear friends. I can spare you the trouble. In the spring the piano faculty will have its annual recital. I sincerely hope you'll attend."

She felt oddly deflated. Her husband, on the other hand, was relieved to the point of telling jokes and toasting Levchenko who was forced to throw back one glass of tea after another. She gazed at Alexander until she felt overcome by an alarming rush of contempt and turned her gaze to the saltcellar on the table. The sight of him suddenly revolted her. He did not care about her, or even Valentin. His own convenience was all that mattered, and each year he grew more self-regarding. As Masha cleared the soup bowls, she let her gaze settle on the younger man, aware of an unexpectedly tender sensation that made her skin grow warm. She pulled her gaze away.

"No more wine for you, my dear," Alexander said with a chuckle. "Your face is flushed."

She couldn't sleep that evening and drifted through their rooms, reading in the living room, wandering into the dining room to stare at the spinet, and then returning to her dressing room to brush her hair while Alexander snored lightly in the adjoining bedroom. She opened her jewelry case and removed the small drawing pencil she'd taken from Astrov on the day they left the farm. She didn't know why she'd taken it, and now it seemed like a silly, girlish thing to do. She took it right before his eyes, telling the doctor she wanted it as a memento. She held the pencil and pressed the lead against her palm until it left a mark, then put it down. A burning sensation started up in her eyes. She couldn't remember when she'd last cried. With Sonya? Each day at the farm had required strength, and she'd remained stoic throughout the four long months. She gave in to it now, unsure if she was crying over the piano or her life.

She quickly took a handkerchief from her dresser and wiped her eyes and blew her nose, but the tears kept flowing quietly. She hadn't given in to Astrov, and now she wished she had. He didn't love her, nor she, him. But there was an undeniable attraction that pulled on her. She would have liked to have had one small encounter, something to remind her that she was still youthful and appealing, that her flesh needed to be touched and held in a way that was not so elderly and dry; for nowadays Alexander was hardly ever interested in her in that way. With Astrov, she'd had the chance to feel the juice of life, and she'd let it go. "Why?" she whispered, hunched over her dressing table. She'd made a vow and was not a person who broke her vows. That much she did know about herself. What she hadn't known was the urgency of her body.

It was Sonya who loved Astrov, even if Astrov loved no one she could see. He was fond of Sonya and perhaps that was enough. But she had contrived to send Astrov away—"for Sonya's sake"—as if the sight of him would be a painful reminder of what Sonya couldn't have. Now her request seemed needless and selfish, an excuse to have her own conversation with the doctor. Yelena shuddered and then looked at herself in the mirror above her dressing table. Crying had made her face blotchy.

Sooner or later Alexander's need for Valentin would end. Then he would begin writing from his copious notes, and the querulous mood would return, lasting until the writing was complete. During this process—by edict, she was sure—there would be no piano playing.

The days that followed took on a purgatorial aspect, affecting her with the urge to flee. Daily she was called upon to help Alexander as he wrote: refilling inkwells, replacing nibs, fetching books, sometimes rereading what he had written with the ostensible purpose of editing when, in fact, he craved praise. She felt as though the air was being siphoned out of the apartment. Eventually, he would finish the article, and they would enjoy the brief afterglow that followed.

Twice Levchenko sent a message that he was unable to come for her lesson or dinner. She wondered if something had passed between the men that had led Levchenko to realize his presence was no longer required. And since Levchenko was a perceptive man, it would take only one pointed word to discourage him. The thought that Alexander may have done just this roiled her emotions and upset her stomach until she noticed one evening that she was sitting in her dressing room with her hands clenched in rage.

On a gray and blustery day, remnants of a negligible snowfall left the streets wet, and she picked her way along Sumskaya Street to catch the tram. When she arrived at the music school, she was overwhelmed with relief. She walked briskly up the steps and into the central hall, glancing to her left. The door to the secretary's office was closed, and she quickly made her way to the main stairway and up, then along the long, dim hallway. Halfway down she heard his piano and caught her breath. She'd hoped he might be there, not wanting to leave a note, and tapped lightly on the door. The playing continued— a Schubert Impromptu. She listened for a moment before tapping again, louder. The music stopped, and she felt a spurt of discomfort. "Enter!"

Slowly she pulled the door open. He was still seated at the piano. "Valentin Viktorovich, I am sorry to bother you."

"Madame Serebryakovna? A nice surprise! Welcome."

She did not at all like the sound of *madame*, especially when she'd finally convinced him to call her by her name.

"Forgive me. I'm out of breath."

"Come in. Come in." He rose and sat her down at the piano.

"I'm devoted to Schubert," he said, showing her the music. "I plan to perform this piece at the faculty recital."

"I'd like to hear it." She rose and stepped away from the piano stool, sitting instead in the instructor's seat.

Levchenko laughed, and the mellowness of his tenor lightened her mood. His voice wasn't heavy like Alexander's baritone. She'd once been attracted to her husband's mature voice since it broadcast self-assurance at a time when she needed assurance in her life. Valentin seemed confident as well, but quietly so, without Alexander's bravura that now seemed so forced.

While he played, Yelena closed her eyes. He performed with clarity, each note carefully articulated and round. It was as if the musical phrase told a story he was sharing with his listener. Nothing overwrought spoiled the playing, and she thought miserably of her own exaggerated volume and tempos. Her musicality was adolescent in comparison. He had so much yet to teach her.

He finished and she whispered, "Bravo... You're gifted."

"Hard work, that's all."

She brought her fist to her heart. "No. Not just hard work but more. Much more... I came to tell you something."

At first she could not look at him, and her voice was scarcely audible.

"Valentin, I am a stranger in this city. A foreigner, in fact. And there are days when I feel I am a stranger in my own home as well. Only music has restored me to myself, and you are the blessed vehicle of that restoration."

She could not remain seated on the piano bench and say what needed to be said. She rose abruptly and walked to the door and stood there, tense and erect as an orator, her hands clasped at her waist. What she thought she might say, the hastily assembled declaration, struck her as commonplace. She threw herself into her feelings until the words spilled out unrehearsed. As she spoke, her voice grew stronger. By the time she'd reached her finale, her voice had stopped trembling:

"Over the course of these few months I've come to realize that to make music, to make art, one must follow one's heart. One must listen with the heart's ear and speak with the heart's words. And so I have come to know that we are allowed, if we are lucky, one great passion, one true love in a lifetime, and I believe for me that is you. I can no longer deny the fact that I love you."

She was staring at the piano and so overcome with the telling that she didn't see the shock on his face or the face carefully recompose itself. He started to rise, and she held out a hand urging him to remain seated. She stepped back—the studio was so small—her back pressed against the door.

"I do not know what to do, my love, because I have no appetite for betrayal." She looked down at the floor. The silence gaped open between them like the steppes, but there was nothing more she could possibly say. Slowly he rose to his feet, stepped aside and gestured for her to sit down. Yelena wilted onto the piano bench.

"Dear, dear Madame Serebryakovna. You and your husband have become dear to me. True friends. But I believe you are confused in your feelings."

She pulled up straight at his words and looked at him. Madame Serebryakovna. She shuddered slightly. The sound of it made her feel as if she'd been thrown down a well.

"You have confused affection and friendship with love of a different sort."

Her hands shook and when he took them in his, she gasped. He smiled kindly, but his eyes were sad, and her heart sank. How had she so miscalculated?

"I sense your dilemma," he continued, squeezed her hands and let them go, leaning away from her. "But what you truly need is a friend. A brother. Yes, you must always think of me as your brother. Isn't that the problem with us mortals? We cannot grasp that we are all brothers and sisters. Dear sister...."

She didn't know how she made it home, nor could she remember ever feeling so hollowed out, until all that remained was this husk. Not even at the farm when Astrov had tried to seduce her and then Vanya had made his own foolish declaration of love—not even then had she felt like this. Yelena went to her dressing room and lay down on the daybed, exhausted. To her relief, Alexander was still at the University. Throughout her life men had pursued her for reasons of their own, reasons she did not always fully grasp but only knew had something to do with her face and her hair and her figure, with some perceived beauty. Her aunt had warned her, but how could she interpret this? It was her face, after all. How did one place a value on one's own face or see what others saw? Besides, she had learned that others saw what they wanted to see and made assumptions about the person behind the face. Yes, she understood what it meant to have *fine features*. She saw them every day in her mirror, had lived with them her entire life. Perhaps she simply did not value them as she might since they were so familiar. On the other hand they had brought her so much grief there were times when she wished they might be altered in some small way. No, she didn't wish to be plain like her husband's daughter. Poor Sonya. Stranded in the country and utterly without prospects. If Sonya had her face would she be married by now? But what if a woman did not choose marriage? Was it easier if she were plain? Her Aunt Katya had been pretty enough to attract a second husband but chose not to. What of her?

Her thoughts tumbled about in confusion. We do not choose and cannot change our features. How much easier might it have been if she did love her own face or felt entitled because of it to all the privileges that once fell at her feet? How would her life have been altered had she flaunted her beauty or indulged in adventures? The fact remained she was not enamored with her looks. And she did not love Alexander and only realized it after they were married. She admired him, needed him, and she had taken a vow.

Then Valentin Viktorovich Levchenko appeared, a man of such inner beauty he practically glowed, the first attractive man in her life who had not pursued her. She'd finally come to understand the feeling that had so eluded her, but it was the wrong man. There had been no love for Astrov, or Astrov for her, only that magnetism pulling them together. Valentin, on the other hand, took her musicianship seriously, took all of her seriously, and her husband as well. For the first time a man was not deranged in her company but remained entirely of a piece and content within himself. And what had she done? She'd pursued him!

She heard Alexander return and opened her eyes, ready

to rise and greet him, then thought better of it. Today his voice repelled her. When they first met, she'd fallen in love with the activity and the aura, the brain and achievements, even his voice, and had confused these with the man. Still it had been her decision. Even now there were times when the old vibrant Alexander came alive and she could find it in her heart to care for him, but not this day.

For several days she considered the note of apology she must write Valentin, but the day would end and she hadn't written a word. When he did not appear on Thursday, she knew she had trespassed further than she imagined, and her mood darkened. She wrote the note quickly and concluded by inviting him to return. She sealed the note with wax and dispatched Masha to the Music School to find him.

Waiting was misery. She could not read, and dared not practice the piano, for Alexander hadn't slept well that night. As soon as Masha returned, Yelena knew she would have to send the poor girl out again for the doctor. Meanwhile Yelena tended to her husband—pulling on his socks, getting his pills and tea—all things she had done many times before but did today as if stones had been sewn to her sleeves and hem. When he complained of her slowness, she snapped.

"You have no idea how unreasonable you can be. Did it occur to you that other people also sleep poorly or not at all? But they get up, go to work and do so without complaint. I don't understand how one man can feel so entitled to bemoan his fate just because he's tired. We are all tired, Alexsya. To be human is to be tired."

He stared at her, speechless. When she heard Masha's key rattling in the rear door, she excused herself and flew to the hallway. Masha greeted her and handed Yelena a small envelope. She felt sure everyone in the household could hear her heart banging against her ribs.

"He wasn't there. I asked the secretary where I might find him, and the secretary said Monsieur Levchenko had gone away but had left you this letter, in case you dropped by. . . . I didn't leave your note, Madame."

The girl returned Yelena's letter. Relieved, she promptly tucked it into her dress pocket, and thanked her, adding, "Please tell Cook there will only be two for dinner."

Yelena retreated to her dressing room. For a moment she sat on the daybed, unable to open the envelope, then chided herself for her cowardice. He had a graceful hand, without a single inkblot.

> *Dearest Mme. Serebryakovna,*
>
> *I am returning to Kiev. My family has summoned me, for they are in need. My father is in ill health with few hopes for his survival. I am sorry to burden you with this news but wanted you to know why I cannot come Thursday to enjoy your hospitality.*
>
> *I do not know how long I'll be away. I am the only son and will need to make all arrangements. I will also be visiting my fiancée, for we have plans of our own, and she has been patient. I have every intention of returning to Kharkov and the Music School. They will be holding my position, and I do not wish to try their kindness. When I return, I hope to call on you and His Excellency. Perhaps even with my dear Eketrina.*
>
> *Very Sincerely,*
> *Your Brother, Valentin*

She closed her eyes and willed herself to breathe slowly, deliberately. She did not know how much time had passed when she finally stood and walked to the window, looking down onto the forlorn side street. She had not expected so much rain. "We have a temperate climate," Masha once told her proudly. She would have preferred snow to this dreary late-winter drizzle. Snow was pure and light and disguised a city, covering the soiled roads until everything, for a time, appeared quiet and clean.

2. Sonya

Kharkov, Ukraine. April 1898.

The air felt frosty when Sonya stepped down from the train car and into her stepmother's arms. Yelena's cheeks were pink from the cold, and she was alone. Yelena made such a fuss over her that Sonya could only believe her father's wife was truly glad to see her. *How lovely you look... I'm so relieved to see you... So much to show you... What fun we'll have!*

"Your father sends his regrets," Yelena explained. "He had a bad night. A turn for the worse, I'm afraid. It's hard on him, you know."

She did know. First the arthritis, then the migraines, and now insomnia. It was also hard on everyone around him. When her father had insomnia, an entire household was forced to stay awake, and Sonya had been relieved when he finally left the farm.

A carriage waited, and the driver kept the horse's pace leisurely while Sonya turned her head to gaze at buildings and carriages, pedestrians and shop windows. As they drove over a bridge, Sonya looked down at a river so muddy and soiled, she couldn't imagine eating anything that had once lived there. She thought of the clear stream on the family estate where the men fished, catching bream for the table. Unexpectedly, the city landscape filled with churches and cathedrals, spires like ornate fingers pointing heavenward. These she liked. When they had the time, she would ask Yelena to take her into one, knowing her father would not.

At least Uncle Vanya seemed pleased about her trip. "Ah! A little junket! You deserve a holiday." The fact that Yelena had invited her had impressed her uncle as well. "You see, darling? Someone besides us old dullards enjoys your company!" Sonya couldn't bring herself to tell him that perhaps some people did not need to take holidays to feel renewed. How did you tell someone so melancholy that every day presented refreshment: a new child in the village school, a lush crop of grapes in the arbor or a warbler in the lilac bush? More than likely he thought that a visit to her father might stave off any plans Papa might have to revisit the farm. She wanted to laugh. Her father would do what he wanted and always had, but she wasn't at all sure it would be pleasant to see him. He'd become a husk of his former self.

Yelena was saying something exuberant about the sunshine. "I hadn't expected so much gray," she said. "But today! Sunshine for your arrival! "

When they reached the apartment, her father was seated in the living room in a wheelchair, a wool lap rug over his knees, a cane at hand. His expression seemed pained, not pleased. The excitement she'd felt at the station flattened into worry. Sonya crossed the room and embraced him while he cautioned her not to squeeze too hard. For an instant, she wondered if he'd arranged himself for maximum pity, Papa the invalid, which only made her feel the opposite. She stepped back, turning away to admire the room. What lovely tall windows! Such exquisite plasterwork!

In the morning she rose early and slipped out of the guest room to take in the apartment alone, hoping to enjoy the view from the front windows. When she turned toward the dining room, she realized her father was already up, pouring himself tea and choosing something from a chafing dish on the sideboard. He had not heard her and was standing unassisted, no cane or wheelchair in sight. Sonya stepped back into the dark living room. Perhaps he felt worse in the evenings. She waited until she heard a porcelain lid clink and then a pause while he sat down at the table. She gathered herself and made her entrance.

"You were never an early bird, Papa."

He glanced up. "But you are, my dear."

She leaned down to kiss his cheek and saw the cane leaning against the table near his chair, just out of sight. He reached for it as she sat down, and a spurt of irritation clouded her mood.

"The English breakfast," she said and made herself look at the sideboard. "Shall I help myself?"

"Please do. There are pancakes and kasha in the covered dishes. Some berries for the porridge. Cook can make you an omelet if you prefer."

A basket of bread stood on the sideboard as well, and she took a roll with butter and poured herself tea.

"I still prefer a light breakfast," she said.

"You take after your mother, then."

"Really? I don't actually remember what she ate."

He smiled for the first time, but the creases and folds that appeared around eyes and mouth gave his face a sad appearance, and her irritation vanished.

"And how is your heath, Papa? Really."

"Oh, a boring subject. I have the sort of ailments that come and go. I'd feel less torment if I could predict their behavior. It's such a backwater! I'm sure I wouldn't fret as much if I could find a decent physician."

Sonya nodded and reached across, placing her hand over his. "I'm glad to see you."

"Thank you, my dear," he said solemnly. "When you turn into a relic, it's hard to imagine anyone wanting to see you."

"Why wouldn't I? I'm your daughter. And Yelena tells me you have colleagues here, and that you go to the University and work."

"Work is the only thing that keeps me alive."

"And Yelena?" She couldn't stop herself. It seemed so insensitive to leave out his wife, especially since he felt so entitled to her help. He was leaving them all out, again. She looked at him with sorrow and thought of her uncle. How could two grown men have behaved so badly, nearly coming to blows?

Her father had suggested selling the farm, and Uncle Vanya had reacted like a madman. Now the behavior of both men seemed utterly absurd. Not everyone deepened with age, she thought; some returned to childhood.

Her gray silk evening dress seemed dowdy compared to Yelena's peach-colored one, but Yelena said they could "spruce it up" with a lace and accessories. Sonya wondered what accessories she meant, since the only jewelry Sonya owned had been her mother's and never left the farm. Now she wished she had brought earrings at least. Yelena was opening jewelry boxes and holding up pearl earrings and a pearl strand and other items until they finally settled on an amethyst set that complemented both Sonya's dress and complexion. The earrings hung like purple teardrops, and the necklace rested discreetly against her throat. Her father would not be coming, and Sonya wondered if she were taking his seat. When she asked, offering him her ticket, he brushed her off with a dramatic show of magnanimity, inventing some reason and finally saying what he meant: the two women should enjoy a night out together, and besides, he was not an admirer of opera.

Yelena's maid darted in and out in a flurry. *Madame, I have your gloves... Let me iron the lace... The hem has come out in back, Madame. Let me stitch it up. No, no, don't move.* Masha crouched on the floor, talking with pins in her mouth, her cap askew, and her cheeks flushed. When the women were ready, Masha dashed off and summoned the carriage that would take them to the Opera Hall. *She's younger than I am*, Sonya thought and wished she had something to give this ebullient young woman.

"We could almost walk," Yelena said. "But your father would disapprove." She smiled at Sonya, as if sharing a joke.

Their seats seemed far from the stage, but Yelena had brought her glasses. During the first intermission, as they wound their way down the stairs to a concession area, two young-looking men approached and acknowledged her. They knew Yelena's husband—"the Professor," one called him. "His Excellency," said the other. They'd met Yelena at a reception. Would the two women care to join them in their box? Yelena immediately turned and took Sonya's elbow, pulling her forward to introduce her. Sonya watched their eyes glide up and down her gown, then around her hair, her throat. Her face. They bowed and greeted her effusively when Yelena told them she was the professor's daughter.

"Ah!" said the taller of the two. "I see a family resemblance." Her heart sank. Her features were her father's—the small eyes and thin mouth and sharp nose. She'd inherited nothing from her lovely mother except her hair and her laugh and her diminutive size. The young men seemed polished and clever and made her feel instantly ill at ease. One rushed off to buy champagne while the taller one offered the women an elbow each and escorted them toward his box in the loge. Soon enough, the other man returned followed by some functionary toting a bottle of champagne and four glasses. "I salute your health," said the taller one with the ornate watch fob. Surely these young men weren't students. Postgraduates perhaps, but what did they do for a living? She would like to know but was at a loss just how to pose these questions.

The young men filled the space with cigar smoke and jokes. At one point the smoke grew so heavy, the air in the box turned gray, and Sonya considered excusing herself for a bit of air but felt too self-conscious to stand and leave. She watched Yelena, laughing lightly, slightly flushed, one hand fluttering up to her earlobe and down again, while the engine of small talk groaned on. When Yelena tried to draw her into the conversation, Sonya had little to say, and what little she said sounded banal. Should she talk about crops or orchards? If the doctor were here, she'd feel emboldened to speak of reforestation or the need to educate the village children, but these young men would have no interest in the countryside, except as a subject of mirth. For them, bread originated in a bakery, not a farm. She could talk about music—she preferred Handel and Mozart and Bach. The opera they had come to hear, *Don Giovanni*, seemed not to interest them at all, except in its risqué references to the Don's exploits, which made her additionally speechless. When they asked her what she thought of "our Russian" composers, she replied she liked Tchaikovsky, but who didn't?

"Did you know Tchaikovsky spent some time here in '93?" said the man with the watch fob.

"Oh, my god, the Tchaikovsky visit!" said the other one. "Tell us about it, Vladimir Ilyich." So the shorter man was the Watch Fob's foil, his personal claque, setting up the jokes and anecdotes and then laughing the loudest. Her dislike for them grew at the same pace as her discomfort.

"The Maestro visited the Music School and gave a master class. I'm told it was thrilling!"

As soon as he mentioned the Music School, Yelena sat up painfully straight and gazed at him with a fixed smile. "Yes, I heard he'd visited. I even saw the photograph."

"Madame, you're a musician?" said the Foil.

"Yes, an accomplished one," Sonya said to her own surprise. "A graduate of the St. Petersburg Conservatory."

Yelena gave an embarrassed laugh, lowered her gaze, took Sonya's gloved hand, and squeezed it. The young men applauded, bowed, toasted again, and as far as Sonya was concerned, made themselves thoroughly ridiculous. She had only wanted to give Yelena her due but was unprepared for such transparent groveling. Since they'd entered the private box, the men's eyes rested continually on Yelena, like jackals on a bone. Whatever notice they paid Sonya was civil and perfunctory, remnants of lessons learned from nannies. They were interested in Yelena, and it flattered them to be in her company, not just because she was Professor Serebryakov's wife but for the Other Reason.

Suddenly, Sonya grew conscious of her tight corset and her shallow breathing. She felt sure her chignon was askew. Perhaps the amethyst earrings looked too rich against her face. Yelena was always telling her how beautiful her smile was, and her hair—reddish brown and abundant—and that Sonya had a perfectly *lovely* figure even if she was a short woman. (So small, she felt like a perennial child.) "Many famous women were petite," Yelena once told her, using the word as if being *petite* could soften the injustice of having an unmemorable face. She sometimes wondered how her life might be different if she had inherited her father's stature and her mother's face. Would Astrov notice her then? But that was fate, and nothing could be done. She preferred not to think of *it*; to do so opened the door to discontent. She seldom felt discontented on the farm. But here, in Kharkov, she was a visitor, a plain woman from the countryside. She felt burdened by this Sonya, as if the moment she stepped into Papa's apartment she became a stranger to herself.

Several days later, a messenger came to the door with a note while they were enjoying late-morning tea. Masha delivered the note to her father on a copper tray. Sonya found both the delivery and the tray ostentatious. She could not remember her family mail being delivered by housemaids bearing trays. Perhaps that was only because she never concerned herself with the mail at all since Nanny distributed the letters by hand when they came. Not that anyone received much mail, except her grandmother, whose incoming periodicals and books occasionally made the table in the hallway look like a lending library.

Her father took a bone-handled letter opener and sliced one end of the envelope, slid out the note, read it, gave Yelena a knowing smile, and handed it to her.

"Levchenko is back in town. He invites us to the faculty recital."

Sonya took this in, gazing first at her father and then his wife, who appeared to have stopped breathing. The only sounds in the room came from the street outside where a vegetable vendor shouted and horse hooves struck the cobbled street as if it were a chopping block. Then a woman yelled down at the vendor. Yelena reread the note and finally folded it and handed it back.

"And who is Levchenko?" Sonya asked.

Her father cleared his throat. "A talented young man who once gave Yelena music lessons. He then arranged for us to receive the piano you see in the dining room."

"He must be a generous person," she said.

"He is," Yelena said. "He helped your father write an article."

"The article isn't finished, my dear. And it would be incorrect to say he helped write it. He provided useful source material."

"He provided all the source material." Her voice had dropped, startling Sonya with its chilliness.

Her father waved his hand and gave a dismissive laugh. "In a manner of speaking, yes. You might say he was the inspiration."

Yelena's expression softened and she nodded. "I'm glad you said that."

"Why wouldn't I?" he asked. "I have nothing but admiration for Valentin." Her father grabbed his cane and stood. "Do you suppose he's brought his fiancée? Nothing about her in the note."

Yelena inhaled slowly, audibly. "If we attend the recital, we're sure to find out."

From their seats in the modest recital hall, they could clearly see the performers' faces, if not their hands. Five pianists were on the playbill, each performing two or three pieces, while the final artist would be performing a Beethoven sonata, *The*

Hammerklavier. Sonya closed her eyes and listened as the first man played a Chopin étude and then a Bach fugue. Her mind wandered during the next two pianists, and she found herself thinking about the farm, about what Uncle might be doing, what Cook would be preparing for dinner, what tune her dear godfather might be practicing on his guitar.

Yelena drew herself up when Levchenko took the stage, and Sonya peered at him with interest. He was extremely blond and mild looking, sporting muttonchops but no other facial hair. She'd seen paintings of Pushkin with just such side-burns and wondered if the poet was the inspiration. When Levchenko sat at the piano and raised his hands above the keyboard, she noticed his long fingers. She'd always wondered if short fingers had impeded her own playing.

He began with a Brahms rhapsody, performed an air by a French composer she'd never heard of, and concluded with a Schubert scherzo. He had great strength but was so restrained in its use that she sensed the energy behind the notes and not in front. And the feeling! There was something else she couldn't put her finger on, a passion, if that was the word, a depth one might expect from a mystic or a poet. He took his bow amid enthusiastic applause. Even if he was the youngest, he was the most accomplished player.

The last performer, the senior member of the piano faculty, took the stage amid sustained clapping. He perched heavily on the bench, eyes closed, for what seemed like minutes, raised his hands and attacked the Beethoven sonata as though he were tearing raw meat with his hands. Sonya felt herself recoil. The bravura was rehearsed, she thought, deliberate, something he'd put on, like a tuxedo, rather than letting it rise intuitively from the music. His fortes were deafening and his pianissimos too faint, as if daring the audience to hear. Were they sup-posed to watch or listen, and since when was force the same as strength?

She leaned toward Yelena and whispered. "Your friend is

the most talented, don't you think?" Yelena turned and smiled, her cheeks ablaze.

At the reception a large, congratulatory crowd circled the senior piano professor, the one who'd bludgeoned Beethoven with his fists. Her family formed a much smaller group around Levchenko. Sonya stood to one side of her father and Yelena while they praised the young man. Several young men patted Levchenko's arm in passing, on their way to the larger crowd. "Well done, Valentin," she heard someone say. "Let's drink a toast later," said another. For a moment she wondered if her father had forgotten her until Levchenko smiled and said, "You are the Professor's daughter, I believe." Yelena recovered and, with a flurry of apologies, introduced them. He took her hand. "At your service," he said.

Before she could offer him her praise, a large middle-aged woman, weighted with pearls and taffeta, swooped down upon them with her entourage—a rail-thin husband and two bored, almost-grown children.

"Valentin Viktorovich!" the woman exclaimed, grabbing him and kissing his cheeks. "We are so very proud of you! Are we not?" She turned to her family, giving each a penetrating look until they mumbled their agreement, heads bobbing, their tepid praise an imitation of the florid woman beaming up at Levchenko, clinging to his arm.

Levchenko turned toward them and introduced them all. "Madame R. is my student and my patron," he said in a gentle voice.

"I hope you're enjoying the piano, Valentin," the woman cooed.

"Yes, indeed. Many people are enjoying it."

Her father and Yelena exchanged glances. Then her father said they would tour the room and return. "We must let your other enthusiasts have a word," he said. He took Yelena's arm and Sonya fell in behind.

At the reception, Levchenko had shared no information about his fiancée, and it was clear she hadn't attended the recital. When Yelena invited him for dinner, she did so, Sonya realized, with the hope of gleaning information about the mysterious "intended." Levchenko arrived punctually, to her father's approval, and took a glass of tea from the maid. She didn't know any men who did not drink alcohol. She'd thought drinking and toasting were masculine rights, something as natural, and inevitable, as fathering children or growing a beard. She wanted to ask him why but since he struck her as refreshingly honest and kind, she had no desire to cause him any discomfort. It would be like asking a man about a prominent scar on his cheek.

Sonya watched him closely. She liked the way he gestured, lifting an arm just so, turning a palm this way or that, graceful and understated, but never unctuous. He didn't bend too far forward or down when talking and tilted his head in your direction while he listened. When her father asked him a question, his reply was factual, laced with a self-deprecating humor. Uncle Vanya would call his *a light touch*. She hadn't formed an opinion of him when they were introduced at the recital. There had been too much hubbub, and all the new voices and faces pulled her attention elsewhere. What had struck her was this: her father's jovial behavior in Levchenko's company and the attractive bloom in Yelena's cheeks. Her family thought highly of him, and on that basis alone she felt inclined to like him.

After they finally sat down to dinner, he looked at her kindly. She'd never thought of blue eyes as soft. Levchenko smiled, his head tilted slightly, and said, "I hear you're a pianist, too."

She felt her face grow hot and bunched her napkin in her lap. "A poor one, I'd say. Yelena is our musician."

"Nonsense," Yelena broke in. "After dinner, you must play your polonaise for Valentin. And I have some new music for four hands."

Sonya had no desire to play the polonaise or the sonatina or any of the other pieces she'd committed to memory. They suddenly seemed exactly what they were—the unchallenging pieces a schoolgirl might learn. She was being humored, her family straining to include her. She yearned to be included but only as a member of an audience, of a group, not a soloist. It was so annoying how shy she became whenever she was singled out. She supposed it would be even worse to sit on a bench beside Yelena and let Levchenko observe not only her clumsy musicianship but her homeliness as well. She couldn't bear it. Her nose was going stuffy and she pulled herself up.

"I couldn't possibly," she said with a laugh. "I haven't practiced in weeks. Besides, nothing would give me more pleasure than to hear the two of you perform." She raised her arms toward Yelena and Levchenko.

She survived the soup and fish, the vegetables and trifle. Still, the tops of her ears tingled with heat, fearful someone would suddenly turn and ask her to play. She was conscious of answering polite questions and asking one or two of her own. When Levchenko asked her about the farm, she replied with enthusiasm at first, then tapered off when she saw her father's scowl.

It came as a bit of a jolt when her father spoke. "Valentin, we were hoping to meet your fiancée, but I gather she has not joined you. Is she planning a later visit?"

In the muted candlelight, Levchenko's pale face grew dark. He must be blushing, she realized, but it took on the hue of a bruise. For a moment he didn't speak, chewing a mouthful of cabbage, and swallowing. She felt as though she were watching the morsel travel down his throat millimeter by millimeter. Levchenko put down his utensils and straightened the napkin in his lap. The silence was disconcerting, and Sonya could sense Yelena grow tense.

"I'm sorry to report that Eketrina broke off the engagement. She didn't want to wait so long to marry. She harbored the old-fashioned desire to marry young and start a family immediately. The prospect of a long engagement discouraged her, I'm afraid." He took a sip from the glass of water Masha had put by his place. "I'm told she will be married soon to an army officer. A surgeon."

"Fickle girl!" Yelena said in a low, savage voice.

"It's her loss," the professor exclaimed. "Her loss indeed." To Sonya's ears, her father's tone, meant to be consoling, sounded false.

Levchenko bowed his head once to acknowledge their support. "Thank you."

Sonya gazed at him. He had been rejected, and that was something she understood. "I'm so sorry."

He smiled at her then, and she saw in his face something open, ingenuous. He seemed to be a man without guile, a quality she would have cherished. Perhaps Levchenko's fiancée was a woman who took transparency as a sign of weakness and found it annoying, preferring bravura and cleverness instead. He was intelligent, not clever, and there were women who were only attracted to cleverness, confusing it with strength. She felt herself expand, as if a shuttered window had been opened.

"We knew each other for so long," Levchenko went on. "Since we were schoolchildren really. I thought this was a natural step. . . . Funny. We think we know someone, and then we learn we don't know them at all."

"Then she would have made you miserable," Yelena added, her voice still husky.

The news had shocked Yelena, Sonya realized, or at the very least startled her. Her father's reply only conveyed surprise, as if he were not inclined to give his response full voice. This is why women are treated as though we are weak, she thought. A compassionate person would allow a full range of feelings, but menfolk—poor creatures—had taught themselves to withhold. Other than her godfather, Levchenko was the only man who had come close to a sensitivity she found appealing. Her father hid his vulnerability behind his gout, giving orders instead. As for Uncle Vanya, she'd once thought of him as caring, but nowadays he drank too much and grew melancholy and then maudlin, which cheapened his feelings. And the doctor? Astrov had hardened himself, laughing things off, numbing himself with alcohol like Uncle Vanya. Only his beloved forests evoked any commitment, and even that was a commitment that seemed to come from his head, more a philosophical posture than an attitude of heart. Yet that didn't lessen her feelings for him in the least. Her heart grew full whenever she thought of Astrov.

At the moment, Levchenko's gaze was so concentrated that she thought she might fall in. Sonya looked down for a second and then up. He was still looking at her and she smiled.

"I'm eager to hear you play again, Valentin Viktorovich," she said.

"Good!" he replied and slapped his thighs, as if putting the perfidious Eketrina aside once and for all. "We should all play. Music is the only salve for the soul. Wouldn't you agree, Your Excellency?"

Her father gave a magisterial shrug. "I believe meaningful work is the salve. For you, it is the piano, and you are blessed in your talent. For me it is ideas and research and writing."

Yelena looked at her husband. "Perhaps what consoles you is thinking about art. Considering its meaning. Contemplation."

"Is that a bad thing?" he said. He gazed at his wife intently.

Yelena looked back with equal intensity and then lowered her gaze. "Not in the least, Alexander. It's what you do so well, isn't it?"

"I thought I detected a note of derision."

"Then you would be wrong. I was only looking for common ground between you and Valentin Viktorovich."

Her father nodded. "And you would find it there... in work."

Sonya held her breath. Levchenko had been looking at her

for some time. When she finally looked back, he smiled but his eyes looked sad. Levchenko broke the silence.

"You're right, Your Excellency. It is all about the work."

Levchenko raised his glass of tea, and her father raised his wineglass, and they toasted to Art while the women looked on. Sonya glanced at her stepmother, unsure whether Yelena's earlier remarks were made to offer comfort or make a point. Her tone, even her voice, was unfamiliar somehow. Hadn't Yelena once told her that she'd fallen in love with Sonya's father only to discover it was admiration and perhaps awe? Papa was not yet retired and still had his good health. Now Yelena looked worn. Worry lines ran downward from her mouth, and another wrinkle creased her forehead. Sonya didn't remember these lines.

Later that evening, while Sonya prepared for bed in the guest room—Yelena's dressing room—Yelena tapped on the door and asked to come in. Sonya had already changed into her nightgown and sat at the dressing table undoing her chignon.

"Your hair is so lovely, Sonya, and so thick. It's a fortunate thing to have abundant hair. Mine is thinning already. . . . Let me."

Yelena took the brush out of Sonya's hand, pulling it slowly through Sonya's hair. No one had ever brushed her hair except Nanny Marina, who tended to pull the brush so vigorously it hurt. Yelena was gentle.

"We have something else in common," said Yelena.

What *other things* could they possibly have in common? The brushstrokes were making her drowsy, and she didn't want to ask, enjoying the moment.

"We are both only children," Yelena went on. "At the time I met your father, I was living with my aunt Katya. May she rest in peace... She used to brush my hair. That was when we had our heart-to-hearts. She was a cultured and intelligent woman. I learned a lot in her house. It was my aunt Katya who urged me to marry someone mature. All the young men I met behaved like silly boys."

Sonya's hair crackled with static and stood up for a moment in a chestnut arc.

"Tell me, dear," Yelena said. "Do you see much of your doctor friend, Astrov?"

Sonya held her breath. His name, spoken aloud, threw her into confusion. She knew Yelena had cautioned him to stay away, but how do you tell the family doctor not to visit? Besides, she wanted him to visit. They all did. He was not just a physician but also a neighbor and a friend to them all. Whenever he walked through the door, the mood in the house lifted. The only time the good doctor relaxed was when he spent a few days at the farm. He used to come once or twice a month and work on his maps, discuss politics with Uncle Vanya, and enjoy the peace and quiet, such as it was.

"Valentin is a special person, don't you think?" Yelena said.

Sonya murmured in agreement, grateful that Yelena had moved onto the subject of Levchenko.

"Perhaps we should have Valentin in again soon. Or arrange an outing."

She knew why her family was attached to him: a surprising ability to bring out others' hidden strengths. An odd gift for a musician. She'd always assumed that great artists were demanding and self-centered, like her scholarly father.

"He's not quite as young as he appears," Yelena added. "Twenty-six, I believe."

Something about this remark made Sonya wonder if her family was matchmaking. She'd never been the subject—or object—of a matchmaker. Perhaps this is what she'd seen at the dinner table when Yelena reacted so strangely to Levchenko's broken engagement.

Over the course of the next week Yelena arranged two outings with Levchenko and another dinner. For the first, she hired a carriage. As soon as Levchenko joined the women, climbing up into the carriage to greet them, he announced, "Dear ladies, you must allow me to be your guide."

With that, he instructed the driver to take them to the venerable Pokrovsky Cathedral with its Ukrainian domes and belltower. He led them through the grounds open to the public and the sanctuary, where they lit candles. He narrated the cathedral's chronology as if he were a student of history, and Sonya asked him if he were.

"When I moved to Kharkov," he explained, "I made it my business to become acquainted with my new home. If you don't visit taverns and restaurants, it's amazing how much time you have. So I filled it with other things. I talked to monks and groundskeepers and museum guards. I gleaned a nugget of history here, an anecdote there. Putting it all together was like building a musical composition. Everything is architecture, you know: sonatas and cathedrals, libraries and fugues, opera houses, scherzos, or even the University gardens. Shall we go?"

And that was only the first day! A second outing followed, with plans for a third.

She'd never had a chaperone, if that was the role Yelena was playing. Sonya had scarcely gone anywhere that required one, unless you included Nanny. She thought nothing of going alone to town or village or countryside on farm business, although Uncle usually accompanied her with a driver. Clearly, Yelena enjoyed visiting the landmarks as much as she did. Perhaps Yelena did not have much opportunity. Since she'd arrived, Sonya had noticed how much her father expected of his wife. When did poor Yelena rest? It seemed so unfair, and Sonya's heart knotted in sympathy. Her father had been most demanding on the two evenings after the women returned from their afternoon outings with Levchenko. Sonya had encouraged him to join them, both times, but he resisted. He had work to do. Or he was planning a trip to the University to meet a colleague. The choice had been his entirely, and still there was that undeniable petulance at the end of the day. He stayed up late and slept throughout the next morning while Yelena was compelled to get up and attend to Sonya.

When they returned home after a third outing with Levchenko—more cathedrals, and a small and charming tearoom on Sumskaya Street—Sonya was exhausted but so stimulated her mind would not rest even though she lay on the daybed in Yelena's dressing room. Her father had spent the day at the University and returned complaining of arthritic pain. Yelena had gone directly to his study to nurse him. With her eyes closed and mind racing, Sonya reconstructed this extraordinary day.

Whenever they climbed stairs or approached a puddle or impediment in the road, Levchenko assisted first Yelena and then herself. Sonya remembered that on the first afternoon, when they ambled along the walkways of the university gardens, Yelena had kept a gloved hand on Valentin's arm. And each day there had been a certain gaiety in Yelena's manner, a flirtatious quality Sonya did not remember seeing before. This wasn't the composed and serious Yelena she knew. She supposed she should be happy for Yelena, that with Levchenko she could let down her hair, but somehow it seemed unnatural. The laugh was a little too high-pitched and her smile too quick. But whenever Sonya dropped back to walk behind them, Levchenko turned and insisted they all walk together. Then Yelena would add, like an afterthought, "Yes, dear girl. Please do."

She was wrong. Yelena was not her chaperone but quite the reverse. With Sonya as company, Yelena could enjoy Levchenko without worry. Sonya felt as though a fist had squeezed her heart.

The evening after the third outing, her father seemed determined to keep Yelena up all night. Sonya heard their raised voices. She put on her dressing gown and went to the study. Yelena was expressing her dismay when her father's voice rose sharply. She didn't like these words or the old man who said them.

"You think nothing of running around with young Valentin while I might need you here."

"You're being unfair, Alexander. We are trying to entertain your daughter, who has honored you with a visit. You are free to join us, you know."

"You know I can't."

"Why not?

"I have no desire to get out and trudge around."

"Mostly we rode through the city. And we invited you each time."

She couldn't bear to hear any more, tapped at the door, and then entered. "Let me stay up with you, Papa. We haven't had a chance to talk, and Yelena needs some rest."

"Don't I need rest?" His face took on a pained and pettish expression.

"Of course you do. But it's this wretched insomnia, isn't it? Let me keep you company this time. I want to."

Her father's face softened. He nodded, apologized to his wife and bid her goodnight. Yelena bent down and kissed him on the forehead.

After Yelena left the study, Sonya asked him what she might do for him. Read? His legs were bothering him so that he wasn't of a mind to do anything at first except lament his fate, his gout, or the incompetence of doctors. What about his recent project with Levchenko, she asked, drawing him slowly away from his pain toward the pleasure of work. He condescended at first. "How could you possibly understand, my dear?"

She was somewhat taken aback but chose not to show it; after all, he was ill. She reminded him calmly that she was, after all, his daughter. She did read. She was capable of interesting conversation. "I am not an idiot, Papa."

Startled, he turned and gave her his full regard. Beforehand, he seemed to be declaiming to the furniture or to an invisible audience, but not to her. She finally volunteered the news that she'd started a school for the village children, and that Doctor Astrov had hoped she might organize another one for the children near his estate. Her father took enough interest in this enterprise to ask how she went about it. Did she teach herself? (Yes, at first). Or did she hire a schoolmaster? (Eventually.)

At one point he said, "You're a competent young woman, I must say." This single scrap of approval would be all she took home.

The evening she spent with her father had produced no revelations or hoped-for intimacy. When she finally went to bed at two in the morning, all she felt was that she'd fulfilled her duty. She'd listened to him, kept him company, and asked the appropriate questions. She thought it sad he hadn't asked after anyone at home. Not even Nanny Marina, whom he liked.

So when Levchenko arrived for dinner two evenings later, at the end of a gray and rainy Saturday, she harbored a sense of completion, of finished business. She had done what she must, or could, for her parent. She had relieved Yelena and given her a reason to get out of the apartment. She had been with her father and Yelena more than two weeks and was scheduled to stay for three, but she had grown homesick. Levchenko's presence relieved the stifling atmosphere and tempered her father's complaints, allowing him to play the learned man that she remembered her father to be. Curious, how Papa never limped or used the chair when Levchenko was present.

After the meal, her father asked Yelena to join him in the study for a moment. "These two young people can amuse themselves for a while, don't you think?"

Yelena protested. "Alexsya, we can't possibly be so discourteous to our guests."

"He isn't alone, my dear. He is with my charming daughter."

And so Yelena reluctantly followed her husband out of the living room. Her barely concealed irritation, her clear desire to stay, troubled Sonya.

From the other side of the table Valentin gazed at her and then suggested they try something at the piano. Papa had made it clear that it would not be intrusive in the least. It was then she decided her father was the one playing matchmaker, an unexpected role for him. Masha had begun clearing the table, and Levchenko asked if they would be in her way. She smiled good-naturedly and said most certainly they would not. She was almost finished anyway."I love to hear it, y'know."

Levchenko shuffled through the sheets left on top of the piano, searching for the music for four hands. When he found it, he placed it on the stand and suggested Sonya take the treble while he took the bass. He flipped through and found what appeared to her to be a fairly elementary piece, a song that would not tax her skills.

"Ready?" he said with enthusiasm. "On three then."

He counted and together they began, Levchenko offering advice, counting the beats aloud when she flagged behind. He followed her lead, slowing down when she dragged behind, "ta-da-ing" like a human metronome that made her laugh. At least they finished the song on the same beat.

"For a moment, Valentin Viktorovich, I was afraid you would arrive first."

Together they leaned back from the piano, laughing, and he suggested they play it again. "You'll feel more confident this time."

And so she did. When they had finished, she said, "Tell me about your students."

"Ah, yes..." The bench was so narrow their arms occasionally touched. She slid as far away as possible, which wasn't far at all. He described first the middle-aged woman they'd met at his recital. "Kind and wealthy and completely lacking in skill."

Sonya covered her mouth with a hand and laughed.

"At least she tries. . . . Then there are my Music School students. Most are skillful. Especially one young man—Stefan from Odessa. Ah! Let me tell you about Stefan."

Levchenko gave a slightly mischievous smile, turned dramatically toward the keys with his arms lifted and played an E major chord, then a curious dark-sounding arpeggio in a minor key, narrating the story of Stefan with musical accompaniment. It became a theme and variations, a light melody in a major key that was, she supposed, the good Stefan, and the dark minor chords and arpeggios for the bad Stefan. It was Levchenko's own version of *Peter and the Wolf*, in honor of a young musician she had never met. By the time he'd finished his narrative, with its improvised musical score, she felt she knew this young man from Odessa, homesick for the sea, lost in smoky taverns, squandering his talent. When he played the final Stefan chord, Sonya applauded.

"You are a splendid audience, Sonya. A gifted listener. I've met so few."

Her checks burned and she turned away. "And you're a wonderful storyteller, Valentin Viktorovich."

"Tell me what you like to do at your farm."

The farm! A rush of emotion filled her, and she laughed lightly. "Almost everything," she said and told him about her beloved household, the planting and haying, the cherry orchard and kitchen garden, the new animals in springtime and especially the workmen's children for whom she'd built a school. She did not know how long she talked, with Levchenko injecting a question now and then, but it seemed an inordinate amount of time.

"I know so little about Russia," he said. "I hope to visit your farm some day. A place that can capture a heart so completely is worth seeing."

Levchenko suddenly took her hands in his. "How long are you staying?" he asked.

She thought her heart had stopped. "A few days more."

"Ah, so little time. I would like to see you again, dear Sonya. I would like to take you out on the steppes. Would you enjoy that? It's a landscape I think you'd appreciate."

The rest of the evening blurred and then seemed to vanish. She did not know how much time had passed when her family rejoined them, prevailing upon Valentin to perform one last piece. There were tears in her eyes when he finished the Chopin, and shortly after he said his goodnights and left.

As she was changing into her nightclothes, Yelena tapped and opened the door. "May I join you?"

Sonya made room for her on the daybed.

"Let me brush your hair," Yelena said.

Sonya stepped over to the dressing table stool and sat down.

"My heart goes out to Valentin Viktorovich," said Yelena, searching for hairpins with her fingers. "I can only imagine his sorrow."

"Yes. A great loss."

"What did you two talk about?" she asked in a soft voice.

"Mostly we talked about the music. He told me the story of one of his students. A young man who seems determined to destroy his own talent."

Sonya felt the tension in Yelena's hands when she pulled the brush through her hair. They fell silent while Yelena continued to brush.

"I have a confession to make," Yelena said at last. "I have a special fondness for Valentin. . . . More than a special fondness."

Dread crept into the guest room and sucked the air from her lungs.

"I am a married woman, but I won't lie to you, Sonya. I cannot say in all honesty that I am a happily married woman."

"I know," she answered, but Yelena did not seem to hear.

"I'm afraid I love Valentin."

The room became uncomfortably quiet. Finally Sonya asked, "And does he love you in return?"

"I don't know. Weeks ago, when I told him the truth, he said I was confused by my feelings. But that was when he was still engaged. Don't misunderstand, Sonya. I will always keep my promise to your father. I will always be a married woman while he is alive. Still...."

Sonya's shoulders and neck stiffened and she jerked forward, yanking her head around.

Yelena gasped. "Oh, dear. I've pulled your hair. I'm so sorry."

"What will you do?" Sonya asked.

"Nothing, I suppose."

"And if he finds someone else to love. . . ?"

"Then there's nothing to be done. But if he doesn't, I am always available."

"As a friend?"

"Of course. . . in any way he needs me."

Throughout the night Sonya stared at the ceiling, her thoughts a jumble of fears. She could not decipher Levchenko's invitation or the tender way he'd held her hands. Was she only a little sister to him or something more? She had no experience with either his words or gestures and could not give them a shape she understood. By morning she was exhausted and told her father and Yelena that she needed a day to rest, alone. She was afraid she might be catching a cold. Masha brought her lemon and honey tea and Cook prepared a nourishing broth. She stayed in bed, glancing through the fashion and art magazines Yelena brought her, dozing on and off, until she grew bored and stiff and moved to the armchair by the window, then over to the dressing table stool, staring at herself in the mirror, then back to bed again. By evening, when her father came in to ask if she felt up to dinner, she had come to a decision. Yes, she told him. If he would give her time to dress, she would very much like to join them for dinner. She felt much improved.

When she walked into the dining room, Yelena rose hurriedly and rushed to her. "Sonya, darling," Yelena said, the new worry lines creasing her face. "I've been so worried."

Sonya embraced her, assuring them she was fine, that it wasn't a cold after all. She'd simply become exhausted by so much new activity. She smiled and offered them a small laugh, to demonstrate her improved health and then took her place at the table. The dinner conversation meandered around the contents of their meal, the suddenly fair weather, a small crisis with the stove, and her father's article that he'd completed that very day. Sonya leaned forward to ask him more about it, but Yelena caught her eye and raised a discreet finger to her lips, warning her off.

"I read something curious in one of your magazines," she commented to Yelena instead, repeating an item in a fashion magazine concerning the construction of hats. She'd never been interested in hats, but the use of feathers from certain exotic fowl and the impact this was having on the bird population had startled her. The magazine had not taken an enlightened position, she thought, but a mercantile point of view, and this had upset her. What could be done to protect the poor birds, she asked? Puzzled, her father and Yelena turned their gazes toward her. If only Astrov were here, she thought. He would have a conservationist's answer.

As the meal wound down and they consumed the fruit and cheese, Sonya drew a breath and made her announcement. She was unbearably homesick and would like to return home no later than the day after tomorrow. She hadn't meant to startle them, and the silence that followed was not, in her father's case, a silence of dismay. He was glad, she was sure of it, and was merely groping for a suitable response. The burden of a guest would be lifted, but first there must be a show of regret.

"Oh, Sonya," Yelena sighed and put her knife aside. "Has something happened?"

"Not a thing, dear friend. I think now I was overly ambitious. Three weeks is too long a holiday for someone like me. I'm not used to it. Besides, a houseguest must be hard on you both."

"It's not," Yelena answered. "It's been a pleasure, hasn't it, Alexander?"

"It has, my dear. We've been delighted. But Sonya is a grown woman and knows her own mind. In that she takes after me. . . . For better or for worse."

The smile he offered was indecipherable. She felt certain he was relieved. Yelena's pleas to reconsider circled the table, and Sonya grew confident she'd made the right decision. Later, as she crawled under the covers, she grasped in full why she couldn't bear to stay. She'd been placed in the false position of a midwife to Yelena's burgeoning love. While her father was matchmaking—and Sonya believed he was—Yelena most certainly was not. Then Valentin entered her head, and Sonya's thoughts grew muddled. What had he meant the evening before last, holding her hands?

Both father and stepmother drove her to the train station and waited with solemn faces as she stepped up into the train car reserved for single women, waiting and waving until the train pulled away from the station. When the city receded and the train slowly moved across the steppes, northward and eastward into Russia, she leaned back in her seat, closed her eyes, and wept bitterly, her body trembling so visibly that an older woman in a glorious plumed hat and veil moved closer to comfort her.

3. Astrov

(Notes from a doctor's journal)
Provincial Russia. May 3, 1897.

It used to be one could visit the Voinitsky household without a whiff of drama. Long hours of stimulating conversation, punctuated by abundant food and drink. But ever since the Serebryakovs' prolonged visit last summer, the household seems slightly off-kilter. A pair of troublemakers, in my view—the gouty retired professor and his bored but beautiful wife. Who wouldn't forgive Vanya for lashing out? Vanya still seems so altered by the experience that I now think twice before stopping by.

Then a messenger knocks, and a new drama unfolds: Sonya is terribly ill. They fear typhoid. Please come at once!

I dropped everything, summoned horse and trap, driving my mare hard the full nine kilometers, only to find a strange young man standing in the Voinitskys' yard. I stopped behind the Tula coach, which had apparently delivered this visitor to their doorstep. Vanya was shaking his hand, ready to guide him into the house. I'd just grabbed my medical bag when the coach pulled hurriedly out of the yard, amid thudding hooves, spattering me with mud. Vanya waved, excused himself from his visitor, and dashed toward me, calling out, "Misha! Thank god!"

He dropped his voice. "We have a guest. What are we to do?"

He gestured extravagantly and dragged me in the direction of the young man, who held out his hand, not waiting for the addled Vanya to introduce us.

"Valentin Viktorovich Levchenko. At your service."

A *khokhol*, I gathered by the name. I had not been so formally addressed in years, and since I am so often at other people's service, his offer had a welcome ring.

"From Kharkov," Vanya said in a rush, escorting us both into the house. An acquaintance of Sonya's. I glanced at Vanya whose eyes widened at the significance of this. It was obvious that the young man knew nothing of Sonya's condition, and I wondered in which wing of this vast and drafty house they would put him, especially if whatever ailed Sonya were contagious. Nanny Marina was waiting for us in the foyer. Indeed, the entire household—family and servants alike—thronged the entry. I kissed Nanny, greeted the family, and then immediately excused myself, following the old woman down the hall toward my patient. What a stir the young man had caused! Sonya has a caller? *Quel miracle!* The family was on tenterhooks.

Sonya was neither awake nor asleep but in that feverish in-between state. No rash or swollen joints or lymph glands that a cursory exam could detect, but her pulse was racing. Nanny said the girl had begun to feel ill less than a week after she'd returned from her trip, at which time they sent for me.

"Yes," said Granny. "A little holiday to Kharkov to visit her father and stepmother."

One piece of the puzzle fell into place.

I complained that we should all have telephones.

Nanny shrugged. "Would that change the fever?"

There were no secondary symptoms for typhoid fever, which, like cholera, roams the district on an erratic basis. If the *khokhol* hadn't shown up to distract him, Vanya would've been in a stew of worry, carrying on about his niece as if she'd never been sick a day in her life. I told Nanny I would reexamine Sonya once she awoke. Since Sonya never complains, they didn't realize she was ill. I suggested an occasional complaint might do her good.

Nanny peered at me as though I'd made a totally preposterous statement and said, "It's not Sonya's nature to complain."

I made my way back to the living room and stopped in the doorway. Telegin sat on a stool near the piano, tuning his

guitar. Vanya won't call the old man anything but *Waffles*—
meant affectionately, I'm sure, but so descriptive of his poor
pocked face that I can't help but cringe whenever any of us
says it. I've even come to think Telegin prefers it. How does an
affable neighbor turn himself into a permanent houseguest?
Waffles, né Telegin, is actually a better musician than we give
him credit for, but he's such an unprepossessing individual we
all tend to ignore him, except Sonya, who adores him. Telegin
was saying something to Levchenko, seated at the piano. At
the other end of the room, Vanya slouched in an armchair,
one foot tapping nervously against the floor until he saw me
and jumped up to welcome me into this soirée of bachelors.
"An impromptu concert!" he announced and then asked after
Sonya.

I was hoping for a drink. Vanya pointed to the other armchair, but I chose to stand for the nonce, rubbing my backside.
Too many miles, bouncing over bad roads.

It was a pity Sonya was too feverish to be told Levchenko
was here. Vanya, who is often flustered but never tongue-tied,
informed me that Levchenko had telegraphed he was coming
by train to Tula and from there by coach. But no one seemed to
know anything about a message. I suggested Kostav had probably held it up since Kostav, our local grain agent, controls the
telegraph office as well as the store and the weighing station.
A complete scoundrel! The man cheats peasants too meek to
complain, selling them dented cookware, broken jars, sour
cheese. Our lives have been reduced to begging for services
from dishonest burghers. Sonya often complains of him—the
thumb on the scales, the bullying sons—and Vanya does a
funny Kostav imitation. With enough vodka, Vanya might be
induced to perform his Kostav again, but I wasn't sure this tall,
young Ukrainian would enjoy the impersonation. He seemed
too earnest.

I'd never seen such pale skin and light-colored muttonchops on a man. If only someone would take his wardrobe

in hand, he'd be quite passable. His suit was evidently new, but the cut didn't suit him—too snug, which only emphasized his height and leanness. Young Levchenko stood up from the piano bench, worrying aloud that perhaps music might bother Sonya, and then asked how she was. Still feverish, I said. I didn't tell them it was no fever I recognized, that perhaps she was simply exhausted.

Levchenko looked pained, and I was touched by his concern. I suggested he carry on. The sound of piano would do her a world of good. The young man turned back to Telegin who was picking out some folk tune. Levchenko smiled a bit too much for my taste, but at least he wore it well, the smile coming out in a natural manner, mouth closed. I hoped Vanya would get around to telling me the details of this visit. Not that the Voinitskys didn't deserve visitors. Vanya often moaned about the lack of company, about how boring their lives had become. When I finally asked him point-blank, with a nod toward the *khokhol*, Vanya shrugged.

"She came home early," he said and gave me a mournful look. Not a good sign, but she claimed she'd had a fine time and only came back because she was homesick.

"Tell me, Misha," he said in that sorrowful voice of his, "would you cut short the first holiday of your life in order to come home and work?"

He threw his hands up and hunched his shoulders. Vanya said they'd had a hard enough time getting Sonya to go. In spite of everything, she and Yelena remain close, and it was Yelena, in fact, who invited her. Not her father. Vanya spat out the word *father* as if it were the pit from a sour cherry. I nodded and let the information drift off. He's taken to calling the professor The Fraud, which Serebryakov is not. He's simply a self-absorbed academic in ill health who woke up one day to discover he was old. How do you explain that to a healthy young wife? The two events—gout, young second wife—converged to make him more imperious than ever. I do agree with Vanya on the one point: the professor seldom thinks of Sonya, and it's to Yelena's credit that she does. I believe the girl was quite young when her mother died. I'd just moved to the area—a young doctor with a new practice. I do remember Vanya had been laid low by his sister's death.

Nanny finally appeared with a tray of bread, cheese, pickles, and vodka, and my mood lifted considerably. "Now, Mishka," she said to me, "make an old woman happy and eat something with your drink."

So I took a pinch of bread as Vanya crossed the large room to invite the other men to join us. When the Ukrainian announced he didn't drink spirits, Nanny's small eyes widened. For a moment I thought she might embrace him. Nanny set her tray down and left the room at a remarkable clip. She'd bring him some mint tea. Then over her shoulder, "Sonya makes it."

"Have you never enjoyed a drop?" Telegin asked in his wheezy apologetic little voice.

Levchenko made it clear that he had nothing against spirits or drinking. He'd simply decided it wasn't for him. As a student, he couldn't afford to study music and drink, too. I pointed out that that had never stopped the students of my acquaintance. Vanya appeared to be considering this as if it were a metaphysical problem, but Telegin nodded and patted the visitor on the arm. I raised my glass and proposed a toast to the health and long life of us all, drinkers and nondrinkers alike. Vanya and I threw back our glasses while Telegin sipped at his as though flinging back a drink would be an affront to Levchenko, who didn't look in the least offended. In due course, Nanny returned with his tea, presented on a small silver tray. I nearly laughed.

Vanya finally gathered his wits and invited everyone to sit. I was consumed with curiosity about Sonya's visitor. I asked Levchenko about his trip, which he described as uneventful, save for the distraction of one crying child. He'd been understandably uneasy when he didn't hear from Sonya, but now he understood why. Vanya waved his arms in profuse apology. *Dreadful... dreadful.* Levchenko must think them hugely inhospitable, not meeting him at the station.

No, he'd only assumed Sonya didn't get his telegram. So calm, so forgiving. My admiration grew, in spite of my resolve to remain detached. Neither Vanya nor I had asked how he came to know Sonya, hanging back, as if to inquire were a breach of etiquette even though the question was foremost in everyone's mind.

"We are so grateful for your interest in our Sonyusha," Telegin said. "You must have met her through His Excellency."

I nearly kissed the top of his balding head.

The young man smiled, offering up the details we'd all been lusting for. The Serebryakovs had become good friends. Madame was briefly his student... a talented pianist. But we must know this. (The three of us nodded like a row of puppets.) She played duets with Sonya, Vanya said, finally zeroing in on the salient fact: the professor and Yelena stayed here last summer.

Levchenko seemed genuinely surprised. They hadn't spoken of it. "How lovely for all of you!"

I turned away, quietly clearing my throat to avoid a laugh. Vanya shot me a look, and Telegin clasped his hands and opened his mouth to speak. I cut the old man off. How did he find them? I asked hurriedly, afraid of what Telegin might reveal.

They seemed comfortable, he said. They had an attractive apartment. Madame now had her own piano, but the professor was not well.

"Yes," Vanya said, pulling out the final consonant. "He wasn't well here either. Gout and insomnia."z Vanya then dropped his voice and muttered to me, out of earshot: "Plus every imaginary ailment known to man. "

"He's working though," Levchenko added cheerfully.

"Always working," Vanya echoed. "The man is a prodigious worker."

"But we were perhaps wondering how he'd met Sofya Alexandrovna?" Levchenko said.

A collective sigh rose up from the male chorus. I coughed lightly into my fist while Telegin clenched his hands together gleefully and trilled, "Yes! Do tell."

It was a recital, Levchenko explained. Since he was on the faculty of the Kharkov Music School, he was obliged to perform from time to time. He lowered his eyes and smiled. Not only a teetotaler but humble as well. How can such a man survive in this world? Didn't he have a single vice, other than no sense of fashion? As I pondered this, the colored chips of the kaleidoscope fell into a recognizable shape, and I nearly grunted out loud. He was perfect for Sonya, if he was a man at all and not a celestial disguised as a man and much like Sonya who is the soul of kindness. I was leaning forward to catch every soft word. Yet something about his presence made me want another drink, and a cigar, and I began fidgeting.

"And how is our Yelena?" asked Vanya in a strange croon.

My god, I thought, he's still mooning over her.

She is perhaps a bit sad, he replied, since the professor's health is a worry to her.

"And a pain!" Vanya blurted out. What followed was an increasingly familiar Voinitsky rant as if he were following a script. First, the abject apology: "Forgive me, Valentin Viktorovich. I don't know you well enough to be so demonstrative." Then the qualifiers: "Neither Waffles nor the good doctor here share my feelings." And then the position: "I'm alone in my bias against the professor." Next, the ostensible grievance, in his case heartfelt: "He neglects his daughter. My niece." And since Valentin (Vanya had moved to the familiar by now) had come all this way to call on her, Vanya assumed it was because he'd observed Sonya's virtues and her great... Beauty. (Uppercase.)

Vanya turned and gazed at me pointedly. For here was the

finale."Beauty is not a word people ordinarily use to describe my niece," says he. "But I can think of no one more beautiful." I was meant to feel chastened, and Vanya's voice caught. He'd had just enough vodka to make him weepy. I cleared my throat and stepped into the fray, speaking directly to Levchenko. "As you've no doubt noticed, the household dotes on Sonya. Nothing would get done without her."

Vanya laughed and daubed his eyes with the back of his sleeve.

Not one to be left out, Telegin piped up. "Did she tell you I was her godfather?"

By this time Levchenko was beaming over so much familial love, and I thought I might have to leave the room. I grabbed the bottle and proposed a toast to Sonya. Vanya held out his glass, but the old man shook his head, covering his with a hand. Telegin was so dazzled by the abstemious Ukrainian he would probably refrain from drink for the rest of his visit. Levchenko raised his tea, and so we drank to Sonya and to a full and speedy recovery.

I agreed to stay for dinner and the night. Nanny Marina sent the girl to fix up the sofa in Vanya's study and then exclaimed, "Ah, Mishka. Ivanchik misses you when you're away!" In the hours since I first saw Sonya, it occurred to me that what I was looking at was a sickness of the spirit. This is difficult for me to say since I'm not a religious man except in the most rudimentary sense. I attend services on certain feast days, let others believe I believe in an Almighty, offer occasional blessings in his name, and say the occasional prayer. But Sonya believed. So did Nanny, Waffles, and probably Vanya, in his way. I believe in very little except work and Nature, in all its ferocity and grandeur.

Later Nanny informed me that Sonya was awake and had even taken a little broth. I asked Nanny to accompany me. As we came through the door, Sonya turned her head in our direction and gave us a small, brave smile. She was clever enough· to know the fever didn't derive from typhoid or chickenpox or anything she'd eaten. I suggested she'd picked something up from one of her fellow passengers. Any Chinamen or gay Parisians on board? Maybe a British soldier home from the East Indies?

"You're teasing me," she said and protested she was better, and didn't I think so? True, the fever had broken, but she wasn't out of the woods yet.

I told Nanny that Sonya could have a boiled egg and bread, if the fever stayed away.

I asked Sonya to let me see her feet and hands. Then I looked again for a rash across her back and throat and the upper chest. She was still young enough to have picked up scarlet fever, but there were no signs of that, either. I gestured to Nanny, and we left Sonya's bedroom and closed the door. When I asked if she knew about her visitor, Nanny shook her head. "And everyone's clamoring to visit," she said but hadn't let them. Good woman, I thought. No nurse could have done better. I asked her to go to the living room and ask our guest to play something on the piano. When Nanny left, I rejoined Sonya, keeping her door open. As soon as I sat down, she asked my professional opinion. I finally had to admit that whatever she had, it was nothing I recognized. She nodded and said somberly, "Me neither."

I took her wrist, removed my pocket watch and took her pulse, reassuring her it was much stronger. I then placed her hand in her lap. Ever since Yelena had her "little chat" about Sonya, I feel awkward whenever I linger in the same room. What was I to do when the girl was ill? Meanwhile, I felt compelled to stay until Levchenko had started playing. When she felt stronger, I said, she must tell me about her holiday. She smiled again, a wan little lift of the lips.

"And you must tell me about your trees, Mikhail Lvovich. I'm eager to see the forest again."

I felt suddenly old. The reforestation project has come too late, but I invited her to see the progress once she felt better. The village needed a school, so I needed her advice. Her gaze settled on me with interest, and she looked healthier than she had only a moment ago. It struck me then. The key to this sweet, plain girl was meaningful work: she had to build and care and keep busy. And this is one thing we had in common. I wanted to ask after her father and stepmother, but this was not the time. Any mention of the fair Hélène would bother us both. If Sonya wanted to talk about her, I would listen, but I would not bring her up. I spoke a little more about the village—a small savage place, although I didn't tell her that.

I stalled but still no music. Perhaps the living room was too far away. I made motions to take my leave, fussing with my bag, telling her yet again that Vanya and Waffles wanted to come and cheer her up. Just as I got up from my chair, the piano sounded clearly. I glanced at her to see if she'd heard it.

How lovely, she said. Was it a phonograph? (No.) Uncle didn't play so was it perhaps Grandmother? (No again.)

"You have a visitor," I said finally.

Her face lost the color it had just regained, and I experienced a sinking feeling. I hurriedly explained that he'd arrived around the time I had. He'd sent a telegram, which never reached the farm. She knew him, did she not? Sonya looked down at her hands and mouthed the name, *Levchenko*. I nodded, and she turned her head toward the windows. She wasn't ready after all.

"I thought all young women enjoyed visits from young men," I said.

"It isn't that sort of visit," she whispered.

This stumped me completely, and I asked what she meant. She didn't answer, and I was at a total loss. Were they to send him away? I wondered if she wouldn't perhaps prefer to see her uncle first. "Perhaps you'll feel up to a visitor tomorrow."

She turned her face in my direction. Another brave smile. Some people were forced to be brave because joy was not available. Sonya often struck me as one of these.

I returned to the living room. Levchenko was still at the piano, and I realized this young man was indeed a professional. When he finished playing, we all applauded and Vanya called out *bravo!* I spoke into Vanya's ear that Sonya was well enough to see him. He apologized to Levchenko and dashed off in a great flurry. Telegin eagerly took out his guitar once more.

Levchenko informed me that Telegin—"my friend here"— was quite a good musician, adding, "We're working up a repertoire of duets."

Telegin plucked a string, asked Levchenko to play an A so he could tune his instrument. I wandered over to the side table and poured myself another drink while the musicians tried out an opening passage of something I vaguely recognized. I sat down in an armchair and watched the two men sort through some additional music. A man did not travel nearly 600 kilometers to make a "house call" unless he had a serious purpose. I found myself intrigued and even hopeful for the girl. They seemed too young to be mere friends. I wasn't yet forty, but at the moment Levchenko struck me as infinitely younger. Vanya once complained that it was his age and lack of appeal that qualified him as Yelena Serebryakovna's "friend." I reminded him that she'd married a man much older than he. Serebryakov must be sixty.

I wandered down the hall to Vanya's study. The accounts table was as cluttered as always. The small table where I always worked on my maps was empty except for one colored pencil that I must have left behind. I opened the map case that I'd instructed young Grisha to bring in with my grip. I took out the current project, spread it out, and secured the corners with weights. When Grisha drove over in the wagon, he told me "the mistress" was sick. I thought he meant Mme. Voinitsky,

Vanya's old mother. But as he continued to give his rehearsed speech, I gleaned it was Sonya, and a queer dropping sensation raked my stomach.

Since the incidents of last summer, I hadn't actually thought of Sonya until I visited later in the fall to treat Waffles for a bout of influenza. Then Vanya drove over in late March during a thaw and spent the night. He'd come to urge me to visit, bringing jams and jellies Sonya had preserved. The Voinitskys were bored and eager for company. Why was I staying away? When I came to treat Waffles, I didn't take the opportunity to share Yelena's confidence. She had urged me to stay away since she believed my presence caused Sonya too much pain. I couldn't grasp why I caused her pain until Yelena told me. I didn't know whether my diminished powers of observation were to blame, or whether Yelena was being disingenuous and underhanded. But I didn't dwell on it.

Vanya's March visit caused us both such discomfort that I could not write it down, putting it promptly out of mind. He'd been in a confessional mood and asked whether I was staying away because of the incident with Serebryakov. (No.) Was I staying away because of the morphine, which in a stressful moment he'd pinched from my medical bag? (No.) Was it because of Yelena? (Here I paused.)

Suddenly, Vanya burst forth, the gist of which went something like this: "I don't know how to talk about friendship, Misha. I have absolutely no tact when it comes to things I care about or that worry me. I simply blurt things out, and it gets me into trouble. I don't know how to carry on a conversation about serious matters by sneaking them through a back window. I only know how to come through the front door. So I must ask you, straight out: Are you avoiding us? Your friendship sustains our household. Without your visits, life on the farm would have no savor. I couldn't bear it. Neither could Sonya or Waffles or Marina. Even Cook has remarked on your absence. . . . There! I've said it."

When he finished what sounded to both our ears like a wrenching monologue, I made some reassuring gesture. He finally sat down. After much throat-clearing, I confessed I hadn't come because I didn't wish to cause Sonya any pain. Vanya replied with the most incredulous look. Sonya looked forward to my visits. "She's surrounded by two old fogies and a tiresome grandmother." (His words exactly.) "You are our closest friend, and not visiting would pain her more."

"This wasn't what Yelena told me," I said, opening the can of worms.

Vanya gaped. "Misha, you leave me completely in the dark. What does Yelena know that I do not?"

Plenty, I wanted to say, but launched, instead, into my classic ramble on "a doctor's life": intrusions and late nights, long absences from home and my own bad habits. (I kept to myself my almost complete disinterest in marriage. Should it ever happen, it would be because I'd found someone I loved unequivocally.) As the litany spun out, Vanya grew visibly impatient. I found myself nervously stroking my mustache. Not for the first time the mustache struck me as the most ridiculous accessory, reaching out beyond both cheeks like two huge parenthetical marks. How had I let it become so enormous? But I couldn't go on. In quintessential Vanya style, he bleated, "Oh, for god's sake, Misha. Spit it out!"

I told him Yelena had said Sonya harbored certain feelings that I couldn't return, and thus my presence in the house was, for Sonya, a chronic reminder and a source of discomfort. . . . In short, Yelena suggested I stay away.

Vanya leaped to his feet. More vintage Vanya: "Absolutely absurd! Of course, Sonya has feelings for you. Why shouldn't she? She has feelings for Waffles and for me as well. It's called *affection*." His voice sat down heavily on the word as if it were a sofa. He declared it utterly ironic that Yelena conveyed this message. This gave him the opportunity to decry her as a troublemaker once again. "Things would have chugged along nicely if it weren't for Serebryakov and wife!"

He was lying, of course. What Sonya felt was clearly more than mere affection, now that it was pointed out to me. But Vanya wasn't finished with Yelena yet. The minx had ulterior motives, didn't I see? Deflect all my attention—my natural affection—away from his niece and over to her. Then when she couldn't handle Dr. Astrov anymore, when the situation seemed dangerous, when she was becoming frightened by such attention—afraid of what she might do—she contrived to send the good doctor packing! Didn't I see?

I'd never heard anything so ridiculous but scarcely had the chance to say so. Vanya's lips were still moving, the words grinding out and up into a thunderous finale: "That woman did Sonya a great injustice!!" Double exclamation points.

And that was just the opening volley to Vanya's March visit. It seemed to have occurred to any number of people that Sonya would make an excellent doctor's wife, and she would. But not my wife.

The light had almost faded by the time Vanya appeared in the doorway to the study and declared, "We thought you'd vanished."

Not a chance, of course. Just me and the bird. Vanya's starling had already settled for the night, fluffed up in a roosting posture on the top rung of its cage. Vanya dropped heavily into an armchair and announced that "our girl" seemed to be out of the thicket, so to speak. Nanny was bringing her some food.

I waited. The bird had settled, and the only sound to be heard in the gathering darkness was Vanya's labored breathing. Vanya turned finally in his chair, leaning toward me. He'd assumed Levchenko was here for the obvious reasons—to ev-

eryone's delight—but Sonya didn't think so. He sighed and fell
back into the chair.

"Her fever has made her melancholy," he announced melo-
dramatically. When had I ever seen her melancholy, he wanted
to know? That was his affliction, not hers. Furthermore, what
was wrong with young men nowadays? She didn't believe he
was here for any other reason than friendship!

"She's wrong," I said. He lurched forward with a smile, relieved to hear me say so. But he was not prepared to hear what
I said next.

"Perhaps she's unable to return his feelings."

This was too much for him, and he burst out, "How could
she not?"

I don't know why he was asking me. He gave me a weary
look and shrugged.

"What are we, Misha," he said, "but a pair of scruffy bachelors!" I at least was young enough to have prospects.... And
here on their very doorstep a prospect arrived for "our girl,"
and how did she respond? The world had gone mad! He leaned
toward me with his creased and weary face, and asked, "What
if she's right? What if he's only after friendship?" He trilled the
word scornfully.

"Then Levchenko is a complete fool."

Still, it was up to his niece to decide her own future. Not us.

The next morning dawned gray and glum until midmorning
when the heavy cloud cover rearranged itself and the sun
peered through. The weather had been overcast for so long,
we were all relieved. Nanny Marina reminded us, unneces-
sarily, that such was the nature of springtime—clouds, rain,
clouds, rain. I felt like a schoolboy and started laughing.

"There you go again, Mishka. Making fun of God's work."

Nanny had assembled a tray for Sonya, which I looked
over, scotching the dairy foods, urging broth instead. This un-

leashed a long lament, concluding with the words, "The poor girl will wither! How can you be so cruel!"

I planned to see Sonya after she had her breakfast so I could determine whether food caused the fever to spike. Vanya and I had stayed up much too late, and he still hadn't appeared for breakfast. Telegin and the young man were already eating. The household has taken up the English method where a sideboard groaned with food and tea, ready for whomever, whenever, each of us helping ourselves. "Very modern. . . . " I told Telegin, who couldn't remember whose idea it was. Levchenko rose and bowed when I entered the room, and I had the dark thought that I didn't like someone so obsequious courting Sonya. Perhaps this was a Ukrainian habit, but I'd always thought *khokhols* were insultingly independent, especially to Russians, or perhaps there was some Cossack in his bloodline: click your heels and acknowledge a chain of command. I nodded back and sat down with my plate. Mme.Voinitsky had apparently already eaten and left the dining room. For this I was grateful. I've never met a more argumentative woman. She fancies herself a feminist and intellectual and is neither.

With his well-intentioned smile, Telegin asked if I'd slept well. One earnest person at breakfast was enough. I didn't know if I could manage two since I'm seldom fit company until noon. He then inquired when I'd be seeing Sonya. He was eager to wish her well if she were up to it. Then Levchenko leaned an arm on the table in supplication. Did I suppose she was well enough for a visit? I promised to plead his case, to his considerable relief.

I struggled through the meal, made my excuses, and left to see my patient. Nanny was with her, having changed her bedclothes and dressed her hair. In spite of the dim light, I detected some color in Sonya's face. A flowery scent infused the room, masking the sickroom odor of the day before. As soon as I stepped into the room, she looked down at her hands, blushing. She seemed shyer than yesterday, sadly indicating improvement. Odd, that the better we feel the more self-conscious we become. Ill and feverish, she'd been more forthcoming. I made my examination, gratified to find that the fever hadn't returned. I conveyed Levchenko's message. She drew back in horror, as if I'd suggested she visit the drawing room in her nightdress, and whispered. "I must look a fright."

She looked lovely, I said, and she glanced at me hopefully and then away.

"Sofyachka, you are like a flower," Nanny said.

"I don't feel like a flower. More like a damp cleaning rag."

Nanny and I both laughed. I suggested she only felt like this because she had no energy. Once she could get out of bed—which she might do briefly—she'd feel much more herself. Besides, it would be a good thing to see him, regardless of how she felt. He'd come a long way. She agreed but only if she could see Uncle Vanya first.

I excused myself promptly and found Vanya in his room. He was just dressing as I came in. I told him Sonya had asked for him, and he perked up considerably, ready to dash off.

"Tell her to see Levchenko," I said, and he looked at me with sudden clarity and gave me a definitive nod. Then I noticed his morning attire. Where on earth does he find his ties? Perhaps from his mother's French magazines. I then said something I ought not to have.

"Don't criticize, Misha. They're my one luxury."

I told him I'd wait in the study since it was far too early for cheerfulness. I went to the map table and examined what I'd penciled in the night before. I'd brought the project that focused on the area around the Voinitsky estate. Here the village, there the farmhouse. Here the fields and gardens, there the woods—or what remained of them. A small river ran through the property, and Vanya fished it, as did the villagers and farm workers. I'd eaten bream from this river. I never think of it as Serebryakov's farm, which it is, until Sonya inherits.

I thought I might measure the woods and talk young Grisha into helping me since I doubted I'd lure Vanya into it again. He complains about the peasants cutting the trees willy-nilly. He needs to put a stop to that, but whether he will—whether Sonya will—remains to be seen. Whatever they decide, serious reforesting will need to take place. If not, there won't be any woods at all in thirty years.

4. Sonya

Her hands trembled when Astrov took her pulse. When he asked to look at her throat and chest for signs of rash, Sonya grew tongue-tied until Nanny came to the bedside and loosened her camisole. "It's all right, dear. He's our good doctor."

That was the problem, wasn't it? How was she to separate Astrov the family doctor from Astrov the family friend? She didn't know how to put aside the feelings she'd sheltered for months and acknowledge him simply as a physician. If only he didn't have to touch her. His fingers were cool, and she didn't know whether this was because she was still feverish or whether his hands always felt cold. He'd checked in earlier, Nanny said, while she was asleep.

At least she knew what this fever was not—not typhoid or chickenpox—but she had no idea what it was. Neither, evidently, did Astrov. So he stumbled around in the odious realm of chat, making silly jokes and treating her like a child. Perhaps that is how he would always think of her. Never mind that she was twenty-one. Sonya felt so muddled she couldn't tell, from moment to moment, if she wanted him to stay or leave. Time slowed until she felt as though she were suspended in aspic.

Yesterday, when someone began playing the piano, her head was too foggy to place the player. Yelena was the only person she knew who played well, but Yelena and her father had left for their new home in Kharkov. Hadn't she just seen them? Then Astrov revealed the pianist's identity, and she nearly stopped breathing.

Today she'd agreed to see everyone—Uncle Vanya, her godfather, even Levchenko. Astrov had made her promise before he left the room. Nanny returned, carrying a bowl of water and towels. "We'll clean you up, dear. Give you a little sponge bath. Your godfather would like to see you, too."

Her heart raced. Suddenly there was a queue clamoring to get in. She couldn't imagine why Levchenko had traveled all this way. Perhaps she'd forgotten something essential, but trying to remember only made her head throb.

"What does he look like?" Sonya asked the old woman.

"Not bad looking. Tall. Young. Very blond, I'd say. Very pale."

"Yes. That's him."

"Perhaps you made a conquest in Kharkov you didn't tell me about." Nanny smiled, her eyes disappearing like currants into rising dough. She pulled Sonya's hair away from her face, pinning it back.

"I've never made a conquest in my life."

"Don't talk nonsense, Sonechka. You're still young. Still lovely."

Sonya laid her head against the hill of pillows. Why would Nanny call her lovely when she wasn't? She was short and she was plain, and that was the gist of it. When people called her lovely, she supposed they meant her manners or smile or temperament. In any event, there was no possibility of marrying if it meant leaving the farm, and there was no one she wanted, except the one who wouldn't have her, the one who'd just left the room.

Nanny passed the damp cloth over her forehead and around her face and neck, paused to rinse the cloth, and started in again along her throat and the nape of her neck. A change of nightgown lay on the chair by the window, and a clean housecoat.

"If you feel up to it, perhaps you'd like to greet your visitors in the chair."

The moist cloth traveled down her arms and then up the inside. She liked the feeling but shivered slightly. The fever had passed.

"How long have I been sick?"

"Long enough. But the doctor came quickly, once your uncle realized how ill you were."

She wasn't sure how long it had been since she'd come back from her trip, but there was no point trying to sort it out until some clarity returned. With each damp stroke of the cloth she felt more herself. Sonya closed her eyes with the pleasure of it and pulled up images of her holiday in Kharkov, if one could call it a holiday. Over and over, in her mind's eye, she saw Valentin at the recital, Valentin at Yelena's piano inventing musical stories, and Valentin holding her hands.

Nanny was right. She felt much better sitting up in the chair. Uncle Vanya had come and gone, embracing her and showering her with kisses and garbled news until she finally sent him away. He smelled of cigars, and his eyes were red. Well, that's what he and the doctor always did when they were together: talked and argued, drank and smoked. Nanny reappeared and said the young man from Kharkov asked to see her.

"Such a nice young man, dear. Don't turn him away."

When Valentin entered the room, she noticed first the new suit and tie. She stared at him, admiring his crisp new attire. The brown suit and vest flattered his complexion. The tie was deep red—carmine, she thought.

"Valentin Viktorovich, what a splendid surprise." She invited him to the companion chair opposite the small round table, summoning up all her strength and hospitality. He crossed the room in three strides, took her hands, and kissed them. The gesture took her breath away. No man had kissed her hands except her relatives and beloved godfather. Perhaps the doctor when she was still a girl. Levchenko sat on the edge of the seat, looking tense, as if he might spring up at the slightest disturbance.

"Please feel at home." She forced herself to smile. "It's a pleasure to see you. But you've come such a long way. And your students?"

"It's the spring holiday, you know. And I've never been this far into Russia."

"Never?"

He shook his head, still smiling. "I can hardly take my eyes off the landscape. I wanted to see you in the habitat you love so much. I see why you wished to come home."

"What did Father tell you?"

"That you were homesick."

"And Yelena?"

"She confirmed it."

For a moment, Sonya closed her eyes. Visiting took so much energy. She struggled to focus, and her head felt heavy.

"You're still not well, Sofya Alexandrovna. I won't tire you for long."

"You could never tire me. In Kharkov you gave everyone energy."

He murmured his thanks.

"It's just that this is the first day I've felt myself."

"I understand. So you'll forgive me if I come to the point."

She laughed. "I like directness in people. But I doubt you would ever offend anyone."

He returned her smile. "I was afraid I might have been too forward when I last had dinner at your father's. I was afraid it was because of my thoughtlessness that you returned home so unexpectedly."

She gazed into the blue eyes that looked so troubled.

"You weren't thoughtless. Papa told the truth: I became terribly homesick. I felt I'd imposed on him and Yelena long enough."

"I can't imagine it."

He didn't know her family. Papa was on his best behavior in Valentin's company. Everyone was.

"I had a question, Sonya. Could I visit you again? I thought we were at the start of a . . . special friendship, if that's the expression. Then you vanished. I came to inquire whether I had misinterpreted anything"

"I'm sorry."

"Never be sorry. I simply came to ask if you would care to pursue this."

Pursue what, and what exactly could she say? If he were inviting her to be his friend, she would gladly say yes. But his hesitance spoke of something larger, and to that she had no answer. Her brain scrambled to assemble her memories of Kharkov and what she truly wanted. And then she recalled the moment on the piano bench when he had taken her hands and invited her to visit the steppes and her heart had climbed excitedly up into her throat and she could not think of a single suitable word. The image collapsed and her mind fogged.

"You must forgive me," she replied. "My head hasn't worked properly for days, and I need time to think."

He gazed at her and what she saw, for the first time, was something she'd never seen in anyone's face, a yearning for her. Sonya was frightened and rang the bell for Nanny. The old woman had been hovering near the door and popped in with alarming speed.

"Yes, my love?"

"We would like some tea."

Nanny left with the same alacrity, and Sonya had the distressing thought that the entire household was hovering and waiting. There was such unspoken expectation in those striving to make the match that she wanted to run away, but where? The farm was her haven, her nest. She'd fled home so that she might be safe. She hadn't been herself in Kharkov. Had Valentin been attracted to a foreign Sonya, a reserved visitor-Sonya? Should she tell him that playing the lady, like Yelena, was not what she did best, that she knew how to put up preserves and pick cherries and mow grain, raise chicks or barter with grain agents? Would he find it distasteful that she entered peasants' huts to treat sick children and workmen, that dirt did not offend but was ever present in her life? She wondered if he'd be aghast to discover that she was more familiar with dung heaps than French perfume or ostrich-plume hats. But then he didn't seem dazzled by hats or perfume either. The dapper young men she'd met at the opera would have found her life hilarious, worthy of crass jokes, but she did not care for them or what they thought. Why was she so afraid?

The tea arrived. They drank one cup apiece in such labored silence that Sonya felt as though they were taking communion. Neither touched the tiny cherry tarts that Cook had prepared, and neither could think of a thing to say until abruptly they both spoke at once.

"I shall return home then," he said just as she was telling him she would write. The tension seemed to drain from his shoulders, and he smiled. "Yes, please write. Perhaps I'll return at a more convenient time."

"But it's so far, Valentin!"

"Not for a friend."

He stood up, took her hand again and kissed it, then promptly left the room. She leaned back in the armchair and released a long, tremulous sigh. Before she could collect her thoughts, Nanny was back to collect the tea things.

"A fine young man. And did all go well, Sonechka?"

"What do you mean, Nanny?"

"With your visitor, of course. Young men do not travel hundreds of kilometers just to pass the time of day... Remember, darling. You would not have to live year-round at the farm in order to remain its mistress."

Stunned, Sonya thought surely she'd misunderstood and groaned. "Nanny, help me back to bed, please."

Sonya threw off her dressing gown and climbed under the covers while Nanny plumped the hill of pillows under her head and shoulders. Was she up for one last visitor, the old woman asked? Her godfather was eager to see her.

"Yes," she whispered. "I would very much like to see my godfather." Nanny left to fetch Telegin.

Did she love Valentin? She didn't know, nor did she know if her heart could move in that direction. Still, the attention he paid her filled her with joy. What she did know was this: it would pain her terribly to commit to someone Yelena also loved. Besides, there was someone else she'd given her heart to, even if he scarcely took time to notice her.

"Darling!" The old man entered the room, his pockmarked face breaking into smiles.

This is love! The realization sprang on her, and Sonya hugged her godfather, holding on tightly, unwilling to let go. How long had it been since she'd seen him? She had no doubt everyone in this household cared for her, deeply. So why did it always come as such a surprise? Could that love ever be enough? What she had on this patch of land was a home and her heart's work and God's grace, and in her weakened condition she did not dare ask for anything else.

5. Astrov

I lost track of time working on the map. Suddenly Vanya was at my elbow, startling me.

I asked if I could once again survey his woods. He bowed and with a sweep of his arm invited me to be his guest, adding he would not accompany me this time. The last time, he'd spent the evening daubing vinegar on mosquito bites. When I asked how he'd found Sonya, he sighed and paced over to the windows and back. Better, he said, continuing his route toward me and back to the windows, sighing and rubbing his beard until I told him to sit down. He dropped heavily into the armchair and crossed his legs, then immediately uncrossed them. Sonya hadn't wanted to see Levchenko at first but he'd insisted. Levchenko was with her as he spoke. He leaned his arms on his knees and clasped his hands. There was something he wasn't saying. One can always tell by the expectant mood in the air. So I asked what the impediment was.

Evidently Levchenko was once engaged, but the fiancée broke it off. I inquired if she thought he was on the rebound.

"No. Worse…" Vanya rubbed his eyes, leaned back in the chair with a groan and added, "Sonya was quite certain Yelena was in love with him."

I was speechless. The only words to come out were *Dear God!*

"But Yelena isn't in the running," I said. "She's married, and from my observation a remarkably loyal wife. Does Sonya think Levchenko loves Yelena?"

"Noooo," Vanya said with great deliberation, and satisfaction. "In fact, she's sure he does not."

I threw up my hands. I couldn't grasp what was stopping her. Vanya elaborated. "First, the Ukrainian has not actually declared himself. And second, she does not think she can love a man that Yelena loves."

I found this complete nonsense. He agreed but reminded me that we were not women, and we had not drunk *Brüderschaft* together. It made no sense.

"What does drinking *Brüderschaft* have to do with following your heart?" I inquired.

"You're asking me, Misha?" he exclaimed, helplessly. There was nothing we could do, he moaned and jumped up and paced again—to the windows, back toward the armchair, to the birdcage, and back again. Finally he walked over to the map table.

"She'll turn him down," he said at last.

I kept my gaze on the map, shading in an area where buckwheat grew. "You don't know that," I said finally.

"No... but I suspect it. Sonya is a woman with strong convictions and tremendous loyalty," he concluded. I kept my attention focused on the map, shading the square and moving onto the adjoining square that demarked the apple orchard.

She wasn't about to accept him if she loved someone else, he said. "Misha, are you listening to me?"

I stood up straight, stretched my back and then looked him in the eye. "Yes."

I had no idea what time it was when Nanny brought in a tea tray. What we both needed was a stiff drink, and Vanya sent her back for the vodka. After several toasts, I continued to work on the map while Vanya worked on the farm ledger, fed his starling, talked to himself, to the bird, and to me. He tried to read but immediately hopped up and paced some more, unable to settle on any one thing.

"You need a hobby," I said.

"I'm not the hobby sort," he snapped. So I turned back to my penciling. Nanny returned to freshen the tea we hadn't touched and announced that our visitor was leaving on the evening train. "I'll take him," Vanya announced in a heroic voice.

The station was five kilometers away, and Vanya was in no shape to drive a carriage anywhere, even if Telegin went with him. Since I'm one of those odd people for whom alcohol has the opposite effect, I felt utterly awake. I offered to drive Levchenko, rolled up the map, gathered the pencils and weights and put them all in the case. It was time for me to leave in any event.

Vanya protested, "It's out of your way!"

"No, it isn't, and that's that." I reassured him that I'd return at the end of the week to check on Sonya. I was certain she was recovering.

"I hate it when you leave," he said. "There's no decent conversation."

His remark brought a knot to my throat.

They brought my horse and trap around after the midday meal and young Grisha put our bags up. Levchenko's topcoat was as old and shiny as his suit was new, and I wondered how music teachers made a living at all. Perhaps there was family somewhere, an old mother dependent on his income. For a moment it occurred to me that Sonya—if she'd made a decision at all—had made a very practical one. What would happen to the farm if she married a conservatory teacher who lived in Kharkov? Levchenko and I climbed up while the household, sans Sonya, gathered nearby. Telegin appeared damp-eyed. It wouldn't occur to any of us that the old man had made a friend. Levchenko had taken a special interest in him.

The farewells and travel advice threatened to go on forever, so I shook the reins, and the trap lurched forward. Levchenko turned in the seat to wave and only turned back around when the house was out of sight.

He gave a huge sigh. "A lovely family."

He remained quiet, and I pointed out the extent of the Voinitsky family holdings, narrating a brief history of the place, mentioning Sonya's mother Anna, who'd been Serebryakov's first wife. Technically speaking, the estate was still Serebryakov's,

but all this would be Sonya's when he died. Most of the profits
and income went to him now, of course. To the detriment of
Sonya and the household. I would've liked to tell him so but
did not. Instead I asked, as an old family friend, what exactly
was his interest in Sonya?

He turned and glanced at me, looking as though he hadn't
slept for days, the skin beneath his eyes dark and puckered.
He'd hoped to explore that subject with her, he said. But of
course he had no idea she was ill.

I nodded. At least he was an honest man. I pointed out that
she wasn't likely to leave the farm, was she?

He'd been dining with the professor and family, he explained, and had made an appeal to her. He knew she was
someone he wanted to get to know better. She then left Kharkov in such a hurry he thought perhaps he'd offended her. He
had to make amends somehow.

"So you came all this way," I said. "That is a significant
amend in itself." I'd hoped to interject a lighter tone, or a grain
of humor, into a situation in great need of it.

Sonya had assured him she was not offended, which he
was happy to hear. "But there's something else, doctor, and I
have no idea what it is."

How could any of us tell him the complicated history? The
family disagreements, Serebryakov's insensitivity, and Yelena's
apparent disappointment—how could I possibly relay what
Vanya had revealed? Where would one begin? I have always
felt the greatest tenderness for Sonya, but nothing romantic.
Any woman who becomes a doctor's wife becomes an unre-
warded housekeeper, and that thought appalls me. Sonya was
a perfect match for the tall Ukrainian but would likely turn him
down, and I couldn't share any of this. Levchenko might as
well have been a visitor from a distant star, and Kharkov was
beginning to feel like just such a place. I gave a little laugh instead. "Ah, it is so hard to know a woman's mind, isn't it?"

My mare plodded steadily along a roadway still pocked from the ravages of winter. The carriage shuddered over each dip in the surface. Since he was about to leave, I refrained from asking him much about himself. Can there be anything more useless than gaining a new acquaintance who will soon exit your life? Perhaps it's a professional flaw, a doctor's shortcoming. So much drama and chaos attaches itself to medicine that a doctor reaches a point where he can no longer bear to express an interest, knowing the pain and awfulness that will seek him out.

We rode on in silence. I'd hoped he might invite a stream of conversation, but he did not. When we reached the station, a porter assisted him with his bag, and I got down to wish him goodbye, asking him to remember me to Professor and Mme. Serebryakov. I then wished him great success in his musical career.

He bowed and thanked me more lavishly than I deserved, offering a weary smile that reminded me of Sonya, an expression completely lacking in guile. Who had lost more, the young man from Kharkov or Sonya? But it's best not to dwell on such things.

"Perhaps we will see you again," I said, thrusting out my hand. And as I said the words, I realized I truly hoped we would. He took my hand in both of his.

"Perhaps," he said, and no more. His voice sounded so doubtful that I was inexplicably overcome and could scarcely look him in the eye. Without further ceremony he said his goodbyes and quickly made his way to the station. I climbed up into the carriage and let my gaze linger on my impatient mare. I couldn't bear to watch him disappear through the gate.

 *PART TWO*

Now We Can All Go Home

(Three Sisters)

1. Irina

Perm, Russia. Early October 1901.

She cannot bring herself to go indoors and remains in the garden with her sisters. They're clinging to her, consoling her, but their words rush by like wind through a broken window. At least she's stopped crying. A breeze travels through the garden, brushing her cheek. The leaves of the maples, scarlet with autumn, tremble slightly. Someone is performing rather badly on the piano in the drawing room, and the music distracts her. Irina thinks she recognizes the tune. "The Maiden's Prayers," isn't it? Over Olga's shoulder she sees her other sister's husband step out onto the veranda, carrying Masha's cape and hat. How tall he seems, and for an instant Irina confuses him with the Baron, and sobs. No one inside the house yet knows. Someone will have to tell them that the Baron has just been shot, that in the time it takes to draw a breath, she's become a widow before she's had a chance to be a wife.

The last person to see her fiancé alive slumps on the garden bench beneath the maple, mumbling an absurd ditty: "Ta-ra-ra boom-de-ay. Ta-ra-ra room, I say."

In this very garden, not an hour ago, the three sisters raised glasses of champagne to the health of the departing officers. Now the garden resembles a thoroughfare. Cadets rush by. Men in field uniform doff their hats or salute them and hurry on their way while a bell clangs from the river barge awaiting the officers. Shouts hang in the air. The regiment is leaving Perm after fifteen years, and most of their friends are leaving with it. Olga's voice sounds far away even though her arms are still circling Irina, tight as a locket. Their oldest family friend, now drooped over the garden bench, will depart tomorrow with the remainder of the battery. Irina gazes at him.

"Ta-ra-ra boom de-ay," he croaks.

Irina breaks away from her sisters and approaches him. "Ivan Romanych, don't. . . Please."

The doctor turns and looks up at her. He seems to have aged since she last saw him, less than an hour ago. His face sags, waiting for her reproach. Irina touches his shoulder, but her hand trembles so noticeably, she pulls it back. "Wasn't there anything. . . ?"

"Nothing, child. The Baron was gone before I could reach him."

Her limbs feel weak. How is she to carry on when her heart is sinking under so much weight?

Ivan Romanych grabs her hand and continues. "Solyony said he was only going to wing the Baron. 'I'll give him a little scare,' he said. Then something strange happened. The Baron took a step forward and to his right and. . . . Oh, Irina! I'm an old fool! I took Solyony at his word."

None of it makes any sense—the duel, the death. All morning her fiancé was attentive; how was she to know his life was in peril? Yes, he was distracted and wouldn't tell her the reason for his "errand." *I must run*, he said. *Be back soon.* Then he asked for coffee to be ready on his return. The thought of his coffee, still waiting, makes her feel even more bereft. Do men who are about to duel consider the consequences? Or is it all misplaced honor and passion? He wasn't the dueling type, and she is convinced Captain Solyony baited him mercilessly.

On the veranda, her brother-in-law Fyodor rocks on the balls of his feet, Masha's hat and cape still in his hands. Fyodor should never have removed his moustache. Clean-shaven, he looks less imposing than ever, in spite of his height. Her hands fly to her face, and she rubs her eyes with her palms. Why is she having these absurd thoughts when a man has just been killed?

"I need to get away," she tells Ivan Romanych. "But not the living room . . . Natasha, you know?"

"Go to my room, child. Rest. . . ."

She clings to him instead, unable to move, lingering like a pet. "Do you remember when you taught Andrei and me to shoot?"

He looks up, surprised. "Did I? I don't remember. . . . I'm sorry."

His face is so creased she finally grasps how old he's become. The battery must have its doctor, but he's done so little doctoring he claims he's forgotten how. . . When this day is over, he'll be drunk.

"My life and light," he says, taking her hands. All her life she's been his life and light, his surrogate daughter, the youngest Prozorov. Now he looks worn and gray, and her mind clings to the one question: why didn't he stop it?

The ringing in her ears began the instant the doctor appeared in the garden and whispered to Olga, "The Baron has been killed in a duel." Now the noise in her head clamors like a fire bell. She pulls her hands out of his and makes her way to the house. As she leaves, she overhears Olga ask him, "Is Irina all right?"

"She will be," he answers. "A few moments alone to collect herself."

"She needs her sisters."

"Well, she knows where to find you," he says irritably. The maple leaves shudder overhead. He has not moved from the bench and whistles the tune she asked him to stop.

Earlier in the day, Fyodor said something about the insult and the challenge until both Ivan Romanych and the Baron shut him up. Now she can only wonder about the meaning of it all while Olga speaks of hope. . . Hope! It isn't love she's lost, but hope.

Irina crosses the veranda and enters the house. The back hallway is surprisingly dark. She seldom comes here. She's always thought of it as a place where servants moved and food emerged and Ivan Romanych rented one large room and Baron

Tuchenbach another. Masha once told her that Ivan Romanych loved their mother. Today such devotion seems extraordinary.

She follows the shadowy hall, remembering how Olga urged her to consider the Baron, suggesting he'd given up his army commission and become a civilian on her account.

"Marry him," Olga said. "You can learn to love Nikolai Lvovich. He already loves you."

Why would a man marry a woman who doesn't love him in return?

"You like and respect him," Olga said. "That's enough. A marriage can survive without love, Arisha, but not without respect. And you both share a desire to work."

Such an unlikely fate for two people reared to something supposedly finer than work. Since the family left Moscow, most of her schooling has gone to waste. Who in this place cares for anything but the price of wheat or linseed oil or real estate? She cringes whenever she thinks of her brother's wife Natasha—cunning and provincial. *This is what we'll be left with when the army is gone.*

Irina imagined the long days of her life with no return to Moscow and knew she could do worse than Nikolai Lvovich—a gentle, humorous man, so easy to talk to, but so plain. Olga scolded her. "Irina, darling, what could be less important in a man than a beautiful face?" He loved her for years; she knows this because he told her. Finally, she accepted his proposal. Tomorrow was to be their nuptials, just as her teaching career begins. Now he is dead, and she sees her solitary life unfold in an endless corridor of classrooms, of reluctant scholars and long hours, tedious meetings and ink-smudged exercise books. *Oh, Olya. It is you and I who will work and work and work.*

Overhead, Natasha's laugh rises over the murmurs of her guests. Someone should have told them by now. Irina is grateful she can reach the doctor's room without encountering the sister-in-law who has so altered their lives. Earlier in the afternoon Natasha criticized her outfit. *That sash doesn't suit you*

at all, my dear. . . . It's not in good taste. She bit her lip when
Natasha said it. What does Natasha know of good taste except
what Olga taught her? How does anyone preserve her dignity
with such a tactless woman? How can Andrei bear it?

She pushes open Ivan Romanych's door, overwhelmed
by the odor of mildew. Newspapers and clothing are strewn
everywhere. She stares, shocked at the clutter, the indiffer-
ence. Why would a doctor, of all people, behave as though his
years on earth were of no consequence? It upsets her, but the
instant he is gone, Natasha will have the room cleaned and
scrubbed with lye, his presence and the memory of his presence erased. Irina glances around the room. He hasn't even
packed, and she thinks of the Baron—Nikolai—so fastidious
and full of life.

What she cannot grasp is why Nikolai would respond to
that unpleasant man's needling. When Captain Solyony first
declared his own love to Irina, she was appalled and remains
so to this day. It still puzzles her that Nikolai befriended him.
And see how his kindness was rewarded? Solyony turned on
him because she preferred Nikolai's company to his. Who
wouldn't prefer the Baron? All that vile cologne, that morbid
sprinkling of hands, Solyony's mean-spirited jokes, and his infatuation with Lermontov! Where does such folly come from?
Ivan Romanych said Solyony believed his hands smelled like
a corpse; but it is Nikolai who is dead, and Solyony, his honor
intact, will march away with his men.

She feels suddenly light-headed and steadies herself
against the doctor's wardrobe. Did her not loving Nikolai
make him careless? And what prevented her from lying? She
struggles to reconstruct their last conversation. His words now
seem important.

"Say something," he said.

"What do you want me to say?" she answered impatiently.

"Anything."

But she lost her temper and cried out, "Stop it!"

Now she wants to take back all her careless words and her impatience. If she knew about the duel, would she have spoken differently?

In torment, she flings the wardrobe open. The doors are so warped, they squeal. Humidity has always plagued them. The house sits too close to the river, and moisture rises with the mosquitoes. This cursed, sleepy town is soon to be emptied of the only friends the Prozorov family has known. Inside the wardrobe the doctor's unpolished boots lie helter-skelter—this boot standing, that one fallen over. Shirts are clumped at odd angles while tunics are wadded up in back. Odd, how women never imagine their menfolk sleeping or bathing or hanging up their clothes. She pushes aside the threadbare garments. Why this man never married, she doesn't know. Did his devotion to their mother prevent him? Masha believes he and their mother were lovers, but Irina cannot bear to consider this. She finds a white silk scarf behind a pair of boots and takes it. A memento, although it doesn't remind her of the doctor but of the Baron, so perfectly smooth and clean. She rolls it into a small ball and tucks it under her sash. As the wardrobe doors groan shut, she fully grasps that they are losing Ivan Romanych also, and more useless tears well up.

She reaches the rocking chair by the window and sits, remaining there for a time. The ringing in her ears subsides, her head clears, and for a moment she forgets why she is here. Outside, cadets call to one another, while upstairs Natasha's guests trill out another toast. Poor Andrei. He was to be their violinist and scholar, but nothing has come of that since his marriage. Nothing has come of anything in this godforsaken place.

She rocks slowly forward and back, watching the river blink through the trees. She still has her sisters and now her work, and for the first time she feels glad to be a schoolmistress. Olga will guide her. Perhaps she might stay with Olga for the time being. Nanny lives with Olga now. What a comfort she will be!

When Irina finally pushes herself out of the chair, she notices the small bedside table with its unblemished cherry wood. It belonged to Mother and to her grandmother before her. She's puzzled how this heirloom made its way down into this gloomy room. Still, she's drawn to it and, when she reaches it, takes a sharp breath. Ivan Romanych's service revolver rests on top like a toad on a jewel. Her fingers travel the surface, through a thin coating of dust, avoiding the gun. She turns away and gazes at Ivan Romanych's unmade bed.

She pulls open the small drawer in the bedside table and discovers a jumble of clipped news articles and assorted medicine bottles. Does Ivan Romanych prescribe medication for himself? If you're a doctor and want to die, do you have the means in a small vial in your medical bag? Do you even carry such things? She supposes all doctors carry morphine, but she hasn't seen him carry his bag in years.

She cannot ignore the service revolver any longer. She imagines he wears it in an official capacity, yet she doesn't remember it. If so, you'd think he might take as good care of it as his regimental saber, but the gun looks neglected. Dear Ivan Romanych. You have let the ground water of this dull town seep in and rust your soul.

She feels suddenly hobbled. Her skirt is too tight, hugging her from waist to ankle. The doctor's slippers rest beside the bed. She catches a whiff of something sour like pickles or German cheese. The odor seems to come from under the bed, and she bends down slowly, feeling the pressure against the seams of her skirt. She finds more newspapers, piles of them underneath, but no food, only an open bottle of dried boot polish and a crumpled pair of trousers. Perhaps it's only the mildew she smells, or unwashed clothing. Even this clutter cannot distract her from the glint of metal on the cherry side table. When she tries to stand, her heel catches her hem. She doesn't so much hear the rip as feel it, a jarring vibration that runs along a nerve through her foot and up her leg. She rearranges herself and stands, holding onto the bedframe. Impulsively, she reaches out and pulls the gun off the table, startled by its weight.

Do certain men, like Solyony, require a gun to feel complete? In its present condition Ivan Romanych's revolver is not an official sidearm but a rebuke. He could have used it, or his status as a doctor, to stop that insane duel. He went as Solyony's second. He could have advised the vain captain to put an end to this useless gesture of broken manhood. But he did not, and she cannot understand why.

More shouts come from the direction of the river. Clutching the revolver in both hands, she lays it like a corpse across the crumpled bed linen, wraps it hurriedly in the white scarf and places it inside her jacket under her sash where it presses like a frozen anvil against her waist. In the drawing room, the partiers grow silent. Perhaps Olga has finally told them.

Irina slips out of the house and onto the veranda. Only Ivan Romanych remains in the garden, still slumped on the bench, staring at nothing, a limp newspaper over his knee. She moves silently down the side steps and across the edge of the garden and into the trees. A person can find the river in the dark by its weedy smell. Today there's been so much foot traffic that dust hangs visibly in the air, mingled with the scent of horses and polished leather. When the regimental band bursts into a march, she starts like a frightened child. They were such little girls when their father left Moscow and took this post, but life without the officers is something she cannot imagine. Who will play the piano, share their dining table and amuse them with jokes and skits, birthday parties and conversation? Who will sing after dinner or play Patience with Masha? Only their brother's wife is glad to see them go.

The din in her ears grows louder. She veers off the path toward the river, moving in among the birches and larches and pines, while upstream several men board the barge. She's grateful for the muted browns of her suit, more appropriate for a schoolteacher than a bride. It bothered Nikolai, she knows, but the matter was out of her control: she had never been in love. Her greatest hope was that, in due course, they would move back to Moscow, that she would come to love him there as he loved her. She promised to be faithful and obedient and even told him how light-hearted it made her feel when she accepted his proposal... How could she have been so heartless?

She pushes through the ragged foliage and stands behind a screen of alders lining the bank. Officers continue boarding the barge. Her boot heels sink into the soft bank, and she steps back. When did they last have rain? Now everyone is saying, *It will snow soon... it will snow.* The sun emerges and glints off the river, making everything too bright. Sunlight only makes the events of the last hour harder to bear.

She glances up in time to see Captain Solyony board with two other men. The sight of him makes her pulse race. Solyony's third duel, Fyodor said, and she wonders if the Baron is the third man he's killed. Solyony used to follow the Baron around the house for no other reason than to make jokes at his expense. How does Solyony, the aspiring poet, reconcile himself to Solyony the destroyer of friends?

Unexpectedly, Solyony appears at the boat railing, and she crouches. She takes the revolver from her jacket and unwraps the scarf, tossing it aside. The military drum pounds as though it isn't on the riverbank but in her head. A horn blares. Men call out as they uncoil the ropes tying the barge to the dock; the anchor chain clanks, the pulley whines, and the boat moves. She scarcely breathes as it drifts in her direction. Her heart is panic stricken, thumping wildly. It was foolishness, taking Ivan Romanych's revolver. She intended to bury it, as if burying a gun might bury the events that have altered her life, but the sight of Solyony so upsets her, she finds herself struggling with a different urge.

When they were young, Ivan Romanych once agreed to teach Andrei how to shoot. She rushed out after them and insisted they take her, too. "What would the General say?" Ivan

Romanych scolded. "What would he do to me for handing his daughter a revolver?" She only wanted to watch and begged Andrei not to leave her behind. And so the doctor allowed her to trail along, to touch the gun, to observe while he showed Andrei how to aim and cock the hammer, how to point and slow the breathing and straighten the arm. *Let me try*, she pleaded. *Let me!* But they were shooting trees, not men. She screamed when she fired, missing the birch, and ran back to the house in shame while the men laughed. This time she cannot miss, or scream. Perhaps for the first time in her life, she will behave like a general's daughter.

The barge floats within range, and she hears a younger Masha scolding Solyony: *You are an impossible and dreadful man!* She once thought Masha rude, but Masha always saw Solyony for what he was, long before the rest of them.

For a moment, Irina loses track of him. The cadets told the sisters he was the only one of their battery allowed on board. The rest will depart on foot. Suddenly Solyony leaps like a monkey onto the low, wide ledge of the barge and looks out along the river. As the overcrowded barge drifts closer, Solyony gazes toward the bank, slender hands on narrow hips. Irina leans out from between the trees on purpose, the gun concealed behind her back. He sees her and spreads his arms wide in greeting, salutes, then removes his hat and covers his heart. When he returns the hat to his head, he gives it a jaunty twist and bows his head in a mockery of respect that makes her furious. With difficulty, she brings the heavy revolver in front of her, counting the meters between them. Just as the band on shore trumpets out a military tune, she breathes in sharply and holds her breath.

Where the river bends, a puff of white smoke appears and then another nearby. She sees it from the corner of her eye and whirls around. An instant later she hears the muffled pop of a gun, then a second pop, and a trio of wood ducks lift up from the opposite bank and fly away. Simultaneously, something at the tree line reflects the sun like a mirror. No one on board appears to have seen or heard, and the smoke drifts back into the trees. Stunned, all she can think is, *who?*

She looks down at the revolver in her hands—unfired and pointed toward the ground. She hasn't even cocked the hammer and knows she never will. It comes to her then: *I should have told Nikolai I loved him.* The only words of comfort he wanted, and she could only offer him a miserly truth. The one time he asked for affection, she replied by losing her temper. Because of her impatience, because she does not know how to love or pretend to love, the only worthy man in her life took a deliberate step to his right.

Three of them are involved in Nikolai's death, not one.

Solyony remains poised on the barge railing like a human statue. Irina raises her hand and waves. She does not feel more kindly toward him, but there is something he needs to know. Then, to her horror, his arms and legs sag and his knees buckle. He crumples slowly, losing balance, and enters the river with the soft plash of a game bird. For a moment he drifts across the river, face down, before vanishing beneath the surface, lost in the boat's wake. Someone yells, "Man overboard!" A chorus takes up the call but is scarcely heard above the din of trumpets and drums. The barge gathers speed and glides downstream. Irina kneels beside the riverbank and slips the unfired gun into the water. Without a sound, the revolver sinks to the river bottom.

Mayhem breaks out on board. Men rush from one side of the barge to the other, peering down, shouting orders. No one looks toward shore. All she can make out is a jumble of uniformed bodies, waving arms and one emphatically pointed saber. The deck becomes a blur of red and white, green and gold, passing her completely on a steadily moving current. In the distance the regimental band urges the troops toward the train station, with a final drum roll and a faint *rat-a-tat-tat.* She gropes for the scarf but cannot find it in the underbrush. In a panic, she tears her fingers on brambles. When she finally sees it, dangling on a thorn, she pulls it loose, rolls it up and tucks it into the sash of her suit, the very sash that Natasha finds so inappropriate—*It won't do, Irina.* She glances down at herself. Dirt clings to her boots. Her hem is filthy as well as torn.

She plunges deeper among the trees, afraid of meeting even one cadet, until she can run no farther. She drops onto a birch stump, panting, and rests her head in her hands. There is no question of returning home, but where is home? A rented room? *Go to Olga's,* she tells herself. *Mend your hem. Put yourself to rights.* She doesn't know how much time has passed when somewhere overhead a cuckoo calls. The notes of its bittersweet song pierce her heart, and she holds her breath, waiting for the woody voice, any voice, to call again.

2. Olga

Late October

Fyodor asked again if he might stop by after classes "to have a word," as he put it. Olga had grown uncomfortable with his visits even if Nanny was always in the apartment. He needed his wife, but Masha had become a ghost haunting every spot she'd ever visited with her Colonel, walking for hours along the river path or through the birch woods while her husband came to Olga for companionship. Now Fyodor visited on the pretext of inquiring about Irina's health.

"A good day, dear?" Nanny asked. She'd kept the samovar hot and handed Olga her tea. A dollop of strawberry jam swam at the bottom of the glass.

"An average day," Olga told her. All her days were too long and too average. It was at this hour that she wished she were somewhere, and someone, else. She was harried by work, weary of classrooms and meetings and tiresome visits from government officials.

She glanced up at the ceiling, to the crown molding, the arched entry leading into the dining room, at Mother's round Persian rug placed in the living area. The district government had taken pains with this apartment to insure a headmaster with family might be induced to stay at the school. Perhaps there had been a time when having a headmistress didn't occur to the school board. Now the district had one of each. Still, there was a consoling spaciousness in these rooms, providing a refuge for Nanny, and briefly for Irina while she recovered from her loss.

Olga gazed through the doorway into the dining room to admire the candlesticks on the sideboard. Even now, the memory of the dispute over the silver candlesticks—one pair for each Prozorov daughter—was distasteful. Their brother's wife was loath to see them leave the family house, and so jealous, she'd fussed and pouted and even wept, forcing Andrei to put his foot down. Even from this distance, the candlesticks shone, and Olga wondered how often Nanny polished them.

Within minutes Fyodor was tapping at the door. Olga asked Nanny to answer it, knowing it would take Nanny longer to reach the door, and in that time she could fortify herself with one more sip of tea. Nanny brought him into the room. She'd felt unusually weary all day and greeted him without enthusiasm. Nanny encouraged him to have a glass of tea. He briefly demurred with a fluttery hemming and hawing that Olga found more irksome than if he'd simply taken a glass in the first place. Finally he settled into the settee opposite, perched there, the tea balanced on his knees.

"How is our Irina?" he asked.

"Better," Olga answered. "You know she has her own small flat. She's there as we speak." The flat was not much more than a furnished room but provided Irina some privacy.

"Ah, good. She's on the mend, then?"

Olga felt suddenly touched by Fyodor's visit. He was more visibly concerned than their sister Masha who had thrown herself into an inappropriate mourning over Colonel Vershinin's departure. For nearly two weeks Irina stayed with Olga to recover. The school had granted Irina a small reprieve to attend to the funeral, after which Irina slept for long restorative hours. Whenever well-wishers other than family came to the flat, Olga gave them tea and sent them away, unwilling to wake her. Not for a moment was she fooled by Irina's brave face.

The new school doctor had attended Irina. He was young and unmarried with somber blue eyes behind a pince-nez. He came back often enough for Olga to wonder if he was developing an attachment to Irina, or the hope of one.

"They found Captain Solyony," Fyodor said.

Startled, Olga peered at him. "Where?"

"He was tangled in some weeds downstream. A fisherman found him."

She'd never liked Solyony. His disappearance and presumed drowning had caused a brief sensation, which she'd refused to dwell on. He was leaving with the brigade in any event. And since Solyony was responsible for the death of Irina's fiancé, how could any of them feel anything but relief at his fate? Shortly after the event, she'd actually heard her brother Andrei tell his wife, "He got what he deserved after that shameful duel."

"That was two weeks ago," she said.

". . . They're saying Solyony was shot."

"What? How could he possibly—"

"They suspect hunters. An accident. There was a bullet hole, anyway. Otherwise he was intact, more or less. Uniform faded, regimental sword still attached to his belt, boots and hat swept away in the current." Fyodor sighed. "Who knows what killed him? It takes only a few seconds for a man to drown."

She shut her eyes and thought of Irina. "Who will miss him?"

"Who, indeed?" Fyodor drained his glass, head thrown back, as if the gesture finalized his feelings on the matter. "I was wondering if Irina might have witnessed his death. By accident. Has she said anything?"

"Not a word."

"It might explain her condition."

"Wouldn't the Baron's death be shock enough?"

"But imagine seeing someone drown, especially someone of Irina's sensibility."

"She hasn't said a word to me."

"And who would care to ask. . . under the circumstances."

She gazed at Fyodor. Why was he so admirable in his concern for his in-laws, yet so unappealing to his wife? He wasn't an unattractive man, his hair thick and well groomed, but his strength was his nose, which gave him an attractive air of resolve until he finally wore you down. What was so incongruous on Fyodor was the sensual mouth. She hadn't noticed until he'd shaved his moustache, and then it took her by surprise. It seemed so out of place on him.

"Tell me, Fedya. Don't you feel Captain Solyony reaped what he sowed?"

When he pursed his lips, she couldn't take her eyes off them. Masha found his lip pursing pedantic, but Olga couldn't agree. Since she wasn't the Prozorov daughter he'd finally married, she felt little need to catalogue his shortcomings. Whatever they were, this was not one of them. Nanny appeared and insisted he have another glassful. He wanted Masha's company but had settled for hers, under the old ruse that schoolteachers understood each other.

Nanny returned with his tea, and he laughed, taking it out of her hands before looking at Olga. "I should have married you, Olechka."

She felt her cheeks grow warm and dropped her gaze. He'd made this joke once too often, and it pained her every time. His early interest in her now seemed so distant. She couldn't remember how, or when, she'd actually turned him away. Had she simply been too aloof, with no sense of how to encourage him? It was only after he'd taken up with Masha that Olga realized how disappointed she was. Once his interest fixed on her younger and more compelling sister, it didn't budge. She'd even convinced herself she was delighted for Masha. . . . At least she no longer dreamed of his attention or the children they might have had, but at the moment her temples throbbed and she felt oddly out of breath.

It was no secret Fyodor adored his wife. Still, Olga wondered whether it was a remarkably balanced nature or denial that caused him to overlook the fact that Masha did not love him. Masha had been impressed with him and mistook this for love, and now it was too late. Olga's heart sank for them all— one mismatched and two unloved.

"We would have made a scholarly pair!" He laughed a bit too loudly. ". . . But I love my Masha." For a moment, her heart reversed itself, and sorrow welled inside her for this lonely man. "And that's another reason I've come, Olechka." He lowered his voice as if he was imparting a secret. "Could you find some time to visit Masha? She's not well, poor thing. Not happy."

He knew why she was unhappy. They all knew. *Oh, you steadfast, honorable man*, she thought. On the day the army left, he had discreetly slipped inside the house while Masha bade her Colonel goodbye, embracing him and weeping onto his uniform. And when she continued to weep and Andrei's wife scolded her, Fyodor came to her defense. "It's all right. Let her cry. . . . Let her cry."

"I'll come Sunday, shall I? I'll bring Nanny."

Olga called to her, sitting near the samovar. "Dear one, shall we visit Masha?"

Deaf as a shoe, Nanny turned as if not quite sure someone had spoken to her and found Olga turned in her chair, smiling. "Is she well?"

"We're going to visit Sunday."

"Thank you. I so miss Mashenka."

"That settles it," Olga told him. How thin his face had become. The changes in town had touched them all. In Fyodor's case, perhaps he'd stopped eating in his worry over Masha, and she'd only now noticed. He stood and left his glass on the side table. She suddenly regretted not serving him some biscuits or bread and jam, a little English tea party, something to sweeten his day. She walked him to the door.

"We're still in upheaval," she said. "The troop departure was so sudden, wasn't it? I miss our dear doctor and . . . all our friends."

"Only time will settle things," he said quietly, took her hand and kissed it and quickly left. Olga closed the door and leaned against it.

It was Irina's fiancé—God rest his soul—who'd said that Fyodor Ilyich was the only man in town happy to see the soldiers leave.

That Friday Irina came for her at three and, reluctantly, they set out together for the old family home, now their brother's. Visiting had become a chore, lessened slightly when the sisters went together. This was an event calling for Fyodor's open-hearted willingness to mingle. Irina told her that she'd visited Masha on Thursday, to remind her of little Sophie's name-day party, entreating her to come for Andrei's sake.

"She became angry," Irina said as they walked slowly along the quiet street. "She ranted against Natasha. And what good does that do anyone? So I doubt they'll come."

"Poor dear. . . just her passionate nature, don't you think?"

"She has no work, Olya. Nothing occupies her but memories of Vershinin." Irina sighed and Olga looped an arm through hers.

"She should return to the piano," said Olga. "Practice. . . give lessons."

They glanced at each other, sharing the thought. For an instant they both seemed enchanted by the idea and looked at each other again with hopeful eyes until the glow faded. Would Masha even try? Masha wasn't a teacher. She would lose patience with young students, even older ones. She would speak her mind and say blunt things.

By the time they reached the garden of the old house, she felt heavy-hearted and in no rush to go in. When they finally entered the living room—that dear old room with its white columns—the first person they saw was not their brother but Protopopov lounging in Papa's favorite chair. Natasha flew through the room while Irina pulled back and turned her head away. Olga clasped her sister's elbow to steady her. She couldn't look at the man, either. Meanwhile, Natasha prated on about "our headmistress and our junior teacher," as if having two teachers in the family was somehow extraordinary and desirable—as long as the women didn't live at home—as if either of them would have chosen teaching if circumstances had been better.

"I miss you so," Natasha crooned to Irina and kissed her cheeks. "You are always welcome here, dear. Even to stay."

The falseness of this last remark made Olga's cheeks burn. Natasha approached, and she braced herself, kissing the younger woman on both cheeks. She suspected that what Natasha really missed was someone to complain to or lord over. Suddenly little Bobik raced through the room.

"So much bother, children," Natasha said and laughed.

She'd been away from the house too long. Both Natasha's voice and her laugh troubled her. The voice was colorless, and the laugh climbed to an upper register and stayed there pounding the air. She felt as if she were being struck.

Little Sophie, barely walking, wanting to chase her brother, tripped on the carpet and fell, bursting into tears.

"Oh, my darling, my darling," Natasha cooed. "Come with Maman. See? You aren't hurt."

Natasha looked up at the sisters with her large, satisfied eyes, and Olga wondered if her sister was thinking what she herself had just thought. Irina was gazing at the baby, now placed in her little chair. There was no Andrei in her appearance and only a trace of Natasha. Masha had more than once remarked at the choice of Monsieur Protopopov as Sophie's "babysitter." He took tea here far too often while Natasha made some excuse: "We can't neglect the chairman of the District Board. He's good for Andrei's career."

What career? Masha said once. Toadying to Protopopov? Signing papers? Gambling? Losing more of his inheritance night after night? It's Protopopov who drags him out to gamble, now that the brigade is gone. Do you suppose Protopopov will eventually own the house?

The sisters lifted their heads at the sound of a violin being tuned.

"Where is Andrei Sergeyevich?" Olga asked formally.

Natasha's eyes went blank and puzzled as if Olga had asked, *where's the samovar?* Natasha shook her head, giving her curls a little toss. Her laugh sounded forced.

"Andrushka? Oh, well, in his room, I imagine. I'm sure he'll join us eventually."

Olga glanced at her sister. Irina's discomfort was palpable. She was perched on one end of the sofa, as far removed from Protopopov as possible. They hadn't taken off their gloves, nor had Natasha invited them to do so.

"I'll fetch Andryusha, shall I?" Olga got up and walked out of the room with a sinking heart, up to Andrei's study. She tapped lightly, but he didn't hear. She tapped louder, the tuning stopped and a querulous voice called out, "Enter."

She announced herself and opened the door.

"Ah, Olga." There wasn't any warmth in his greeting, and he looked as though he hadn't slept, his face as baggy as his clothes. Olga was overcome by a bewildering emotion. What wife would allow her husband to look so shambling?

"The party is beginning, Andryusha." She smiled at him, crossed the room and kissed his cheeks.

He embraced her and then stepped away, taking up his violin and playing one long and tremulous note before lowering the instrument. It wasn't like him to be so remote.

"Who's here?" he asked.

"Irina and I have just arrived. Masha and Fyodor will be here later. Hopefully."

"No one else?"

"Mr. Protopopov."

"Of course." He raised the violin and played the opening bar of a tune so melancholy she wondered how he could bear to play it. He repeated the notes, the vibrato widening, drawing his bow across the strings so slowly it sounded like breathing.

"You know, I'm not supposed to play when 'guests' are here." He gave a small, bitter laugh. "Then I realized—no one can hear from this distance. . . . Enjoy the party, Olya. I'll come later."

He turned away, her little brother, walked to the windows and repeated the same heart-rending refrain. He continued the piece this time, and she waited until the song was finished, thinking perhaps it was Tchaikovsky. He remained facing the windows without turning back. Before closing the door, she said, "Please come. Irina would love to see you."

His appearance appalled her. His shirt cuffs looked frayed. How could a wife allow her husband's garments to go unmended? Several servants circulated through the house, although Nanny said they weren't happy. Natasha kept losing them to kinder mistresses. Natasha couldn't relax around her help but lurked and brooded and fussed at the slightest error. No one was allowed an ordinary mistake without a scene. Nanny told her that one poor maid lasted only a day because of a spot on Mr. Protopopov's wineglass. It was too upsetting to dwell on, and she felt relieved she wasn't here to watch.

Over a year ago, Natasha's threat to dismiss Nanny Anfisa had left Olga's stomach in knots and her heart in revolt. Nanny Anfisa had spent her life caring for the Prozorov children, and Olga had always intended for Nanny to remain with them, end her days with them as well. When she was offered the head-mistress' apartment, she took it without a second thought and brought Nanny with her. It pained her even now to remember Natasha's heartless comment: *Why do you keep her? She's useless. You should turn her out!*

She felt weighted down and rejoined the others in time to see Protopopov swing little Sophie high up in the air. He then lay a hand on Natasha's arm and let it linger there while Natasha's laughter hammered the air. In Olga's absence, Irina had still not removed her gloves. When she entered the room, all eyes turned toward her.

"Andryusha will join us in a bit," she lied.

Protopopov grunted and sat down in Papa's chair while Irina's eyes beseeched her.

"Still no Masha?" Olga asked and regretted it, adding quickly, "You know how she is about time. Always unaware of the hour."

"I'd think she'd want to see her niece and celebrate her name day," Natasha said with a pout.

"Don't be disappointed. She has her own troubles, as do we all."

"But isn't it a shame for poor Fyodor. The way she's carrying on."

Irina bristled. "Carrying on?"

"Everyone knows she was sweet on the battery commander —I've forgotten his name. What's his name, Olya?"

Olga was speechless and floundered.

"Masha's lost many great friends," Irina said. "As have Olya and I—all of us. Ivan Romanych is gone to Poland, not just the Colonel. All of our good friends are gone. She has every right to feel melancholy. And the Baron—"

It was too much for Irina, and she lowered her head and cried quietly.

"What did I do?" Natasha asked. "What did I say?"

Protopopov snapped to attention in one nimble move as though some inner spring swept him to his feet. He removed an immaculate handkerchief from his suit pocket, crossed the room like a dancer, seemingly on tiptoe, and offered it to Irina with a small bow. Olga drew back, amazed. One didn't expect grace in a man so large and top-heavy. His response was quick and his body suddenly fluid. For an instant he became appealing, and she had to remind herself who he was. Irina thanked him but declined, taking a small handkerchief from her sleeve. "Please don't worry," she said. "I'll be myself in a moment."

"The strain has been too much," Olga added. "Perhaps I should take you home, dear."

"But the cake!" Natasha pleaded.

"Please forgive us, Natasha dear. We'll return soon and enjoy the babies another time. As you can see, Irina still isn't well. It's too soon."

Irina's crying tapered off. Olga took her arm and nodded to Protopopov, who bowed deeply, reached out for her hand, suddenly effusive with sympathy, and kissed it.

"You must allow her feelings," he cautioned Natasha in a low, dramatic voice. "She has been widowed."

Olga glanced at her sister-in-law and realized Natasha's disappointment precluded any sympathy for Irina.

It was still daylight when they left the house, and a breeze had picked up during the short time they were indoors. In the garden the last of the maple leaves shivered on the trees. Fallen leaves rolled ahead of them before coming to rest against a paving stone or a clump of grass. They walked arm in arm along the avenue lined with evergreens their father had planted, the very trees Natasha was so eager to cut down. Now the wind moved through the firs in a low moan. Any day the weather would turn, and the first snow would arrive. It was as if the brigade had taken the remaining sun with them, leaving them with gray skies and certain winter. Olga wondered if she would have noticed the weather change sooner if she didn't spend so much time indoors. And who would have thought a visit to Andrei's would have laid them so low?

They turned onto the street leading toward the school grounds. Leaves and twigs crackled underfoot.

"Come for supper," Olga said. Nanny was pleased when any combination of sisters gathered in one room. Irina nodded.

Nanny greeted them at the door. "Was it a nice party, my dears?"

Irina removed her hat and gloves, dropped them on the entry table with a sigh, and then wilted into the old rocker that Ivan Romanych gave them before he left. Nanny brought her tea. Irina took it gingerly and rested the glass on the side table, stood to embrace Anfisa, clinging to her.

"Whenever I see you," Irina said, "I think of Father and all the good times we four children used to have. Do you know, I can scarcely remember Mother?"

"There, there," Nanny whispered. "We are still together. If not in the same house, at least in our hearts."

Nanny untangled Irina from her neck with a laugh, and Irina sat with a thump and explained, "Protopopov the Terrible was there. What more can I say?"

"And Andryushka? How is he?"

"Invisible," said Irina. She picked up her glass and stared at it.

"Yes, it was awkward," Olga said. "I went to his room to ask him to join us, but he didn't. It would have been better if he had, but who can blame him? He looks terrible. I don't think he sleeps."

Irina leaned into her hands and began to cry once more. Nanny bent over her with her handkerchief in her hand.

"Seems like everyone is offering me their handkerchief to-day." Irina took Nanny's with a sniffle. The weeping passed, and she dried her eyes and blew her nose and smiled weakly, her eyes still red and unhappy.

"Olya?" she asked. "Do you remember what you said just before we learned about Nikolai?"

She shook her head.

"We were in the garden, we three. Remember? Masha had just asked for her hat, and Fyodor went indoors to fetch it, and you said, dearest, 'Now we can all go home.'"

"Yes. What of it? We were all leaving."

"I thought you meant we could all return to Moscow. That it was time. That we were now free to leave this awful town."

"I don't believe—"

"—Don't you remember how we planned to return the year after Father's death? Nothing is as it should be because we are here. Masha doesn't play piano anymore, and Andrei cannot play, and I am so tired... I want to go back, Olya. I want to go."

"But we've lived here for so long. For better or for worse, this is our home, isn't it? You haven't been to Moscow since you were a child. How would you manage?"

Irina broke into sobs, and Olga rushed to her and knelt beside her chair and held her. First the Baron, shot in a duel, then her champion, Ivan Romanych, forced to leave with the troops. Why wouldn't she want to return to Moscow? There was a time when they all shared Irina's dream, but Olga hadn't thought of Moscow in months. What fantasy had entered her sister's head?

"Listen to me, Arisha. Don't forget what you said, dear one. You said we must live and we must work. And you are doing both. Here at the school. We two sisters together. We must look out for Andryusha and Masha and each other."

Irina nodded and wiped her eyes on Nanny's handkerchief and whispered. "Work. . . yes, work. . . . Remember what you used to say? 'Ah, to live!'"

"Winter will come," said Olga. "And we shall be busy pulling on boots and laying fires. Then spring will come and our spirits will lift as the days warm and the leaves bud. Then summer will arrive, and we'll all complain about the heat and the mosquitoes, as we do each year, as if we had forgotten them for nine months and discovered them for the first time. But there will be picnics and hikes along the river and through the woods, some with our students who will laugh and pull each other's hair ribbons. And we shall invite Andryusha to bring Bobik and Sophie, and Masha will join us and we'll drink a little wine and the air will be soft and the breeze gentle, and you'll say as you do each summer, 'What a beautiful day!'"

Early the next week, Fyodor stopped by her classroom in the late afternoon. His face drooped like Andrei's, and the skin under his eyes looked withered. While their brother grew fat with unhappiness, Fyodor grew thin. He clasped his hands behind his back and rocked on the balls of his feet. The effort to appear jaunty only made him seem less so. Would she be available for dinner tomorrow evening, he asked? Again Olga felt herself warm to him, and she wondered if she would have made him happy. Would Fyodor have loved her as much as he clearly loved Masha?

"I must attend a meeting," he explained. "I don't want my Masha to eat alone another night."

The following evening she was struck by how quiet the streets were since the troops had departed and the officers' houses were mostly empty. A few families remained, waiting to be summoned to the new post, including Vershinin's wife and daughters—one reason for Masha's continued distress.

The night air was crisp and her mind cleared. She supposed it didn't matter where one lived as long as there was work. Each day was so full she didn't think so much these days about tomorrow. She only wanted the present day to have its full measure. She also worried for Masha, always alone and with so little to fill her time. She felt as though an enormous cape, the color of night, had dropped across her shoulders, large enough to enfold her sisters and Nanny and Andryusha. How silly! She must have once dreamed the cape.

She followed Masha into the dining room. Olga sat down at the newly set place, and Varka served the soup. Steam rose in a reassuring vapor. Masha threw herself back in her chair.

"So tell me about Sophie's party."

Olga looked down at the table. "We didn't stay long. Natasha said something tactless to Irina. Then Andryusha wouldn't come out of his room, and Mr. Protopopov played host instead."

Masha put her spoon down, glowering.

"There's a good reason that overweight bear is so attentive to Sophie. Don't you think?"

"Yes, I've thought the same, but the subject is so disagreeable I can't talk about it." She gazed at the shreds of beet swimming in the soup.

"Anything to do with Natasha should be put out of mind," said Masha. "At least Bobik looks like Andrei. But the boy is terribly spoiled."

If only Andrei would take a firmer hand, but how could he? Andryusha was as appalled by a scene as the rest of them, and Natasha ruled the house by causing scenes: stomping her feet, crying out and rowing with the servants. It made her shudder, but Masha was not so finicky.

"She's changed," said Olga. "She was actually rather sweet and naïve when she first came to the house. Don't you remember?"

Masha gave her a pointed look. "No, I don't. And I think producing an heir has brought out what was there all along. . . . two children, two different fathers—"

"Masha, don't!"

"Why can't I say it? I know you think the same."

"Please, darling," Olga whispered. "Servants talk to each other."

When Masha placed her hands on the table, Olga saw how chapped they were and wondered if Masha had been leaving the house without her gloves. Her sister poked at the meat dish and the cabbage, scarcely a forkful reaching her mouth. Masha's lack of appetite only increased her own. Olga's stomach rumbled, and she reached for the bread and butter, which she seldom ate, dipping a small crust in the meat gravy and nearly swooning from the fragrance.

"Masha, have you heard from—"

"—No. . . The wife and children are still here."

"Of course." Olga chewed the meat slowly. The pleasure of the meal stood in pained contrast to the words she felt compelled to speak next. "Wouldn't it be better to make a clean break?"

Masha's look pierced her, and Olga regretted broaching the subject at all. Masha remained silent until she'd collected herself. Oh Masha, she longed to say. You were always the strongest and the most passionate. Before the Colonel left, he'd asked Olga to check in on his wife and daughters in case they needed anything. She'd visited twice. The first time she was politely received, but the second time the woman turned her away with a harsh word, and Olga decided it would be best not to return.

How she struggled to understand Masha's attraction to him. It was much easier to grasp why Vershinin was attracted to Masha. He was even older than Fyodor and could put one to sleep with his sad, philosophical talk in his gravelly voice. There had been evenings when she wondered if Vershinin would ever stop talking. He seemed so nostalgic and hopeful, yet weighted down with the drama of his family. Surely it wasn't simply the medal-laden uniform, something Fyodor would never have.

"I haven't cried since he left," said Masha. "And I won't now. Either Vershinin will write me or he won't."

The maid returned and placed a decanter of red wine on the table. Masha waited until the maid was out of the room before she reached for it and poured some in her glass, thumping the decanter back onto the table without a glance in Olga's direction. She took a sip and realized she was drinking alone.

"Olga, I'm so sorry. Please join me." She poured a second glass for her sister.

Masha had traveled so far away Olga was unsure what to say. "Masha, darling, forgive me. . . ."

Her sister lifted her head, her dark eyes boring into her.

"It's a hopeless situation, isn't it?" said Olga. "Vershinin is not likely to leave his little girls. Why not aspire to a friendship in letters. After all, there's Fyodor to consider."

Masha grabbed the decanter and refilled the glass. "To your health, Olga."

They lifted their glasses, and she took a sip while Masha drained her glass.

They were distracted by a clatter in the foyer as Fyodor entered and removed his hat and coat. At the sound, Masha's spine drooped like a collapsing reed, and she hooded her eyes with a hand, leaning for support on her elbow. The maid rushed out to greet him and take his coat.

"My two dear sisters," he said, striding toward them, rubbing his hands. "Have you been having a good time?"

Masha sat up and twirled her empty wineglass by the stem.

"Pay no attention to me, my dears. I'll slip into my study here and leave you alone."

The study was in fact no larger than a broom closet, but Fyodor was proud of it. He hovered briefly, waiting for a small word of reassurance, but Masha was oblivious, and suddenly Olga felt weighted down by Fyodor's unhappiness as well as her sister's. The maid, who'd returned to the kitchen, emerged with two cream puddings and asked if he would like a pudding as well.

"No, no, I couldn't."

"Why not, sir? There's plenty."

"Very well, then." He smiled with evident delight and pulled out a chair and sat.

Olga glanced at Masha. If only Fyodor had stayed away twenty minutes longer. Tears welled in Masha's eyes. He saw these and couldn't let it go, covering her hand with his.

"My dearest Masha. Wine always makes you sad. Perhaps you should drink less."

She gently slipped her hand away from his and stood.

"Olga, please forgive me. I've had a headache all day. But don't run away. Stay and keep Fedya company."

Masha came around the table and leaned down to embrace her. Olga held onto her, and they kissed until Masha pulled away and retreated down the short hall and into her room. The door closed with a small click.

He looked at Olga with sad eyes and shrugged while an embarrassed smile flickered across his full lips. "Ah, well."

Fyodor escorted her home. She was hard-pressed to speak of the matter that so concerned her. She'd hoped to impress on him the need to find some useful work for Masha, but her mind kept veering off onto a different track. In spite of his evident love for his wife, he didn't seem to grasp what she needed or what she felt at any given time. Masha was only eighteen when she married him, and Fyodor, the most interesting man she'd met. Olga was not convinced Colonel Vershinin was the better man, only the more ardent. Would she have become bored with Fyodor, too, had she married him? Olga couldn't imagine it. Her expectations had never been as high as Masha's, nor her passions. She was as dull and dutiful as Fyodor. She would have devoted herself to him and to their children and perhaps lived in the small home he now shared with Masha.

Olga shivered and drew her cloak more tightly around her. Who were we to challenge our fates, to weave stories of lives we might have had if only. . . ? Such a waste of time! She had a life, and it was hers alone. If it wasn't what she'd imagined when she was a young girl, then whose fault was that? Providence decided, not Olga Prozorovna.

As they walked and Fedya made small talk, the strange thoughts that had been incubating took solid shape.

"Come inside," she said when they reached the apartment building. "There is something I wish to discuss with you."

He followed her indoors. Nanny greeted them, and Olga dispatched her for tea in a preemptory tone that startled them all. "Please, darling," she added in a softer voice. "There's something important I want to share with Fedya."

The old woman tottered away in good humor, and Olga took his hat and coat and put them up. When he was comfortably seated, tea glass in hand, she went into her room and returned with her father's army Inverness and hood. Fyodor gazed at her.

"Stand up, Fedya."

He stood, and she handed him the great coat and asked him to put it on. Her father had had the traditional garment fitted with a hood to accommodate the dank Perm climate. It fit Fyodor across the chest and down the sleeves but in length was two inches short. "Nanny will lower the hem."

"Do I dare ask what this is all about?"

"Of course," she said and smiled. "I have been thinking seriously about your plight. The trouble with our Masha is this: she is a romantic. Romantics aspire to something pure, perhaps spiritual. And romantics require wooing. She is attracted to mystery and poetry and longs for what I believe is called *a soul mate*. You must find a way to play that role."

A surprised laugh popped out of Fyodor's mouth. "You want me to be something I am not? Olya, you know who I am—a schoolteacher. A man of reason. A Latinist."

"Stop! I want you to draw on a well deep inside that you do not even know is there. Surely you must remember what it was like when you first courted Masha. Only this time perhaps you must embellish."

"I'm completely confounded. What are you asking?"

"What I am asking, dear brother, is that you woo your wife again."

The puzzled expression did not leave his face. "And how does the coat figure in?" he asked finally and turned in a circle, still wearing the Inverness. He lifted his arms, resembling an enormous bat, and burst out laughing.

She helped him out of the garment and asked him to sit. "Our Masha has taken to walking along the river as far as the bridge, even along the esplanade."

"So I've been told."

"She prefers to walk in the fog or snow."

"No wonder she looks unwell . . . and I can't imagine why she wants—"

"Fedya! You're hopeless! You must think as she thinks. The weather both underscores and conceals her emotions. She is in a fog. But she adores the fog because it is . . . *poetic*. Are you beginning to follow this thread?"

He was staring at her, his great brown eyes serious. Then he smiled, a sad twitch upwards of the lips. "I would never have expected such invention from you, Olya."

She looked at him directly, pointedly, and he lowered his gaze. When he raised it at last, his face bore an expectant look, and she continued.

"You will probably find her near the bridge. The coat is your disguise. Your costume, if you will. A handkerchief over your mouth might alter your voice. The hood will conceal your face."

"Are you telling me she won't recognize my voice? Really, Olya—!"

"I've considered that . . . here." She handed him a soft, dark- blue handkerchief, one of her own. "Place it over your nose and mouth. Like so, and tie it behind"

"You're turning me into a bandit?" A laugh popped out, and for an instant she wanted to cane him like a schoolboy.

"You've also lost a loved one. Isn't that true? Perhaps, at first, you should only let her see you. Then you might approach her with concern. After all, why is a woman of her class wandering about? . . . I'm sorry. Am I being too obvious?"

He sank down into the settee and shook his head. "I can't do this. It's like asking a custodian to play the prince in a school theatrical."

"Are you so eager to lose her?"

"How can you say that?"

She'd shocked him. "It is our nature to protect the things we love. Children, trees, Nanny . . . your wife. You can do this! Think of it as an intellectual game of cat and mouse. Except make it . . . *soulful*. You are luring her back."

"'Fyodor Kulygin, the mysterious stranger'? Forgive me, but I don't know whether to weep or laugh."

⚔

3. Masha

She once considered sending a cake to Colonel Vershinin's wife and daughters but thought better of it. Before he left, the Colonel had asked Olga to look out for his family, and Olga had tried. During the second visit, the wife became truculent and called her a "foolish do-gooder, feasting on the pain of others." Truth be told, Vershinin's wife frightened her. The woman had created so much drama during his tenure as battery commander: suicide attempts, depression, constant disagreements with her husband, and public scenes. How he must worry for the children! Yet no one spoke much of the families waiting to be summoned.

Masha passed the house often and stopped once, intending to speak to a woman shaking a rug on the step, assuming it was a maid. As she approached, Masha realized it was the wife, her blonde hair tied up in a blue handkerchief, her dress protected by an apron that covered her sleeves. Masha veered away before she could be recognized, vowing not to come back.

Vershinin used to say, we must work, and only our descendants will be happy. She hadn't had an interesting conversation since Vershinin left and the Baron was killed. Olga found the Colonel a gloomy man. Yet when Masha was with him, she didn't find him gloomy, only thoughtful, and those thoughts seemed to come from a deep and soulful reserve. Was it melancholia they shared or only inadequate marriages? She was glad she had no children to neglect, and she'd stopped wondering if children would make a difference. They hadn't blessed Andrei. Children had only made his wife more troublesome than ever.

Her thoughts were muddled, and she needed to leave the house to sort them out. She called Varka and told her she was taking a walk. If Fyodor returned before she did, Varka was to serve him supper immediately. She dressed quickly, forgetting her gloves, and headed toward the river through a heavy mist. In spite of her resolve, her feet turned in the direction of the Vershinin home. It was nearly dusk, but the house was dark, and the front door stood open. A small pile of boxes was stacked to one side of the gate, which also stood ajar. Most of the dwellings on this street housed army officers' families but appeared occupied, with smoking chimneys and windows yellowed by lamplight. She was breathing in shallow bites and crossed over and stood by the fence, staring through the gate. An elderly workman appeared in the side yard, and she called out to him. "Excuse me, grandfather? Do you know if the family is in?"

"Nay, Madame. The Colonel sent for 'em. They left last evening on the coach. In a hurry, I'd say. Couldn't even bother to take all their belongings." He nodded toward the boxes stacked near the gate, and sighed. "We'll hafta send these on."

She asked if he might tell her the destination, but he shook his head. With the incurious tone of a peasant, he said he didn't know where they were going. Someone else took care of it and would return for the parcels. Her face grew hot, and her temper flew out of her mouth.

"Did you bother to ask?"

To her chagrin, he removed his cap and bowed. She was stricken with shame.

"Sorry, Madame. I'm an old man. The family is not my job, only the property." He remained stooped, cap in hands, and she cursed her temper.

"Forgive my error, please," she said. "Who then might I ask about their welfare?"

"I don't know his name. But he'll be back for these."

He pointed to the three rectangular boxes, one atop the other and tied with rope. The old man bowed again, turned abruptly and limped inside the house. She watched him go, still ashamed and unable to move, until she heard a different door at the rear of the dwelling open and close. Her surprise flattened into disbelief. Vershinin had sent for them without a word to her. When she finally turned away from the gate, she felt as vacant as the house. She drifted away and for several blocks had no idea where she was walking until she recognized Olga's building ahead. It was nearly dark by the time she reached her sister's apartment, and her ill temper had returned. She flung her coat onto Olga's settee and dropped into the old rocker, face in hands.

"Masha, what on earth?"

"They're gone. Sent for."

"Who?"

"The house is empty."

Masha looked up, and Olga hurried to the settee, pushed away the discarded wrap and sat down, reaching over to take her sister's hand.

"Tell me," Olga said. "Slowly."

And so Masha told what little she knew, and then more than she might have chosen if she weren't so upset.

"So . . . This confirms the rumors I heard in school." She patted Masha's hand. "Families of the officers are finally being sent for."

"But where?"

Olga shook her head. "Poland is all I know."

"I want to hear from him just once."

Olga rose slowly. Her taffeta skirt rustled like the dead flower stalks in the old family garden, like the dry clack of winter cattails by the river, sounds so sad she didn't believe she could bear it. Olga walked to the sideboard in the dining room and returned with a glass of tea and handed it to her.

"Dear Masha. You shouldn't hope so much."

"But hope was all I had."

"Then find a different dwelling place for your hope."

She sat up and stared at Olga, perplexed. "I don't understand you."

"Perhaps you've been given another chance."

"Another chance? Was there a first one? You're confusing me, Olya."

"A new start with Fyodor."

Her stomach sank, and she was overcome by a dark feeling, as if she'd been cut adrift from herself as well as everyone she knew. "I don't love him."

"Perhaps not, but you did at first. Or thought you did. Irina didn't love the Baron but planned to marry him anyway . . . until the tragedy. Love sometimes comes later, little one, not before."

"What drivel!" Masha jerked forward, splashing tea over her skirt. She set the glass down and pulled out her handkerchief, dabbing at the spill. "Only someone who isn't married could believe that!"

Olga turned away and walked slowly back into the dining room to the samovar. *Bite your tongue!* Masha scolded herself. No one on this earth is as kind as Olga. Her sister poured water into the teapot, waiting for the tea to steep before straining it in. Without hurry, Olga returned to the living room, sat on the settee and leaned back, gently rolling the tea glass in its silver holder between her hands to warm them.

"I always thought I would marry and have four children," Olga said. "Like us Prozorovs. I thought my destiny was to be a mother and the mistress of a busy house. . . . But that was long ago."

"Not so long," Masha said in a small voice. "It's not too late for you."

"It is too late. I'm well over thirty. But frankly, I don't care. I'm so tired by the end of the day I think how splendid it is to have silence. Time alone. No students. No sulking house staff. No quarrelsome faculty or meetings . . . only quiet."

Olga got up again and walked behind the settee to the French windows, looking down toward the misty street. The clock on the sideboard chimed five—their father's clock, rescued from the old house. The day she moved out of the family home, Olga had slipped it into her trunk, telling no one. *The one bold act of my life*, she thought. Slowly, she turned toward Masha with a weary smile.

"Your husband is a decent man," she went on. "He is bright, sometimes charming, and has an honorable profession. So what if he isn't the dashing soldier of your dreams? He adores you. Treasure that, Masha. It's something I'll never know."

By the time she left Olga's, it was dark. Mist rolled from the river and penetrated her wool wrap until she felt utterly chilled. She moved hurriedly in the direction of the river. The old agitation had returned, and there was no possibility of returning home in a decent frame of mind until the tumult had settled. What a strange fall. Instead of the usual early snow, the weather remained chilly and fog-bound. She sensed the bridge ahead and looked up. She could make out a few lanterns on barges, blurred globes glowing through the mist. She grasped the railing along the esplanade and counted the lights. They reminded her of June fireflies.

From the corner of her eye, she caught a glimpse of something dark, and turned. This was the third time she'd seen him, standing near the footbridge, a tall figure in a military cape. The garment reminded her of their father's cloak, the hood pulled over his head. She hadn't found his presence odd the first time she saw him, but the second time she became curious. She was certain it was the same man. She hadn't lingered to see if someone joined him, and in a moment of levity made up names for him: the Ghost General, the Jilted Soldier. But the battalion had left for Poland. Perhaps he wasn't a soldier at all. She only knew of the battery officers who had become family friends. Perhaps other soldiers were stationed nearby. She would have to ask Fedya.

She continued to watch him until she realized he was moving toward her. Masha caught her breath and stepped back. At a distance of several blurry meters, he stopped. She couldn't make out his face, lost in the recess of his hood.

"Madame? I don't wish to alarm you, but are you well?" The voice was oddly muffled.

"Yes . . . thank you."

"One worries when one sees a woman alone."

"I'm quite fine, thank you. I enjoy walking."

"Ah. . . . As do I. . . . Perhaps I should escort you home?"

"No, that's quite unnecessary. But I appreciate your kindness. Good evening."

He nodded solemnly while Masha turned, frightened and thrilled, and hurriedly made her way back along the river path and home.

4. Fyodor

He was afraid he'd come too close, but there was no recognition in her face. What would happen if one evening he appeared on the esplanade just as a wind blew the fog away?

On the walk back to the school grounds, he considered the probable sequence of events. When Masha alerted Varka of her departure, Varka must have run to Olga's apartment and spoken to her maid, who then dashed off to his classroom with the news: "Your missus is taking her walk." Varka would not come directly to him for fear of seeming disloyal. Besides, he doubted Varka knew any details of his playacting. What a web we weave… With a certain fluttering near his diaphragm, he'd retrieved the hooded Inverness from his classroom wardrobe and set off toward the river. He had seen her twice but had refrained from appearing curious. Instead, he'd nodded solemnly in her direction, as any officer or gentleman would do, and then departed. On both occasions, he'd managed to arrive before her, taking up his post near the bridge. This evening, however, she'd arrived first, and he felt as stealthy as the mist, hiding in the gloom until her attention was focused on the river. He slid out of the shadows and sensed her turning to gaze. He didn't look her way but moved through his role on instinct alone, for his strategy was borne of terror, not planning. He felt her watching him but continued to take no notice.

Olga had suggested he imagine a purpose his character might have for being on the bridge, such as a rendezvous with a debtor or client or beloved. He'd rolled his eyes. "You want me to play the role of a spy? Can't I be myself?" Now her remark seemed utterly sensible, and he decided thus: Masha would not be Masha but "the sad and mysterious woman." And he would imagine himself as an officer longing for a faraway home.

But this evening his heart had pounded. What if she had agreed to an escort home?

In his dark classroom, Fyodor removed the cloak. It was damp, and with a rag he rubbed it dry before placing it back in the cabinet. If he rushed he might arrive home before Masha, but now that didn't seem desirable. Varka would be keeping the dinner plates warm, not to mention the dinner. Cook would be ranting that the meal was ruined. How can you cook for people when you don't even know when they'll be home!

He pulled on his own topcoat and left the school. The mist had diminished, leaving only patches floating in the air like tattered gauze. He slowed his pace so he might compose himself before arriving on his own threshold. He'd made an effort to drop his voice, which Masha once told him rose up too high whenever he became excited. The Colonel's voice was not so pleasingly pitched, if he remembered correctly. It had a rough, raspy quality that wore on a person. But this did not seem to deter his wife who listened to Vershinin expatiate for hours on end.

Soul mates. He didn't know if this could happen within a marriage or was fated to take place outside. He'd never considered the necessity of such a person. It seemed an invention, an act of the imagination, and that was not a place where he chose to dwell. But Masha did, everything infused with imaginings of what might or should be or what one ought to believe in, ought to do. He'd once thought Masha loved him for his practicality and his modest scholar's knowledge and the life this could afford them. Perhaps she had imagined him as someone else since nowadays everything he did or said annoyed her.

He entered the foyer and removed his coat, shaking the moisture off.

Varka appeared and took his wraps. "Welcome home, sir. The missus just sat down, sir."

He did not call out a greeting as he usually did. He'd become self-conscious about his two voices—his own and the voice of his new persona, the cloaked stranger. He pulled down his vest, glanced at himself in the small hall mirror, and smoothed back his hair. When he entered the dining room, he quietly greeted his wife.

He leaned down to kiss her cheek, whispering, "May I?"

She did not pull away as she often did. Instead she looked up at him with interest. This evening she seemed less distant, more at home. Beside her plate was a small book, her place marked with a hairpin. He took his time pulling out the chair, seating himself, unfolding the napkin. Since he had begun his second role, he'd reached the conclusion that it was eagerness that put her off. With distance came mystery. Wasn't that what Olya claimed his wife craved? Fedya, could it be possible that your Masha is drawn, irresistibly, to what she cannot have? In some eyes, the unattainable fruit is the sweetest.

"Pushkin?" he asked and indicated the book.

"Yes. I never tire of him."

He picked up his soup spoon and slowly slid it into the broth. "Perhaps you would read some to me after dinner."

She looked at him, her head tilted at an angle. "You're interested?"

"It would be unpatriotic not to love Pushkin," he said. A smile flashed swiftly over her lips and was gone. "I must make more time for poetry, and not just the Latin variety. It's so easy for teachers to allow exercise books to run their lives. Don't you agree?"

A small silence opened up, and for once he did not rush to fill it but waited for her. She leaned toward him.

"I've often wondered what it must feel like to be a schoolmaster. Three of my family members are teachers, including you. Does teaching make you feel more at home in the world? More steady?"

"I can't speak for everyone. I don't know any other profession."

"You know facts, pedagogy, formulas. Your head is full of Latin. Is that enough?"

He thought briefly before answering. "On my better days I like to think we are offering something to the future, that somewhere along the way our students learn to behave properly and to think for themselves. *Non scholae, sed vitae discimus.* I suspect most schoolteachers approve of the former, but not the latter."

Masha barked out a sharp laugh. "I wouldn't have expected you to say that."

Her gaze grew intent now as if there were something she needed to know and would remain unsatisfied until she did. "But do we ever learn what's important, Fedya? If a person doesn't know why they're born or why geese migrate or why rivers run to the sea, what's the point of it all?"

Her words had all the earmarks of a Vershinin monologue, as if she'd fallen under the spell of his philosophical musings and confused these with eternal Truth.

"Masha, dear. Can we really know? Can't we accept the mystery?"

She shook her head. "I know less than ever."

Varka reappeared and placed on the table a platter of buttery potatoes and a small joint of meat. After the meal, he would request Varka bring their tea into the drawing room, ask Masha to read. At the moment, his head was in turmoil. *Come, Fyodor. Think like your homesick officer. Screw your courage to the sticking point.* He cleared his throat.

"Perhaps what you are looking for lies there." He pointed to the volume of Pushkin.

c⟞⟞⟞o

5. Olga

November

She was putting up her wrap when she heard Nanny Anfisa cough, went to the old woman's room, and peered in. Nanny never closed the door, afraid that in her deafness she wouldn't hear Olga call. Olga asked if she could bring her some honey tea.

"Nothing, child. How was our Mashenka?"

She answered briefly, coming into the small room with its narrow bed, trunk, its single chair, and small table. Nanny reminded her of a twig wrapped in bed linen.

"Shall I call the doctor?" Olga asked.

"But Ivan Romanych has left us, hasn't he?"

"No, no, dear. The school doctor."

"So much fuss for an old lady."

"Will you drink a little honey tea? For me?"

"Of course, my dear. Anything for you." Her voice sounded faint and scratchy.

Olga found the maid, asleep in the back room, and asked if she would make some lemon and honey tea for Anfisa, waiting up so that she might take it to Nanny herself. The room was too cold, and perhaps this is why she left the door open, to catch the heat from the main stove. Olga felt a draft as well and asked if Nanny had enough blankets. Another quilt perhaps?

"Nothing, dear."

The old woman's hands shook holding the cup. Olga reached over and held it for her, her arm circling Anfisa's diminished shoulders. The tea seemed to soothe Nanny's throat and relax her. Olga sat beside her in the old cane chair until her breathing sounded less ragged.

"Nanny? Do you remember me as a child?"

"I remember you all."

"What was I like?"

"Ah, Olechka. . . You were sweet and quiet and helpful . . . A very dear child."

Exactly as Olga imagined, and still it was disappointing. She'd never felt Irina's joyful fire or Masha's bursts of passion. She never played a boyish prank that she could recall, not like Andrei who'd once put a frog in her wardrobe. All she'd be remembered for was obedience.

"Nanny . . . ?"

The old woman had dropped off to sleep. Olga left the room, sent the maid away, and prepared for bed. Sometime in the night Nanny's coughing woke her, sounding far worse, a deep rattle. She lay awake, listening, until she couldn't bear it any longer. Wrapped in her shawl, she contrived to heat water for more tea. The process took her far longer than she expected, and she grew anxious. Nanny was already awake and feverish when she brought in the tea. She propped the old woman up against a pillow.

"So much trouble I cause you, Olyusha."

"Hush, now. I'm going to fetch someone."

Olga hurried down the rear stairs to the servants' quarters. The smell of cooked cabbage made her nauseated. She hadn't thought to bring a light and pressed one hand and then the other against the narrow stairwell, afraid she might fall. At the bottom of the stairs a ribbon of light glimmered under the first door. She stopped and tapped and whispered the maid's name, but there was no answer. An older woman poked her head out, finally, and inquired what she might do for her, and she explained.

"Not to worry, Madame. I'll find the doctor for you."

Olga was so relieved that she bathed the woman with thanks, unable at first to place who she was until it finally came to her that this woman was the head cook. *You have lost touch*, she chided herself. As headmistress she was so removed from the fray, no longer aware of who was who or who worked where. She'd become oddly helpless. At the old family home, she always knew. She had even carried the keys to the cupboards and pantries until Natasha demanded, as mistress of the house, the keys be turned over to her.

When she returned to the apartment, she considered whether she should summon her sisters and Andryusha and then decided she was being overly dramatic. The doctor first, but the pendulum of her worry kept swinging. Anfisa was over eighty years old, her joints and back stiffened with arthritis. Her long years of service came back to Olga in colorful images. Nanny had fed and washed and carried them all, tucked them in at night, sewn for and loved them. Was there anyone kinder than Nanny Anfisa? With Mother's illness and early death, she became their mother, and so indulgent, leaving the discipline to Father. How Nanny and Ivan Romanych spoiled them!

When the doctor arrived, Irina trailed in after him.

"Darling!" Olga exclaimed

"The maid came to me first," Irina explained. "Together we fetched Ivan Petrovich." She nodded toward the young doctor.

Olga turned back to him and led him into Anfisa's little room, observing the crucifix hanging above her bed. Surely she'd noticed it before, but at the moment she couldn't recall it and stared at the simple wood icon. She left the doctor and returned to Irina in the living room. The head cook was still standing in the doorway. Olga thanked her and pressed a few coins in her hand and asked if she would be willing to prepare whatever the doctor needed for Nanny. The cook readily agreed.

"Your maid will be here within the hour," she said, and Olga nodded, sorry that she was pulling the girl away from whatever home and whatever sleep she was enjoying. Some other servant must also have been roused from bed and sent to fetch her back.

She sat with Irina in the living room, saying little, waiting for the doctor to emerge from Anfisa's room and tell them what to do. Irina had removed her hat, and Olga marveled at her hair as if she'd never before noticed how golden it was, like the angels' hair in the church paintings. No wonder the young doctor had taken an interest in her. He'd attended to Irina during her mourning and depression. Olga sensed a relationship about to bloom and felt a strange compulsion to warn Irina against such a match. A doctor would never be at home, and they would likely always be poor.

Oh, why wasn't she able to sit still? She hadn't been seated with Irina five minutes when she felt the urgent need to ask the cook to prepare the samovar as well as a meal for the doctor. The cook left immediately. She glanced at the clock, but the minute hand appeared frozen, and she asked Irina if they should send for Masha.

"We don't know anything yet, and it's after midnight."

She couldn't get the sound of Nanny's cough out of her mind—dry and deep. More pictures came back to her—of a young Nanny swinging Irina, singing with Andrei, listening to Masha prate in her child's voice the stories and poems she had written and only Nanny would listen to. She'd taught the younger girls how to embroider, how to prepare the samovar and serve a cup of tea, how to boil an egg in an emergency, how to slice cake and cut the flowers in the cutting garden. Where had she learned all these useful lady-of-the-house things, a woman who could scarcely read or write?

Olga's nerves felt frayed, and she'd reached the point where she would rather stand than sit. Meanwhile her eyes glanced again and again at the old clock on the mantel. When she looked up, she discovered only three minutes had passed. She couldn't bear it any longer and went to Nanny's room and asked the doctor if there was anything she might do to help. He was almost finished, and she stayed to cover Nanny in her camisole and then a wool shawl. The old woman was too weak to help herself, and no man's hands were as gentle as a woman's. The lace on her nightcap had been mended, Olga noticed. Nanny never allowed an inch of lace or hem to remain torn, and Olga suddenly wondered if her own tilt toward fastidiousness had come from Nanny, not Mother. Olga prayed silently that Nanny might rest and recover.

The doctor snapped his bag shut and glanced up, gesturing with his head that they should leave the room. His bedside manner seemed a bit solemn. What he lacked in humor he made up for in care and solicitude.

"More water, dear?" she asked Nanny, who could scarcely open her eyes. She touched the forehead and found it oddly cool.

Olga left the bedside and followed the doctor out. He suggested they close the door. Olga shook her head. "I doubt she'll hear. She's deaf." But what if Nanny could hear everything? She'd once heard that the dying had acute hearing. Olga escorted him down the hallway to the living room where Irina waited, perched on the edge of the settee. When she saw them approach, Irina stood while the doctor gestured for them to sit.

"Pneumonia, I'm afraid. Clean bedding if she sweats, blankets when she chills. Make her comfortable."

Irina glanced at Olga, then back to the doctor. "Of course. Anything else?"

He sighed. "She's an elderly woman. She'll survive the infection or she won't. I'm leaving these small packets. Mix the contents with warm water or tea. They'll help with the fever and restlessness. There is so little to do in these cases."

"What cases are you speaking of?" Irina asked.

"Someone without the strength to fight back. . . . Someone old." He stared directly into Irina's eyes until she looked away. "I would contact her family if I were you."

"We are her family," Olga said and his eyes widened slightly. "There is no one else."

"Then be prepared," he said quietly. His eyes looked sad as he gazed at Irina, and Olga's opinion of him improved.

Irina left with the doctor, and Olga returned to Anfisa's room and spent the remainder of the night in the bedside chair, afraid if she were anywhere else she wouldn't hear the old woman call out. She drifted off and when the maid awakened her, Olga saw the first gray light of day gathering in the windows. She leaned over and, to her relief, found Nanny asleep, but her frail chest was heaving slowly as if straining to do its job. She took her hand and whispered her name, but Nanny didn't reply. Her mouth was slightly ajar, as if this were the only way she could breathe. A full glass of water rested on the bedside table. Olga picked it up and then put it down again. She would have to waken the old woman first. She noted for the hundredth time how cold the room was and tightened her shawl around her shoulders. Perhaps this was why Nanny had become ill, sleeping in a chilled space, without enough quilts, behaving as if the most meager accommodations were all she wanted or needed or deserved. Her humility brought tears to Olga's eyes, and suddenly she couldn't stop weeping, muffling the sound with her shawl.

Questions flooded her mind, things she'd never asked but now felt an overwhelming need to know: When did you come to us. . . ? Tell me about your life, Nanny. What did you do as a child? What did Mother look like before she died? What color was her hair. . . ? Is it true she loved Ivan Romanych as well as our father? Nanny dear, why didn't you ever marry . . . or have children of your own?

She pulled away and left to find the maid, asking her to contact Irina again and then Masha. One of them would reach Andrei while she remained with Nanny. The maid left immediately, and Olga poured herself tea. She didn't know how much time had passed when the cook let herself in through the back entrance, carrying a pan of broth and bringing a cupful to Nanny's bedside.

"It'll do her good," she said and placed it on the bedside table.

When Olga attempted to raise Nanny up, she realized she was beyond drinking soup or even water. She felt weightless, her breathing still jagged, struggling in her final hours. Olga slipped a few damp tendrils of hair under Nanny's tidy cap.

"Poor darling," Cook said. "She's already on her journey, isn't she?" The woman knelt, crossed herself, muttered a prayer and ducked out of the room.

With a handkerchief, Olga moistened the old nurse's lips with water. She hadn't expected Nanny's departure to be so swift. She remained where she was, moistening the cracked lips, unable to leave. Cook's remark had nicked her heart. No one should have to take this journey alone, and if she had to remain by Nanny's side for a week, she would do it.

So many departures in so short a time! She couldn't think of them without the deepest pain, and now Nanny. One would think they were being punished, but for what? Natasha had once carelessly said that having to care for Nanny in her old age was distracting Olga from her duties. A preposterous remark! Olga had had to get up and leave the room after Natasha said it. To his credit, Andrei came to her defense. *My dear, Olya would never let anything distract her from her duties. Besides, Nanny helps Olga around the apartment.* Nanny had cared for them all, until this very moment. Why was this so beyond Natasha's comprehension? Perhaps she'd not grown up with a family nurse. Perhaps the new merchant families in town didn't treat them like family members, the way the Prozorovs had.

Masha was the first to burst through the door. The maid muttered something to her, but Masha didn't stop, flying through the apartment until she reached Nanny's room, her cape still clinging to her shoulders. She'd come without a hat, Olga noticed, and her dark hair stood out around her head, wild and windblown.

"Olya?" Masha knelt beside the bed. "How could this happen so quickly?"

"I know, dear. . . . nothing to be done."

"Irina has gone for Andrei."

She was suddenly afraid they wouldn't make it in time. In the course of twelve hours, Nanny had been robbed of her life, and she couldn't take it in. Nanny was their fulcrum and strength, even in these last years. Masha's wrap drifted off her shoulders and fell to the floor in a puddle of cloth. She was still wearing black. Olga looked down at herself, dressed in her school uniform, a dark blue suit and white blouse, as proper a headmistress as one could be. Only the brooch was missing. She didn't remember getting dressed. How ironic that her life had come to parallel dear Nanny Anfisa's: no children of her own, with other people's children in her daily care. Oh, Nanny, did you wish it for yourself? A house, four children, gardens and meals and visitors, the full spectrum of a mother's life?

The clock on the mantel ticked as if the sound were amplified. She asked Masha if she would like some tea or something to eat. Masha shook her head, unwilling to take her eyes off their old nurse. The maid came to the doorway to report she had sent for the doctor again—for whatever good it would do, but Olga thanked the girl. Her eyelids felt weighted and dropped shut.

"Go to bed," Masha said. "I'll wake you if anything changes."

"I can't."

"But you must. I promise I'll wake you."

Suddenly Irina stood in the doorway, crossed the small space in three steps, knelt beside Masha, and whispered, "I can't believe this."

"Where's Andrei?" Olga asked.

"He'll be here."

"If Natasha doesn't bar the door," said Masha in a weary voice.

"He'll be too late," said Olga.

No one spoke after that. From time to time they looked at one another and then returned to their vigil, charting each breath, hoping for a flutter of eyelids, a smile, a final word. Occasionally, one of them got up, took a step around the room, and sighed.

Olga pulled her shawl tightly around her shoulders. She would have to send for the priest soon. . . . She'd stopped listening to the clock, listening only to Nanny.

There was a sudden loud inhalation, and the three women inhaled in unison. Nanny drew another sharp breath, and stopped. The sisters stopped, too, and waited, but there was no more breath coming in or out of Nanny Anfisa. None of them could utter a word. How strenuous dying was! How abandoned the living felt! Not once did Nanny's eyes open. Now her hand went limp in Olga's, and her mouth remained open. Finally, Irina stood and reached down and delicately closed Nanny's mouth and held it shut for a moment before kneeling down. Masha, who seldom wept, was the first to cry until the room filled with the sounds of weeping. *Poor Andryusha*, Olga thought. *Late again.*

6. Masha

Andrei had not yet arrived. *As usual, the last,* Masha thought. She was still upset that he'd missed the Trisagion service at Olga's, failing to join the procession to the church. When, ten minutes ago, they'd filed in behind Nanny's casket for the funeral, Olga whispered over her shoulder, "He won't come." The choir had already sung the first *Lord, have mercy,* and the priest was leading them in the initial chant: *Blessed are those whose way is blameless, who walk in the law of the Lord.* And still no Andrei.

Olga had taken charge, sparing no expense: the best incense, candles for each mourner and clergy and choir member, a fresh wreath laid on Nanny's forehead and a cross in her hands. Masha thought it unfair that the dead weren't here to enjoy the fuss made at their parting. But Nanny would have been embarrassed, even if no one deserved such attention more.

Fyodor clasped her arm as if he thought she'd crumble without support. If she eased out of his grip, he took hold of her again. Between her husband and the intolerable incense she was afraid she might suffocate. Again the choir sang *Lord, have mercy.* The priest chanted the second part of the Psalm while the mourners replied: *Have mercy upon thy servant.* There was no ventilation, and Masha stared in misery at the clergyman, a man she had never liked. His stained cassock stretched over a broad torso, his beard shabby and his eyebrows so overabundant they cast a sinister shadow over his face. Her thoughts turned to her knees now pressed against the unpadded bench. Why do we ask the deity to bless the dead and release them from pain while inflicting pain upon ourselves? It made no sense, and thinking on it only made her more distraught. If this were a lesson in humility, she rejected it. She'd loved Nanny Anfisa and would have done anything for her, but she detested groveling, even before God.

She glanced at her sisters kneeling in the pew ahead, their bodies rounded in prayer. She didn't know the mourners who arrived late. Servants, perhaps, like Nanny. She recognized several teachers from the school, here to impress Olga or console Fyodor, who'd displayed surprising emotion at Nanny's death. It still seemed a pitiful showing. Had the battery been in town, the church would be filled with officers. Ivan Romanych would be sitting with them, as well as the others . . . Perhaps even her Colonel.

How insufferably dull the town had grown since the army left. The Prozorovs were alone and adrift, stranded among civilians. They'd once been military children, but what should they call themselves now? Masha lifted a corner of her veil and dabbed her nose and eyes. She couldn't bear the incense much longer.

The priest completed the chanting of the psalm just as Andrei arrived, out of breath, his wife conspicuously absent. He walked hurriedly to the front and pushed in beside Olga, who lifted her head and stared through the black mesh of her veil as if she didn't recognize him. Poor deaf Ferapont trailed in behind him and stopped beside Fyodor, hat in hand, head bowed, leaning toward Fyodor who made room.

The choir took up the hymn: *O Christ-God, who from a Virgin didst shine forth upon the world.* . . . The priest began his recitation of Psalm 50, but all Masha heard were the familiar words, *make a clean heart, O God, and renew a right spirit within me.*

The funeral service stretched out painfully. She could not keep her mind on it but traveled back to the hours spent with Vershinin. Perhaps she was wicked not to be thinking of Nanny, but there was nothing she could do to stop the sweep of memory. Happiness is something we never have but only long for. How often had Vershinin said this? Perhaps as often as the priest's calls for blessings and the choir's repeated song of mercy.

She was aware of the chanting of the psalm and then the mourners' response: *Alleluia.* From time to time Ferapont leaned toward her husband and mumbled, "Whadde say?" At one point the old man was overcome with weeping, and she could scarcely hear the scripture. Then, to her relief, the choir sang again, drowning out Ferapont's sniffling. Olga had told her recently that Andrei's wife wanted the old man sacked, but Andrei refused, reminding Natasha that Ferapont worked for the District Board, not her.

Not one of them knew how to respond to Natasha's incivility, not even Andrei. His wife didn't even have the charity to come to Nanny Anfisa's funeral, sending her husband on alone. On one occasion Masha had permitted herself to stand up to her sister-in-law—perhaps a bit too bluntly but at least honestly. Yet Fyodor had chided her later. "It isn't necessary to reply to ignorance with rudeness," he'd said. How was she supposed to reply? Natasha herself had been rude. She didn't for a moment believe Natasha was ignorant, only selfish. She couldn't now remember the occasion or even what she'd said. Apparently, a Prozorov was not allowed, regardless.

Masha's attention threaded its way back to the service as the priest called the mourners forth to say their final goodbyes. She had been dreading the moment. As if reading her mind, Irina turned in the pew and gave her a sad smile. The church had grown increasingly smoky, and the old servant, Ferapont, couldn't stop coughing. Andrei left Olga's side, took the old man by the arm, and escorted him out.

Time compressed and then lengthened. People walked by them slowly and returned to their places, and then it was the moment for the family to come forth. Her legs turned to water, and for once she was glad for Fyodor's support. The four of them gathered while her husband stood back, each kissing Nanny's hands that held the simple cross. She didn't recall reaching the pew, and when she turned back to face the altar, the priest was already reciting the parting prayers, *Pardon thee, O spiritual child, all thy deeds done amiss in this life, both voluntary and involuntary. . . .* What deeds had Nanny done that were remotely amiss? Nanny's life had been a long blessing on the Prozorovs. Now an irrevocable change had taken place, a turning of the corner, but toward what?

The priest placed a small copy of the prayer into Nanny's hands. Men she didn't recognize stepped forward and sealed the coffin, hammers ringing so vigorously that she winced. Then Andrei and the other pallbearers lifted it and proceeded up the aisle and out of the church as if they were carrying a pillow. The family followed first, Olga leading the way. Eyes smarting, Masha had never felt so eager to leave a sanctuary. Outside, she took a deep breath. The air had never smelled so clean. Beside her, Irina whispered, "Oh, the insufferable fumes . . .! Now I can breathe."

The pallbearers loaded the coffin onto the wagon. When at last poor Nanny's box was positioned, the driver cracked his whip, and the ponies pulled forward along the rutted track. Suddenly, the wagon lurched and tilted. The coffin slid to the very edge, and the mourners gasped. Andrei rushed forward with another man, but by the time they reached it, the cart had righted itself and the coffin settled back. Voices behind the sisters murmured in relief. Again Olga took the lead, and the group followed the wagon the short distance to the gravesite.

Andrei drew up beside her, and Masha reached out and grabbed his sleeve. He turned and embraced her, and they clung to one another. He fell into step beside her.

"You never visit me, brother. I miss you."

He put his arm around Masha's shoulders and pulled their heads together. He had grown so stout that she had difficulty reaching his cheek. She became aware of a hollow feeling, reminding her of the day Colonel Vershinin left with the regiment.

"I'm seldom free of the house," he said. "The children require so much. . . . "

"And your wife?" She instantly regretted her tone of voice.

"Don't start, Masha. Please."

He gave her a pained look and let go of her shoulders, trotting ahead to join Olga. She didn't know why her tongue raced ahead of her good will. She'd only wished to offer support, but he was sensitive these days to any criticism of Natasha. She found it hard to be rational about the woman who had "stolen" their brother and turned him into a bloated shadow of himself. How ironic, that Natasha judged the sisters nowadays and found them lacking. Andrei had a sensitive and creative soul, and his wife was trying to shape him into something he was not—a district politician—by cajoling and manipulating and throwing tantrums.

Fyodor moved closer. "Andryusha doesn't look well," he said.

Masha nodded. "How could he? Living with that woman."

"Please, my love. Not now."

"Why is everyone shushing me today?" Her voice wobbled with anger.

He shrugged, and in that shrug she saw the Fyodor she didn't like, the same ineffectual man as Andrei. She hadn't yet become used to her husband's clean-shaven face, and without his moustache, the full and sensual mouth startled her. When he patted her gloved hand, she was afraid she might scream.

"But I'm angry, Fedya. Natasha didn't even have the courtesy to come to the funeral," she said. "That really is beyond the pale, don't you think?"

Fyodor shook his head and again took her arm. She was too tired to resist.

"Why, then, Mashenka, are you behaving exactly as Natasha might?"

Her eyes blurred, and she pulled her veil back under her chin.

In the days following Nanny's funeral, Masha grew weary of Fyodor's hovering concern, but this evening he sent word he would be late. Varka had already set the table, and when she asked if Madame would like to dine alone, Masha sat down to consider. The house felt barren. Even with Varka and Cook present she was lonely and bored.

She glanced up at the maid. Varka had turned out well, she had to admit, but was rather slow and so thin one couldn't tell her age. Young, she supposed. Fyodor told her Varka was thrilled to become a housemaid—something Masha couldn't imagine. The young woman bowed when spoken to and plodded stoop-shouldered from room to room. When Fyodor appeared, she stood straighter and moved faster. It hurt Masha to think it was only with her that Varka slouched, which only provoked unjust thoughts. Varka's face, when you could see it, was plain and colorless, her eyebrows too thin. On the one occasion Masha saw her smile, she understood why Varka didn't smile more often: her wide mouth held a jumble of mismatched teeth. Still, Masha grudgingly admired the maid's calm disposition.

"I'm going for a walk," she told Varka. "If Kulygin returns, tell him I'll be back soon."

"But it's dark, Madame."

"It's always dark. It's winter."

Masha rose from the table and went to the foyer for her wrap, calling over her shoulder, "It's all right, Varka. I don't need help."

"Remember your gloves," the maid called back. Masha sighed. Varka was beginning to sound like Olga.

She should have warmed herself first with a glass of wine, but the cold air would have made the wine go directly to her head. Her boots crunched through the packed snow as she walked through the small garden to the street. All day the sky looked as though it wanted to snow again but did not. She hastened toward the river path where gaslights stood at inadequate intervals, providing a semblance of light. A few lamps along the bridge and the esplanade, created more shadows than illumination. She hadn't anticipated the bitter cold and was thankful she'd worn her gloves. Fewer barge lanterns than usual winked off the river, and she wondered where the boats had gone. She used to stand at the railing and guess the cargo for each passing barge: *oil in that one, grain over there, housewares and muslin and fine linens* . . . .

A figure stepped out of the shadows, and she inhaled quickly. The ghost general wandered a short way up the footbridge, leaned slightly over the railing, and gazed out. Her pulse quickened, and her face grew warm. She didn't wish to appear too curious but turned her body slightly to keep him discreetly in view. She'd rather hoped he'd appear. She'd begun to wonder if it would be considered forward of her to inquire of his wellbeing, as he had inquired once of hers. Surely this tall figure, wrapped in wool, had a story to tell. An aura of sorrow hovered over him, a sorrow she understood only too well. She would like to hear of someone else's misfortune, for she was growing tired of her own. Perhaps Olga was right, but she still couldn't accept it, stubbornly clinging to the hope that Vershinin would write once the wife and children had joined him in Poland.

Her breathing grew shallow as she considered a course of action. Then, conscious that her legs were trembling, she walked slowly toward the footbridge. He didn't appear to see her come. Olga would consider her gesture the greatest folly. What if he's insane? A criminal?

"Good evening, sir," she said and stopped within three meters.

He turned, took a step back and bowed. When he spoke, his voice sounded as though his mouth was padded in cotton. "A good evening to you."

"It has occurred to me, sir, to inquire if you are well."

He gave another bow. "I'm touched by your thoughtfulness. Yes, I'm well. *Compos mentis*, as they say..." He cleared his throat. "I find great solace here at the river. I grew up beside a different river."

"So did I! In Moscow. . . . And you? Tell me."

"St. Petersburg. On the banks of the great Neva."

"How thrilling. But you're a long way from home."

"Indeed. But it is not always in our power to choose where we reside."

"I guess you to be a military man. My father was a military man."

"Then you must understand the soldier's peripatetic life."

"Somewhat. I would prefer to be in Moscow."

"And I would prefer St. Petersburg. But I take solace here. There is majesty in the Kama, in any river. . . . A sense that you are connected with all the water in the world as well as your homeland."

"I've never thought of it quite that way. . . . But we're too provincial here." Had she become so dull that the only things to come out of her mouth were pettish complaints? If she'd been speaking with someone she knew, she'd be ashamed.

"Are you assuming," he asked, "that each and every resident of a great city is a sophisticate? I can assure you, dear lady, they are not. Peasants and merchants live everywhere."

"But what of culture? Here we make do with second-rate everything. It's discouraging."

"Ah, I don't have an answer. Perhaps it's a question of access. Of distance. Given the same opportunities as a Muscovite, perhaps the musicians and actors of our small city would do just as well."

"I thought all the soldiers had left," she said abruptly.

"I am retired."

"And elected to stay?"

"St. Petersburg is a great distance away."

"I understand. . . . I imagine you've seen the Bronze Horseman then."

". . . Of course."

"Oh, do describe it for me!"

The man fell silent and turned away from her briefly. She had yet to see his face and did not wish to stare. His hood was pulled forward so severely, the face seemed to reside like a marble bust in a recessed alcove. Perhaps he suffered a disfiguring scar—that she could understand.

"What can one say?" he said finally. "It has remained steadfast through weather and warfare. The symbol of our great city."

Pushkin had been in her mind from the moment he mentioned St Petersburg. She searched her mind and found the opening scrap of the poem she'd learned so long ago. "'Alone, upon a sea-washed shore, he stood—'" she quoted.

"'His thoughts aloft,'" the man replied, "'his gaze far off.'"

"And gazed afar," the man replied. "The northern river sped on its wide course him before."

She was suddenly in high school again, required to declaim an opening passage that a classmate completed. And when everyone had grown and graduated, the same call and response took place at dinner tables and drinking establishments throughout the nation. What was it Fedya recently said? *Non scholae, sed vitae discimus.*

"Someone I know once said it was unpatriotic not to love Pushkin."

The ghost general laughed for the first time, a high-pitched chuckle, a sound she thought she recognized from another place.

"*Thee I loved,*" she recited, the first poem that came to mind. "*Not yet love perhaps is in my heart entirely quenched.*"

"*But trouble let it thee no more,*" he replied "*Thee to grieve with naught I wish.*"

"*Silent, hopeless thee I loved,*" she answered. "*by fear tormented, now by jealousy.*"

"So sincere my love, so tender," he concluded. "May God the like thee grant from another. . . .' You see?" he said. "It doesn't matter where you live. We Russians learn the same poems."

This is not what she wanted to hear, and she felt herself plunge down into that dark place of discontent. How tired she was of that dreary hole! She turned away.

"I've upset you," he said quickly. "Forgive me. I only meant to console."

"You did console. For a few moments I could believe there were still civilized people in this town. Thank you . . . I must go."

Salt stung her eyes as Vershinin's words filled her heart: *Except for you I have no one—absolutely no one. . . . I even dream about you... You are the most splendid woman. . . ."*

Masha nodded her farewell to the man and walked quickly away from the esplanade and the bridge, taking the lesser river path until it cut through the birch woods and onto the road home.

7. Fyodor

His forehead felt moist. He'd begun to perspire the moment she quoted Pushkin. Fyodor untied the handkerchief covering his nose and mouth—like a wretched highwayman—and wiped his face. His head was hot, flushed from the effort of maintaining the disguise. When she mentioned the famous statue he thought his heart would stop. What did he know of the Bronze Horseman except what everyone knew: it was large and bronze? Catherine the Great's tribute to her famed predecessor, Peter, dressed as a Roman on a rearing horse. In a school primer an etching of the horseman accompanied Pushkin's eponymous poem all schoolchildren read, committing scraps to memory. *Non scholae, sed vitae discimus.* Not for school but for life we learn. He'd always had a good memory, which he attributed to the Latin, but never before had he been so grateful for it.

Yet he'd upset her at the end, and he couldn't discern why. All the Prozorovs believed that their stay in Perm was temporary, in spite of the fact they had lived here for fifteen years. What did his wife remember of Moscow except a young girl's burnished memories of landmarks that had surely changed? Hadn't their own town grown? Hadn't it prospered? He had always been a contented man—with his town, his work, his wife, even the small house subsidized by the government. He enjoyed his in-laws, even his students, less so his colleagues but that was to be expected—faculty envy, he supposed, but they meant well for the most part. His policy had always been to remain on good terms with all men, even if his wife disapproved.

For the first time he deliberately pondered Masha's unhappiness and was unprepared for the pain. Her sorrow seemed to come from some obscure, subterranean source only briefly ameliorated by passing fancies. Surely Vershinin was one of those distractions. Olga spoke of soul mates, and he was troubled that Masha had made of Vershinin such a person. Vershinin was so unhappily married, no wonder he had turned to Masha. Had Masha not been there, the colonel would have found someone else equally sympathetic— educated, musical, honest, and bored. Olga had confided her opinion that the colonel would not have time to correspond, that he had "moved on" of necessity. But what of Masha? Clearly she had not moved on. Perhaps she only needed more time to heal, and he must be patient.

She has no work, Irina told him, repeatedly. Without work, there is no life. But how could he coerce his wife to work? Besides, a married woman would be hard-pressed to find a position in this town, unless she ran a business, and it was as likely for a Prozorov to run a business as it was for geese to fly north in winter. If only she had continued her music. . . . He did not know how long it had been since Masha had played. She'd once performed lovely duets with the Baron.

The school was dark by the time he reached it, except for the headmistress's room where a light shone. Poor Olga, whatever life she might have had was eclipsed long ago by her school life. He entered his own room and lit a lamp, methodically wiped the cloak with a rag until it felt dry and hung it up before putting on his own topcoat. Just as he left, he grabbed a stack of exercise books from his desk. His alibi.

Thee I loved; not yet love perhaps is,
In my heart entirely quenched. . . .

Masha had shoved Pushkin into his mind, and now he couldn't rid himself of the man. Of course, he loved her still. The flame would never be extinguished. A man must remain loyal to his wife, regardless. There were different lines from Pushkin he liked more, from the more mature, less rapturous poems, but his wife preferred the poems from the heart, penned by a very young poet.

The front gate squealed as he pushed it open and closed. In the foyer he removed his hat and coat and gazed at himself in the small mirror, scrutinizing his face. The mustache was showing signs of life. Masha had done nothing but complain since he shaved it off. *Why do you do everything the headmaster does? A shaved face does not suit you.* Well, the headmaster was still clean-shaven, an absurd statement of fashion from that redoubtable old man. He, Fyodor Ilyich Kulygin, would reclaim his facial hair because he loved his Masha. The maid's face suddenly appeared beside his in the mirror, and he turned away quickly.

"Let me help you, sir."

A smiling Varka took the coat out of his hands, and he thanked her. What a comfort to find one pleasant voice in his house, one kind word.

"The missus is waiting for you in the drawing room."

"You mean she hasn't eaten?" It was after nine.

"No, sir. . . . I'll bring the soup directly."

Cook would not be happy. He went in and found Masha seated in the brocaded chair, reading. She looked up when he entered the room.

"My dear, you must be famished."

"I wasn't hungry. I thought I'd wait."

He made a show of putting the stack of exercise books down on a side table. "I'll return to these after dinner."

"Shall we?" She rose and walked slowly toward the dining room. He grabbed her hand as she passed, and brushed it with his lips before letting it go, following her into the dining room. At the table, he pulled out her chair, waiting until she was comfortably seated. He wanted to touch her but pulled his hands back before his fingers reached her shoulders. The last time he attempted to caress her neck and shoulders she complained that his hands were cold. *Don't, Fedya. I can't bear it.* Slowly he seated himself, reached out to the decanter of wine, and poured them each a glass.

"To you, my dear." He raised his glass and sipped.

"I've had the most interesting series of encounters," she said at last.

"Oh? Tell me." His back grew tense.

"In the last month, over the course of several evening walks, I encountered a man who turned out to be a retired officer."

She was gazing at him with unusual intensity. . . or perhaps it was only his imagination.

"Do any batteries remain in town?" she asked.

"None I know of. But I heard some are stationed in some outlying towns." A complete lie.

"Ah. . . . He was from St. Petersburg, evidently. But I never once saw his face."

"How is that possible?" A vein throbbed in his neck.

"He was wearing a hooded cloak. And of course it's been cold."

"Curious, indeed."

"It reminded me of our father's Inverness. Do you remember those?"

Fyodor nodded thoughtfully.

"You know, Fedya. When Irina's Baron resigned his commission and became a civilian, I didn't like the look of him in a suit. He lost something . . . God rest his soul."

"Perhaps he gained something as well."

She gazed at him with interest. "Well, now he's lost it all."

They fell silent. On this matter, at least, they were of one mind: Irina's life was forever diminished by one gunshot.

"Andrei was right," she said at last. "All duels are immoral. But I'm glad Captain Solyony is dead. No one deserved it more."

She'd blurted out the words as though she couldn't hold them in any longer.

"Shhh, Masha. I know you say this for Irina's sake. I know how much you feel her loss, but 'two wrongs. . . .'" They say it was an accident. A duck hunter or someone cleaning a gun."

"I don't believe it, do you? Solyony killed a decent man. And someone decided to hold him accountable. What I cannot understand is why the Baron agreed to the duel in the first place. He was the kindest man I knew." Tears lined her eyes.

Fyodor looked down at the empty plate and then up. "I was there. . . . Solyony insulted his and, by implication, Irina's honor. I will spare you the exact words since they're not fit for any woman's ears. Captain Solyony imagined himself in love with Irina, you know. And when he insulted the Baron. . . . Of course the Baron could not allow anyone to soil our sister's reputation. He had no choice, Masha. With military men, honor is everything."

"But he'd resigned his commission." Her gaze made him uncomfortable.

"He was a trained officer. And he was in love. . . . *'Thee I loved you; not yet love perhaps is in my heart entirely quenched . . . .'* Even in death I imagine his love for Irina lingers."

Varka served the soup while his wife stared at him, a startled look in her eyes. He quickly refilled their wineglasses and smiled sheepishly. Remarkably, this woman, who seldom smiled, smiled back.

"It's not like you to drink so quickly," she said.

How true. He was the one who cautioned her about her consumption, throwing back one goblet after another. Now the expression on her face alarmed him: She'd become a hound on the scent.

"*In vino veritas,*" he said and took a sip. "I must fortify myself, my dear. Never have I corrected such dismal essays. It's enough to make me doubt myself as a schoolmaster." He nodded in the direction of the drawing room where he'd left the exercise books.

"You never complain," she said, and the rare smile turned ironic. "Perhaps you should read a few aloud for our amusement."

He shook his head. "The thought depresses me."

"You, Fedyusha? Depressed?"

"Seldom, that's true. It's only the papers."

He grabbed the wineglass and drank it down. How had things come to such a pass? Invention upon invention, lie after lie. He should feel remorse but did not. Quite the opposite. An unusual boldness rose to the surface.

"What would you say to a little holiday party for the language teachers?" he asked. "A soirée with champagne? Something to liven the season?"

"What holiday?"

"Our own. Something to bring a festive mood back into our faculty."

"What 'festive mood?' These people can't be something they are not, and they were never festive."

"I thought hosting a party might cheer us all up and create good will."

"Oh, Fedya! Not here! I'm not up to such an event. Forgive me for saying so, but I don't like your colleagues, except of course Olga. You'll be required to invite the headmaster, and he's insufferable. I especially don't like that old fraud of a French teacher. Osip Karlovich will bore us all to tears. He'll wrest your party away from you—or try to. Fedya, you know he's an outrageous ham. He'll become the table-talker and grow pink and drunk as the evening wears on. Picture him, please!"

She leaped out of her chair, wineglass in hand, spreading her shoulders out like that swaggerer, Osip Karlovich, moving the wineglass from side to side. "One toast and then another and then a little anecdote in French that the rest of us can't understand—which is the point, of course. 'Fe fe fe, monsieurs et madames'."

She put the glass on the table with such a thump it wobbled.

"No, I won't have Osip Karlovich in my home. Or his plump wife either. She reminds me of potato pirogie."

She dropped into her chair, threw back her shoulders and rounded her arms as if she were holding a balloon, inflated her cheeks, bobbing her head and arms to one side and then the other like a doll.

"That woman is always too rouged and overdressed. Laughing at her husband's jokes as if she hadn't heard them a hundred times. And Herr München? He can't stand the competition. He'll grow dour behind his manicured beard. He'll fiddle with his monocle as if he didn't know which eye it belonged in. Imagine him, Fedya, squinting until he cuts himself with his own eyepiece!"

She popped up again, so abruptly her chair tottered behind her. She threw her shoulders straight back and saluted, then grabbed a teaspoon off the table and clamped it against her right eye, holding it tightly in place by squinting—a trick Ivan Romanych once taught them. She saluted again with the spoon affixed to her eye and spoke in an exaggerated guttural accent.

"Herr München's back vill go ramrod straight, stiff to zee breaking point. Picture it, please! Herr München snapped in half out of envy. Herr München, zee nutcracker! We'll use his heels to open our valnuts. His salute vill break our almonds." She threw both arms above her head and clapped her hands, at the same time clicking her heels together. The spoon dropped onto her plate with a clatter.

"Herr München, the nutcracker, pretending he's qualified to teach German because he has a German name and a German monocle."

She fell back into her chair and reached out to him, her arms resting on the table. "I haven't the strength, Fedyusha. I implore you."

Fyodor threw back his head and howled with laughter until his eyes leaked. He pulled out his handkerchief and stood up from the table and turned his back to blow his nose.

"Forgive me, my love." He regained control of himself and sat down, taking both her hands, until another fit of laughter caused him to lurch up again, as if he were having a convulsion. When he finally sat down, he cleared his throat, a long catarrhal rumble that was as hilarious as his laughing fit, and she giggled.

"Who knew we humans could make such funny noises?" she said.

"Indeed!" He dabbed his eyes. "Masha, I didn't know you had such a gift for caricature. Disrespectful, of course. . . ." He barked out a cough and finally caught his wind and wagged a finger at her playfully. "'Two black marks for bad behavior!' Oh, my. . .!"

The laughter started up again, and she joined him until he was suddenly aware of the maid, hands clasped over her narrow chest, standing in the doorway. Masha followed his gaze. Varka's mouth was open in a wide smile. For an instant, they saw a loveliness they'd not noticed before, a brightness in Varka's eyes.

"May I bring you something?" the maid asked and closed her mouth self-consciously.

Masha cleared her throat. "Yes, please. I believe we're ready for the trifle."

Varka bobbed a bow and disappeared with amazing speed. Masha gazed at him, widening her eyes meaningfully. She cocked her head in Varka's direction. "Did you notice?" Masha whispered, leaning toward him. "Our Varka, how smartly she moved? And all this time I'd thought she was a tortoise."

His wife peered at him then. "Excuse me, Fedya, but. . . . have you bruised your lip?"

He lifted his hand to his mouth, then used his napkin to dab away any smear, but clearly that wasn't what she saw.

"Ah, well." His face grew warm. She was peering at the shadow growing above his mouth. "I decided the clean-shaven look didn't suit me." His eyes were fixed on his napkin, which he folded and unfolded and finally laid across his lap.

"You're growing a mustache?"

"Re-growing. Yes. . . . Do you approve?"

"If that's what you want, of course."

"I'd hoped you might." He gently touched the fringe above his lip.

"A mustache suits you, actually. I've always thought so."

He felt too embarrassed to return her gaze. While she was giving his upper lip her full attention, Varka reappeared with the dessert. They turned in her direction and exclaimed in unison, "Ahhh!"

Varka had put the stub of a taper in each dish of trifle and lit it. Masha looked at him and briefly held his gaze. Then they both turned and watched the maid's slow, illuminated progress from the doorway, across the dining room to the table. With great care, Varka placed the trembling desserts in front of them, each in turn, while the tiny candles blinked and danced.

8. Andrei

December

The jangle of harness bells drew Andrei to the study window. A troika stood in the yard with some poor child holding the horses. Had his wife known what he could see from this very window—her illicit comings and goings, and those of her "guests"—Natasha might have thought better of moving him into this back room. Protopopov slowly emerged from the carriage, adjusting the buttons on an expensive topcoat, and lumbered toward the house.

Each time the man arrived, he struck Andrei as more ursine than the week before—a heavy, bearded head atop a heavy body, balanced on startlingly narrow feet. Andrei no longer bothered to use his name. As soon as Protopopov's carriage pulled up to the house, he thought, the Bear is here again. In the beginning, Andrei had actually believed the man was extending the hand of friendship, until Natasha's fluttering laughter put such foolishness to rest.

Andrei glanced at his watch and smiled. Any minute and then, bliss!

Within seconds Andrei could make out Natasha's laugh, the sound lurching up the stairs, down the hall and into his room like an inebriated guest. He couldn't remember his sisters laughing with such wantonness, nor could he remember them dressed in bodices cut so low that one was forced to stare at a hillock of flesh. Andrei sighed and turned away from the window. Why deny it? His wife made him shudder.

Luba knocked on his door, waited for his summons, and entered, staggering under the weight of the tray. "The missus said you'd be wanting your tea, sir. She sent up the new seedcakes, too."

He thanked her and pointed. She placed the tray on the round table under the window. On her way out she stopped, folded her hands over her apron, and recited in a loud whisper, "The nursery awaits you, sir."

"Tell the nursery I'll be there anon."

A tricky business, these furtive visits, for he must time his appearances to coincide with that fraction of an hour in which Nanny Galina took his son to the drawing room to join Natasha and "guests" while baby Sophie napped. Andrei counted to twenty, slipped out of the study, moved quietly down the dark hallway to the nursery, and opened the door. Sophie's nurse was sitting in the rocker near the baby's cradle, knitting. When he stepped into the room, she looked up and smiled, and he thought he might drown in a torrent of longing. Nelly! How lovely she was! And so young, with fair hair and skin and rosy cheeks, diminutive features, and small hands.

He'd paid little attention when his wife first informed him she'd hired a different nurse for the little girl, except to regret the expense. "Why two nannies?" he'd asked his wife. "We Prozorov children only had the one."

Natasha shook her curls—had she been standing, she would have stomped her foot—and announced, *because that's the way it's done nowadays.* For six months he scarcely knew Nelly was in the house.

"My dear," he whispered and the young nurse put away her knitting and stood. He came to her and took her soft, dry hand, so unlike Natasha's moist one. "Is she asleep?" he asked.

"Yes, but the missus will call for us in less than an hour."

"We have an hour!"

"Luba will warn us."

"Come to my room."

"I daren't . . . safer in here." And the girl nodded toward the adjoining room, which she shared with Bobik's nurse.

A great peal of boyish laughter reached them. The Bear would be playing with Bobik now, and he felt a flicker of anger until he raised both the girl's hands to his lips and kissed them. She blushed and lowered her gaze. He pulled her into the small adjoining room, and they sat together on a narrow bed. He touched the blond tendrils that had escaped her cap and then ran his hands down her back, circling her waist and pulling her towards him. She trembled when he kissed her. She smelled of flowers, of spring. She was too young to be confined to the lifelong chore of nursing someone else's child. She must have children of her own. When he'd first asked her how old she was, she told him she was twenty. It couldn't be true. She couldn't have been over seventeen, eighteen at most. He'd fallen in love with her the moment she first spoke: *Sir, will you come and play for the children?* So innocent and completely unaware of how Natasha loathed his violin.

His wife had moved his study about the house, room to room, until he finally landed in the doctor's old quarters. During a rare family event, Olga protested, as did Masha's husband Fyodor: How unseemly to have the master of the house ensconced on the same floor as the scullery! In what was once a rented room! Natasha had been so abashed—the only time in their married life Andrei had seen her thus—that she promptly moved him upstairs, into the pokey room at the end of the hall adjacent the back stairs. He might have found his migration through the house amusing, except for all the bother of packing and unpacking his books and papers. What was more astonishing, laughable even, was the cause of his frequent relocations. His wife found his music-making so objectionable that she even kept him to a strict schedule, behind closed doors. Thus the back bedroom, he assumed. "Now you won't wake the children, Andryusha."

The violin didn't wake the children. How could good music do anything but soothe? He was a skillful violinist, one of the few things he felt certain of. He was allowed to play when the maid was cleaning up the tea things or whenever his wife was out of the house, which had become more frequent with each passing year. On one occasion Luba, the maid, sent a message that Natasha was away, and Andrei went to the nursery to serenade the children. When it became clear that Galina disapproved, he didn't return except when she, too, was absent. (How had he missed the fact Nurse Galina was in his wife's camp?) Of course, it was perfectly acceptable for Natasha to plunk away on the piano.

Since the Bear's arrival, the ban on violin music was in effect even if no one indoors could possibly hear him. What with the Bear's basso, his wife's robust laughter, and little Bobik's squealing and running, no one in the drawing and reception rooms could possibly hear a thunderclap. From time to time, Andrei played anyway. It was his family home, after all. Once when she complained, he'd simply glared at her and announced, "*Tant pis!*"

He would never have guessed, six months ago, that he would one day welcome the Bear's visits. In those stolen minutes, he told Nelly stories of his childhood in Moscow, his growing up, and begged her to tell him stories of herself. She was reticent at first, shy and wary, until he finally realized she was awaiting that awful event, when the master of the house forces himself upon the maid. In a flash he saw himself as that dreadful creature—that cartoon—the importuning head of household, the satyr in a silk vest. His body trembled with the shock, as though he'd just entered an ice house, and for an instant he despised himself. At that moment, he moved away to give her breathing room and said, "I will not take advantage of you, Nelly. But let me be with you, talk with you. You and the children are the only pure things in my life." She looked up, and for the first time he saw trust in her eyes. Some weeks later, when she'd slipped through his unlocked door after midnight, he believed he'd been truly blessed.

Thirty minutes passed before Luba stuck her head through the nursery door with a *ppssstt*. Nelly jumped to her feet and ran out of the side room, leaving Andrei in a state of joyful misery. Through the half-opened door he heard Nelly protest. "But the poor lamb is still sleeping. It isn't good to wake a sleeping child."

"But the missus wants her," Luba said. "Whatever you do, Nelly, do not cross the missus."

Luba left, and Andrei slipped out the nurses' chamber into the hallway and returned hastily to his study. The baby fussed as she was roused from her cradle. He heard Nelly coo and console, her voice causing his heart to leap and his imagination to soar until Sophie's cry brought him back to earth. Poor child. He knew the reason for this waking: The little girl must be paraded before the "guest." He also knew what his sisters whispered among themselves but had decided to give it no credence. How could he, when the child lived under his roof, attended by the celestial Nelly? He sat at his desk, trying to work, while his mind took off like a foxhound on a trail.

He lost track of the hour until the stomping and whinnying of horses in the yard distracted him once more. He got up and peered out onto a twilit yard. The footman held up a lamp as the Bear climbed back into his carriage. There was a time when the man drove his own carriages, but that was before financial success (and usury) put servants in every room of his house and atop his sleighs and troikas. Natasha, in a shawl, was bidding him goodbye with one-year-old Sophie in her arms. Andrei peered at the little girl. She was wearing her knitted cap, but was otherwise scarcely protected from the cold except by his wife's shawl. Where was Nelly? The driver shouted, the whip snapped like a gunshot, the mares bolted smartly ahead, and the Bear exited with the same clamor that accompanied his entry into any space.

The yard cleared, and Natasha came indoors. Andrei made his way down to the drawing room to have a word. She'd put the toddler down to play, directly in the path of the busy maid who was endeavoring to tidy up the tea things.

"Watch the child," his wife barked. "Be sure to wipe the little side table, will you? And don't be a lazybones about the carpet."

He didn't know how Luba would be able to sweep up the invisible crumbs since the little girl was tottering through the very area she had been ordered to clean. And should Luba pick her up and place her elsewhere, both mother and child would set up a wail. What really chafed was his wife's inability to utter a single *please* or *thank you*. Natasha believed her servants had nothing better to do than to connive behind her back and that only a stern demeanor would keep them in line. Unfortunately, what Natasha considered stern, the Prozorov family would consider rude. His wife must have sent Nelly back to the nursery.

Andrei swooped up the child and gave her a little toss (as the Bear often did), and Sophie giggled. How heavy she was now. He hugged her and chucked her chin and cooed and set her down away from the spot Luba was tidying.

"My love." He approached his wife. "I happened to notice that Sophie was rather exposed when you said goodbye to our guest."

"Exposed? What do you mean, Andryusha?"

"Not wrapped up on such a chilly day."

Her eyes beaded. (Never a good sign.) "Are you saying I don't care for my own child?"

"Not at all. You're a superior mother. Just an oversight, I'm sure."

"And why were you spying on me?"

He laughed out loud. "That would not be possible, Natasha. Why would I want to?"

"But you did!" (A little foot-stomp here.) "You're always spying!"

He burst out laughing again, and Sophie looked at them with an expectant smile. Papa laughing?

"Perhaps you protesteth too much, my dear."

Her face darkened, the mouth drawn down in a frown. With any other woman he would take her words as the product of a guilty conscience, but he did not believe his wife possessed a conscience. Did a fox feel guilty when it filched an egg? Did a crow brood with remorse over a scrap of carrion in the road? It was criticism that enraged her. There was a time he dreaded her fits of pique. When had he started to take this perverse satisfaction in provoking them?

Natasha's hands were balled into fists, and Luba looked at them with discomfort. He turned and lifted the baby up again, clucking and cooing, and then put her on his shoulders where she squealed with delight. Natasha's fists unclenched, and she reached out to them.

"Be careful, Andryusha."

"Of course, my love. I'm always careful."

Her large green eyes followed him while he and the babe promenaded the room. Shortly, he dropped down into Papa's old chair and turned his leg into a hobbyhorse. The little girl shrieked with glee and suddenly belched, expelling a large yellow blob, which rolled off her chin, across his trouser leg and onto the Oriental rug.

"Andryushka!" his wife wailed. "Now see what you've done! Nelly! Nelly!"

She bore down on the child who remained on his knee totally recovered and composed. Simultaneously, Luba dove to the floor to remove the ejected food.

"No harm done, madam," Luba said, glancing at him with sympathy.

"What do you mean, 'no harm done'? I'll decide that!" Natasha grabbed the child from his knee as if reclaiming a stolen garment.

"Yes, madam." Luba picked up the mess and vigorously cleaned the spot with a rag.

"My sweet darling!" Natasha clamped Sophie to her bosom. Suddenly confined, the little girl began to fuss. "Get the nurse," his wife ordered Luba, who fled the room.

A child was not just flaxen hair and sweet-smelling flesh, he thought, but a sac of fluids prone to spill at any time. Women seemed better equipped to handle these surprises. But the fact he'd made his daughter laugh was the highlight of his day. Then Nelly flew into the room.

"I'll take her."

"Please do. Her father made her spit up."

His wife released Sophie with a series of kissing sounds that Andrei found revolting. He glanced at Nelly and smiled.

Gently, Nelly took the child out of Natasha's arms and, smiling, spoke in a sweet singsong voice: *Did we have fun with Papa. . . ? Did we ride the hobby horse. . . ?* His wife wasn't listening, he realized with relief, her attention now focused on Luba who had just reentered the room. Luba stopped halfway to announce old Ferapont's arrival.

"Oh, really!" Natasha moaned. "Not again."

Not for the first time, Andrei was glad the old man was deaf, and a picture of Nanny Anfisa rose up and pinched his heart.

"Sorry to bother yous," Ferapont began. He was carrying a valise from the District Board.

"Please take him to your study," said Natasha.

He gestured for Ferapont to follow him. Had the old man worked for the Prozorov family and not the District, he would have been sacked by now, for no other reason than he was elderly and hard of hearing.

As he passed his wife, she whispered, "Why they keep him on, I'll never know."

Olga had invited him and his little sisters to have tea in her apartment. On the day of the party, he took unexpected pleasure in dressing up. Until Nelly became a factor in his life, he'd preferred comfort to style, which once took the form of sagging trousers, socks that puddled around his ankles, unstarched collars. Nowadays he took care in his appearance, even curtailing his consumption of tea cakes in an effort to regain his lost shape.

He was translating into Russian a famous English memoirist's history of London—a city he had always wanted to visit. This undertaking so impressed Natasha that she gave him some peace. The project was real—he'd even located a publisher—but progress was slow, and his ambition wavered. It was only in these little gatherings where his sisters encouraged him that he found the will to carry on. He hadn't mentioned his work to Nelly, assuming a servant girl—even one he believed he loved—would take little interest.

Andrei invited his wife to join him, but she declined, as he knew she would. Only when Olga had an official gathering did Natasha agree to come. These intimate little Prozorov affairs bored her. She claimed it made her uncomfortable that his sisters didn't know how to dress. "Oh, Andryushanchik, our dear sisters are so . . . *je ne sais quois* . . . unstylish?" Whenever she said this, he had to stifle a laugh. Olga was the one who'd taught his wife how to build a wardrobe. Yes, Masha always wore black, but then Masha looked good in black. And if Olga now wore conservative suits in her role as headmistress of the high school, that was hardly a fashion blot but an expression of her rank. It would do his wife a world of good to pull her head out of her French magazines, stop popping into the milliners or summoning her dressmaker.

He was adjusting his tie when he heard a strange thwack in the distance, a sound that yanked him back to childhood. Every Christmas, when they were children, one of the young battery officers would take him and Irina out to the forest to cut an evergreen. He waited now, but the sound did not repeat. He stared back at his reflection. His hairline had not receded, but a bald spot grew wider by the year so that his crown would one day resemble a monk's tonsured head. Not even a starched collar could disguise his thickened neck, and he felt newly resolved to take exercise and improve his life, for Nelly's sake. When the army was still here, there were so many more opportunities for exercise.

By god, he missed the officers! Masha was right. The civilians of this town were a dull lot. The only decent conversations, the only worthwhile musical evenings included the officers who once poured through this house. He felt sad and suddenly afloat, as if they'd just left when, in fact, they'd been gone for weeks.

Andrei straightened his tie, and the sound rang out again. *Thwack!*

He found Natasha planted outside on the veranda, supervising the destruction of the firs. Flabbergasted, he rushed to her and shouted to the woodcutters to stop.

"What's happening here?" he asked.

"The fir trees are coming down. They're so unsightly."

"Unsightly? My father planted those evergreens. He took great pains to provide a graceful avenue to this house and a route to the river. Look. What an impressive sight! Why didn't you consult me?"

"I told you long ago, but you weren't paying attention."

"You have my full attention now, and I'm not happy."

She whirled in his direction, hands on hips. "They're unsightly, Andryusha. Everyone thinks so." Her voice wavered.

"Who is this 'everyone'? As long as I live, there will be trees! Are you planning to kill me, too?"

She burst into tears, and for the second time in as many minutes, he was undone.

"You are not running the house," she blurted out. "You aren't taking the responsibilities and solving the problems and dealing with servants. You aren't, Andryusha!"

He lowered his voice. "Listen to me, my love. You are free to make whatever decisions you feel proper inside the house. But please leave the grounds to me."

She stomped her foot, and he quickly put his arm around her shoulders and pulled her to him. "Whoever told you the evergreens were unsightly did not tell the truth. Look at that avenue of firs! It's majestic. It improves the house . . . increases its monetary value."

He felt as if he'd swallowed ashes, but there was no more effective appeal. To his wife, the world was an enormous market, an attitude he'd failed to notice before they married.

"But the maples must go." She pointed to the loveliest trees in the garden, one living and the other admittedly dying. "I can't stand the leaves and seeds. They clutter the garden. I want flowers, Andryusha. Flowers!" She was sobbing now and leaned her head against him.

Where had she learned to cry? It was uncanny and exhausting. More vexing still was this constant rediscovery that his wife had no more love of natural beauty than a hen. And why must he rediscover daily that everything he and his sisters deemed valuable was of no consequence whatsoever to his relentlessly ambitious wife?

"Do you see that branch?" He pointed to a strong, slightly bent limb on the living maple. "Wouldn't it be grand to put a swing for the children there? We children had a swing."

Natasha turned and gazed through wet eyes at the splendid maple. In summer it shaded the veranda. Olga loved this tree.

"No, Andryusha. Swings aren't safe. Besides, I want flowers, and nothing can grow in its shade."

Later, he would regret what he agreed to: "Very well. We shall cut the old maple. All right? But promise me, we'll keep the evergreens. They won't affect your flower garden. Truly. Look. They're too far away."

He turned her toward him. She rested one hand on his chest and looked up at him. Her eyes had taken on a pleading cast. For the first time in months he felt himself tumbling into the eyes that had once been so alluring. For a moment the old attraction fluttered, reminding him of when they'd first met. She'd seemed so sweet and admiring. In those days she'd even listened to him. Andrei gazed in longing at the maples and noticed for the first time the three woodcutters standing next to the veranda. One had knelt down to whet his axe. The other two stood elbow to elbow like puppets: one man was no larger than a child and the other was tall and gangly. Both were clenching greasy caps and grinning. He did not see more than five teeth between them.

"I heard cutting," he said.

"You did?"

"Where?"

"They might have trimmed down some branches." She pointed in the direction of the nearest fir. He peered at it. The tree looked as if a giant had taken a large bite from the foliage nearest the ground. He hurried over to the men and had a word. Natasha was blowing her nose when he came back and told her he'd instructed the woodcutters to wait for his return. He was still scheduled to have tea with his sisters; perhaps he might convince Olga to return with him since Olga was the one Prozorov Natasha still respected, so long as she didn't live in the house. He reminded his wife that she had been invited as well, but she brushed this off with an impatient flick of her hand. He urged her to go indoors.

"You will have your flowers, my dear. But it's too cold for you to remain out of doors in a shawl."

She allowed him to escort her indoors and smiled, the irresistible dimples forming. He forced himself to look away.

"I can't linger, my dear. Olga is expecting us, but I'll be back directly."

"Shouldn't you take the carriage?"

He was only going a short distance, and who knew how long it would take to summon the boy to hitch up the poor nag and bring it around?

"We Prozorovs like to walk, my dear. Our father's discipline."

She stared at him as if he'd said *we Prozorovs like to crawl.* He quickly kissed her cheek, and she laughed in surprise. On his way down the veranda steps he passed the woodcutters honing their blades.

"Wait for my return," he hissed, and the tall one nodded.

The small flush of attraction vanished. He didn't trust her and found himself speeding up, eager to reach Olga's and bring her back. Before he'd gone far, he felt winded. Olga's apartment on the school grounds was a ten-minute walk, but he felt as though he was moving through custard. His good trousers chafed his thighs, slowing his pace. The tie was too tight, and his head felt hot. Before the building came into view, a sharp pain stabbed his side. He stopped and bent over.

All his thoughts gathered at the base of the doomed maples. For the six years they'd been married, Natasha had never felt the need to listen to his pleas for courtesy. *Darling, one doesn't yell at servants, one asks . . . My love, why do you want to remove the needlepoint seat on the little rocker? Ah, I see . . . . It's Irina's.* It hurt him that she wished to eradicate every trace of his family, while jealously guarding the more expensive heirlooms. What a scene she'd made over the candlesticks bequeathed to his sisters. He'd felt so embarrassed. Either she didn't know what was right or she didn't care. She did exactly what she wished to, snatching at opportunities as if they were migrating birds she could pluck right out of the air. He supposed it was the profoundest folly to expect a spouse to change. After all, he hadn't become the entrepreneur she'd dreamed of. So why did he still cling to the hope that he and the woman he'd married would, occasionally, see eye-to-eye?

When he reached Olga's apartment, he was winded. His neck felt moist. He knocked, and Olga opened it, startling him. They were so used to Nanny.

"Andryusha, darling! Come in."

Olga took his arm. Masha was reclining on the settee, her black skirt spread dramatically around her. Irina, like a blond feather rising, floated toward him. "Brother!"

He crossed the room and embraced them. "Olya, my wife is determined to cut down the maples. I've stalled her, but I fear she'll take advantage of my absence."

They stared at him. How pale their faces were, he thought. And why didn't they say something? Were they holding him accountable for this as well? They seemed to blame him for everything nowadays. His head throbbed as if a cannon volley had gone off in the room. He turned to his oldest sister.

"You're the only one who could talk her out of it."

Olga went into her bedroom and returned covered in a cloak and headscarf. Masha didn't move. When he looked at her, she dropped her gaze and shook her head. Masha had not set foot in the old home since the day the army left.

"I'll stay with Masha," said Irina. "Please come back for tea, brother. We miss you."

Sweet, considerate Arisha! He embraced her again.

"We'll be back soon, won't we?" Olga turned to him, and he replied, "Of course."

Outside the air was bitter but windless as they hurried away from the school grounds.

"I'd forgotten she wanted to cut down the trees," Olga said at last. "She spoke of it the afternoon the Baron was shot."

The Baron! He hadn't thought of Baron Tuchenbach in weeks. Now Tuchenbach came back to him with unexpected force—a man whose laugh could delight a room. He hadn't enjoyed the sound of the piano since the Baron last played it. Nor had he enjoyed a card game since Ivan Romanych left with the battery, and it was already December.

Why couldn't Natasha wait until spring to devastate the premises? How had she come to feel so entitled? Without the maples, the garden would look forlorn at Christmas. And how could dahlias and tea roses take the place of trees? What could he say of his life when all he had to show for it was loss heaped upon loss? His own helplessness pressed down upon him like a millstone.

His legs grew heavy as bricks. The remnants of last week's snowfall lay here and there like clumped and tattered sheets. Winters in Moscow seemed so much jollier, with sleighs pulling through busy roads and lights blinking and great fires in hearths and the rush and tumble of busy citizens and the aroma of roasted meat and chestnuts. Maybe this was only a child's memory playing tricks. He stopped and called out, "Olya, a moment, please."

His sister turned back, tightening her cape, her hands tucked in. In her haste, she must have left without her gloves, which wasn't like her at all.

"There's something I wish to say. In private."

"What is it?" She seemed impatient to get on, and he could hardly catch his breath.

"I'm in love. . . . I had to tell someone, and you're the only one."

She stared at him. "What are you talking about?"

"Sophie's nanny. Nelly. A precious, lovely creature."

Oh, Brother. Be careful. If Natasha gets wind of this, she'll sack the girl. And that would be terrible for Sophie."

"I know and I'm afraid."

"And does this girl love you?"

". . . I don't know."

"But Andrei. . . . A nurse? A working girl?'

"She loves music. She brings the children to the study to hear me play."

Olga looked at him with sympathy and slipped her arm through his. "First things first."

They turned a corner and a faint thwack sounded in the distance. His heart skipped a beat as they approached the house, and the fir-lined avenue came into view. They glanced at each other. Her forehead was creased with worry lines— dear Olya, old before her time.

"At least we'll still have the evergreens," he said, and she nodded.

They came around the veranda to the garden and saw the remnants of the good maple lying on the ground. Two of the woodcutters were sawing the main trunk into segments while the third man hewed off smaller limbs with his axe. All that remained standing was a pitiful, foot-tall stump he couldn't take his eyes off of.

Olga sighed. "What's the point now, Andryusha?"

"I told them specifically to wait. I told them to do nothing until I returned!"

He was pounding his right fist into the open palm of his left hand. He had never felt so enraged. He took out his pocket watch. Thirty-four minutes had passed. Anger like black smoke gathered into a dense and treacherous cloud in his head. He could scarcely see and imagined his eyes blood-red.

Olga grasped both his arms and pulled him around. "Come back with me. We never see you, and there's nothing to be done here."

He couldn't look her in the eyes or face his sisters. He knew what they thought, and he couldn't bear it. Poor Andrei. How dull he's become. All those debts, and now this.

"Not now. I need a serious word with my wife."

He couldn't bring himself to tell the truth: he respected his wife as the devoted mother of his children, but he did not like her. In a Prozorov world, Natasha wasn't a likeable woman; she was infuriating. Not once during their courtship and early marriage did he question the qualities that now disturbed his peace of mind. Ivan Romanych had laughed and said, "smitten with love and robbed of sight." Be that as it may, he would not allow anyone to speak ill of Natasha in his presence; and Masha, for one, couldn't leave the subject alone. Olga nodded, kissed his cheeks, and walked slowly away.

⊙═╍═⊙

It snowed again soon after Natasha had the maples cut down. At breakfast one morning Natasha informed him—in her new, singsong voice—that Monsieur Protopopov would pick him up in the afternoon so that they might drive together to the District Board meeting. He glared at her, finished his breakfast in silence, and returned to his room to work on the translation. He had little to say to her since she'd destroyed the trees behind his back. He shunned her whenever he encountered her in the hall or the living room or on the stairs. His mealtime remarks were directed to the help, never to her. For once he was too disgusted to fear her, and to his immense gratification, his behavior was not lost on Natasha. She adopted a girlish tone. (He was not soothed.) She trilled a little "An-DRYU-sha!" whenever she wanted to draw his attention to some little favor she'd done. (He grunted in reply.) He spoke directly to Luba whenever he wanted tea brought to his study or laundry collected. On the one occasion his wife protested, he told her cuttingly, "I think I know when I want my tea." In irritation, he'd twice referred to her formally as Natalia Ivanovna, and this produced a most satisfying silence. He couldn't say whether the lingering anger or his love for Nelly had emboldened him.

He also observed that in recent days his wife wanted him to agree to everything the Bear proposed. *It's for your career, Andryusha.* What passed for a "career," in his view, resembled a pitiful, unwatered houseplant. He still couldn't reconcile himself to her expectations. But how on earth could he toady to a man so crude he allowed food to remain in his beard after a meal? Her standards for what made good company depressed him. She'd drawn back from the army officers as if she found them rough, when in fact they were the most refined and affectionate people in their lives. She invited Olga to the house only because of Olga's status. She patronized Irina and was both scornful and afraid of Masha but would like Masha's husband Fyodor to stop by and amuse her. After all, he was a schoolmaster, and one never knew when that connection might prove useful.

But the Bear's visits were a different kettle of fish altogether and, while suspiciously frequent, at least had the satisfying effect of keeping Natasha out of his hair. Nowadays, a mischievous urge hopped up, and Andrei would play his violin as loudly as possible in spite of his wife's rules. He began to look forward to her irritation, the pink flush of her vexed face that followed "our guest's" departure. *Andryusha, how rude! And you're frightening the children again.*

Absurd! Why not finish the job and throw away all the books in the library. Give Masha the piano and remove the family portraits hanging in the hallway, toss out the oils in the drawing room and Mother's lovely watercolors on the stairs. In their place Natasha could frame bucolic pictures from her fashion magazines: a French milkmaid and cow, over here; a French hat the size of a river barge, over there; a French corset, dangling on the stairs.

The week before Ivan Romanych left with the army, Andrei told him all his tribulations as a married man. Hard now to believe he'd spoken so freely, even though he'd known the doctor his whole life. Ivan Romanych's reply startled him: *Here's what I advise, old boy. Take your hat and walking stick and decamp . . . and don't look back. And the farther you go the better.* Typical of the doctor, Andrei thought, a bachelor who took nothing seriously, a spendthrift who had lured him to one disastrous gambling table after another. And why the doctor did not stop that shameful duel, he'd never know. It was moral failure, from a man who should have known better, and it had tarnished Andrei's feelings. But with each passing month, the doctor's advice returned to torment him. He once awoke from sleep with the doctor's words on his lips: *Leave, and don't look back . . . .* His own voice woke him, and the startling awareness of tears on his cheeks. Had be forgotten Nelly?

He put down his pen when the hubbub in the yard grew too distracting: the Bear had made his appearance. Andrei deliberately dawdled. He cleaned his pen, put up the manuscript, stacked the pages, stretched to the ceiling and down to his toes ten times, and then pulled on his suit jacket. When he finally left his room, he found Natasha waiting by the door, his topcoat in her hands.

"I was just coming to get you," she said in her new eager voice. He slowed his gait, yawned audibly while thrusting his arms through the upheld coat sleeves.

"I hope you don't yawn at meetings, Andryusha."

She handed him the white neck scarf she'd purchased so that he might resemble the Bear, like matched chess pieces in their dove-gray topcoats, matching leather gloves and white scarves—Protopopov the king and Andrei Sergeyevich Prozorov, the pawn.

She held out a cheek to be kissed, which he ignored, fussing with his gloves instead, and strode purposefully out the door.

The Bear let out an enormous greeting and instructed his coachman, a man thinner than a weather vane, to hoist Andrei into the sleigh. Once he was seated, his host threw a furry bearskin rug over his knees. Andrei wanted to laugh at the appropriateness of the gesture, and the rug. Once he was settled, the Bear signaled his waiting driver who cracked the whip, and the sleigh lurched off across the fresh snow, his mares stepping smartly, as if the coachman had spent all the previous day teaching them how to lift their feet. A cold wind swirled around them so vigorously that the earflaps of his cap threatened to fly away, and his nose turned icy.

He soon realized they were not taking the usual route to the district offices but seemed to be on a leisurely tour of the countryside. He gazed around for landmarks. The Bear directed his man to stop the team, and Andrei made out the cemetery off to his right and the old church, St. Alexander Nevsky, where he had been married. His cheeks were burning, yet the Bear, unhindered by the cold, began his familiar recitation of self-importance—the man who'd traveled from rags to riches. Andrei would have liked to express his annoyance. Instead he nodded at the appropriate intervals, gazing out at the graveyard and church and the fields beyond.

When the sleigh started up again at a walk, the Bear turned to him and grinned. "Andryushka," he began. Andrei drew back at the condescending diminutive. "Look around you."

Dutifully, he looked around at the bland, snow-draped landscape.

"This is what frugal investments will bring a man."

Andrei sat up, suddenly attentive.

"Sober living can produce immense results," the Bear intoned.

The statement was so obvious that he could think of nothing to say. He knew Protopopov's intended reference and found it especially offensive since it was a sly pass at Andrei's gambling debts. And what hypocrisy! The Bear had had a hand in those debts. For the hundredth time, Andrei lamented that his wife had brought the man into his sphere. His pulse quickened as he tried to sort out Protopopov's purpose here. The only picture that appeared was that of his breathless wife holding up his topcoat and murmuring, "Monsieur Protopopov is waiting."

My, my, Mikhail Ivanych! Andrei thought bitterly. *All the waitresses between here and Moscow, and a colleague's wife as well!*

He shifted his gaze back to the unremarkable pasture-land his host had made clear belonged to him. What else did Protopopov own? What country store or trading company or brickworks? He'd never had Protopopov's, or his wife's, head for business. Indeed Natasha's practicality had been one of her attractions: an industrious and sensible young woman, so unlike his own family. Masha had dismissed her as petit bourgeois, which he'd considered unjust at the time, even if it were true. Perhaps something was missing in the Prozorov temperament, something that might place them in tune with these new mercantile times. Recently, he'd wondered if he should have taken a commission with the army after all, following in his father's path, but his father had never encouraged it. "You'll do a university course," Father said. "Or else you'll be o ur musician." Nothing had turned out as expected.

The Bear sighed, the most contented sound Andrei had heard in weeks. Andrei leaned forward, eager to seize on the man's good mood.

"Mikhail Ivanych," Andrei began. "I have a favor to ask."

"Of course." The Bear was still smiling.

"The District should provide an annuity for Ferapont's old age."

In late January, fierce snowstorms left mounds of snow until the cookhouse disappeared except for its roofs. The men dug and shoveled for days on end. Andrei remembered such days as a blessed time. Their father attached the pony to a small sled and pulled all four children around the neighborhood streets of Moscow. Here, in Perm, he remembered sledding and ice skating when the river froze. But Natasha had become protective, unwilling to let the children out of doors. Poor Bobik was growing ill-tempered.

Nelly took the children on "voyages" through the house, playing games of hide-and-seek and See What I See. He heard them in the hallways, traipsing through the house. The girl pushed Sophie in her little pram while Bobik ran ahead. Galina took advantage of these reprieves. She claimed to suffer from sick headaches, which Nelly informed him were not migraines but the result of drinking bouts with Cook. Two weeks ago, she brought the children to "Papa's study" to hear his violin and to play with his toy soldiers, shake the snow globe and pet the tortoiseshell cat. Andrei implored her to return with the children.

Today, the snow remained deep but the sun shone. Still the edict stood: the children were to remain indoors. He was buried in his books when a tap on the door distracted him.

"Enter."

Bobik flew into the room with Nelly behind, pushing the pram. "May the children spend a few minutes with you, sir?"

He rose quickly from his chair. "With pleasure!"

Andrei spread his arms for Bobik to jump into, a new game Mother would certainly disapprove of. He kissed his son, placed him in the desk chair and asked the boy, "Shall we have a little dance music?"

"Yes!" the boy trilled and clapped his hands.

Andrei removed his violin from its case and tuned it. The baby peered out of the pram and raised her arms. Nelly picked her up and carried her to her father, who kissed her, then set her down to toddle around. He did not dare touch the nurse with the children present. One innocent word from Bobik and they were finished.

"Where is Galina?" he whispered.

"In the scullery. I offered to take Bobik off her hands, and she accepted."

Gleefully accepted, Andrei assumed. He resumed his role as host.

"Here, Nurse. You and baby Sophie should sit in the rocker. Bobik may remain in the desk chair like a true man of the house."

The little boy laughed.

"And I will perform a dance."

With a sharp attack he brought the bow down across the strings and began a cheerful peasant dance, followed by a sweet Beethoven lullaby and finally one of Brahms' Hungarian rhapsodies that brought the boy to his feet to dance around the room. Nurse and Sophie clapped their hands to the music. The atmosphere was so festive that no one heard the footsteps churning down the hall until Natasha pounded on the door.

"Andryusha!"

She flew into the room without waiting for his permission. He could not let that pass. "Madame, this is my room. I ask that you respect that."

For a brief moment the cyclone of wrath stalled. She took a step back. The occupants of the room counted the seconds.

"Andrei, I go to the nursery to see my children—"

"My children as well."

"What is the meaning of this? No one is in the nursery, and I hear this dreadful scratching at the end of the hall."

"Scratching? What on earth are you talking about?"

"That... your violin."

Andrei forced himself to laugh deeply, loudly. "I thought you said you were up-to-date on the new childrearing practices: on safety and diet and two nannies instead of one. How could you have missed the information about music improving the mind— especially in children—and enlarging the soul? Classical music prepares a child to excel and makes a child a better student. I'm surprised. Surely you knew this?"

His wife's eyes enlarged, her mouth formed a small O. She was preparing to back out of the nursery when the look of indignation returned. With a vengeance she bore down on Nelly. "And where is Nurse Galina?"

"I'm so sorry to have upset you, Madame. I'm responsible. Galina is suffering a sick headache. I offered to take the children out of the nursery. Just for a brief while to let her recover. I should have asked, but the poor woman seemed so ill, Madame."

"But she is not in her room."

"Perhaps she went to the scullery. Cook prepares an herbal drink for sick headaches. Very healthy, I'm told . . . . I'm so dismayed to have alarmed you."

Nelly's eyes were downcast, her voice a thin thread of remorse. Had she not been holding the child, she might have gone down on her knees. His wife plumped up with satisfaction. She loved nothing more than a servant willing to abase herself, for Natasha hated haughty servants who made excuses.

"Have the children come here before?" Natasha asked him.

"Oh, I believe once before," Andrei said. "The last time Galina was ill."

"I don't want—"

"Stop! I do want them here. We will enjoy music. Here or in the nursery, if you prefer—"

"I do prefer."

"Very well. But on this issue I must insist. The children are not allowed to enjoy the snow. In springtime they will not be allowed to enjoy a swing on the maple bough because the maple no longer exists. Therefore, we *will* have music."

His wife stared at him. Andrei scowled and narrowed his eyes menacingly. (What a good teacher his wife had been!) Then he took a step forward. She leaned away from him.

"We shall speak of this further," she said in a muted voice and left the room.

Well into the new year, he kept mostly to his room until, in April, a sudden thaw sent snowmelt through fields and roads. Other people's children played in the streets and gardens, muddying their boots, their small sunflower faces turned skyward. For a week, the gloom lifted and the air warmed. Windows opened, and the mood in the house brightened with the lengthening sunlight. Tentative smiles replaced the servants' glum expressions while a single thought played in everyone's mind. *Spring!*

Andrei's head filled with plans. He would finish the translation, take up walking again, and visit his sisters afoot. He would encourage Nelly to relieve Galina and bring the children along.

It was time Bobik learned the names of trees and plants and birds. Natasha had no such interest and Galina was hopeless, but Nelly cared. He was poking around in the old family study—a dark and neglected room now devoted to storage—when he discovered his father's elaborately carved walking stick in the wardrobe. He didn't know how this cabinet had escaped Natasha's notice. Over the years she had taken on the Prozorov family home as though it were a patient in need of a good bloodletting. Yet there it was, hidden away, a thrilling artifact from his boyhood.

The change of season made him restless and sharpened his ardor. When next he encountered Nelly he inquired of her afternoon off, abashed that he hadn't asked before. "Thursday," she told him. "I visit my father."

He slipped a piece of paper in her hand. "Meet me here before you visit your father." He'd drawn a map, the path through the birches that would take her from the cookhouse to the old church. No one would see her.

On that afternoon, he left the house as shadows leaned gently across the soggy lawn. A mild breeze carried a rich, loamy scent, and the green tips of Natasha's bulbs poked through the mud. He strode away from the house along the conspicuous main road, his father's walking stick in his right hand, a crystalline-blue sky growing slowly bluer. He moved in the direction of afternoon birdsong and one distant, lowing cow.

When the steeple of the church loomed up, he realized he hadn't visited Nanny Anfisa's grave since her funeral. How quickly she'd passed. The angel of his childhood and the bulwark of his youth. By the time he reached the cemetery, he was awash in memories. Olga would not allow her to be separated from the family—*Where else should she rest?*—and had planted flowering shrubs around her gravesite so that they might bloom this spring. Evergreens lined the northern edge of the cemetery, and a grove of spruce sheltered one corner of the old church. A sturdy lilac marked the southern limit of the family plot.

He was eager to tell Nelly how important the nanny of his childhood had been. Perhaps she would turn out to be such a person in his daughter's life… if she stayed.

A flat boulder thrust out of the ground east of her gravesite and was often used as a bench. He sat here and looked out over the headstones and fences. He turned his head toward the old church in time to see a late strand of light strike the copper steeple, and the sight filled him with tenderness. Within moments he saw movement beyond the church, and Nelly emerged from a break in the trees, dressed in her soft green coat, the veil of her hat pulled down over her face. When she saw him, she ran toward the rock, and he rose to greet her.

"Dear one," he whispered, folding her into his arms. "Sit with me."

He took out his handkerchief and opened it for her, laying it against the rock.

"I can't stay long. My family expects me."

"Please tell me about them."

And so she did, describing the beloved mother who'd died of cholera, the father who worked for the railroad and played the fiddle, her responsibilities as the oldest. She'd gone willingly into service, and he wondered if a job in the Prozorov household was a reprieve from a small house in a dreary workmen's neighborhood. He understood now where her love of music came from, but where had she learned to read and write?

"Our mother taught us." Nelly smiled with pride and straightened her back. "And there was a small school, you know."

He didn't know. Perhaps Olga did. How had this happened, and in such a place? He felt a renewed rush of warmth for this young woman. It was easy to fall in love with beauty, but to discover the object of one's love was also admirable—he was suddenly overcome, tongue-tied.

Thirty minutes easily passed, and they were so lost in conversation he didn't notice the encroaching twilight or hear the carriage arrive. Two voices interrupted them and trailed off again. Andrei didn't turn but only registered the sound as though cataloguing a birdcall. Then a laugh ripped the air, a sound so familiar that he caught his breath and whirled around on the stone seat to peer through the gloaming. He caught a flash of pale cloth as two figures stepped down from a one-horse carriage. The first figure loomed, bulky and top-heavy, assisting a smaller one, swathed in light-colored garments. Natasha laughed again and said something in her fluty voice he couldn't make out.

"Lord, have mercy!" Nelly whispered. "The missus!"

They slid off the boulder and crouched behind it. To Andrei's horror he realized the intruders were picking their way around the gravesites toward this very seat.

"I must leave," Nelly said. "Alone."

"Run to the spruce grove," Andrei instructed, pointing. "Then behind the church and back the way you came. They won't see you. I promise."

Still crouched, they darted behind a nearby headstone, and then further back behind the boughs of a pine. Quickly, he kissed Nelly's forehead and whispered, *now*. She dashed nimbly toward the rear of the church and soon vanished into the trees. By this time his wife and her lover had reached the flat-topped rock where he'd sat with Nelly only moments before. His heart was a mallet beating against his ribs. He strained to see, peering through the spiny limbs of the pine. In the gloaming they appeared as two figures against a pale surface. The figures melded, whispered, then separated as the smaller one laughed and pushed the other away. Then the Bear reached out and pulled his wife toward him. Andrei heard a moan, then the revolting sound of smacking lips.

"Mikhail Ivanych," Natasha said in a voice pitched high like a girl's. "You are so hasty."

This he clearly heard.

"You know what I want," the Bear grunted, followed by a gravelly chuckle.

Indeed, he knew! The thought he might have the opportunity to witness this caused his mallet-heart to beat harder. A white hat sailed through the air. Then a pale garment flew after it and landed nearby while his wife tittered and panted. Grunts followed, a man impatiently wrestling with fitted garments. Suddenly, the Bear's backside reared up, hugely visible to Andrei in his hiding spot. When the Bear dropped his trousers, exposing striped underwear, all cognition stopped. Andrei ducked closer to the ground and brought his hands together in front of his lips and imitated the sound of a forest owl. *Twoo whoo. Twoo whoo!*

"What's that?" his wife said and instantly sat up.

"An owl. Pay no attention."

"Bad luck, Misha. An owl at dusk is bad luck."

"Don't be superstitious," the Bear said with irritation.

Natasha had always been superstitious, and Andrei hooted again. *Twoo whoo!*

"Stop!" she hissed.

Hunched over, Andrei darted behind a corner of the church. Shielded by spruce trees, he hooted again: *Twoo whoo!* Then, before he could stop himself, a loud, demonic cackle escaped his mouth, and his wife shrieked.

"Get me out of here," she screamed. "Out! Out!"

She sprang to her feet, and white flashes of petticoat flapped through the twilight. He could discern a figure on its hands and knees, groping for the far-flung garments. The Bear rolled clumsily off the stone, tugging at his trousers still wadded at his knees, and stumbled after her toward the carriage. The patient horse did not move as his wife flailed her arms, her coat flapping, unable to climb into the carriage without help. Up and down, up and down she bobbed and fell. Her failure to reach the seat had Andrei in stitches, and he ran quickly behind the church to the other corner where the view was better. He peeked around the brick wall and repeated the cackling, maniacal laugh.

"Highwaymen!" she shrieked.

The Bear finally reached her, gave her bottom such a shove that she flew into the carriage, then clambered up behind while she railed at him in a fury. During the course of the argument, she grabbed the reins and gave them a fierce swat against the animal's withers. Thrown backward onto the seat, Protopopov roared in anger. The carriage bolted out of the graveyard, spitting rocks. Andrei dropped to the ground and laughed uncontrollably, great chuffs of air rolling out of him until he heard one long trailing cry of misery. . . .

The streets were unbearably quiet when he finally made his way home. He felt strangely weightless, as if in the course of one evening he'd shed a hundred useless pounds. It wasn't a bad feeling, if he thought about it.

A night watchman called out, and he replied, moving into the glow of a street lamp. When the old home finally rose out of the dark, its windows lit, he stopped, acutely aware of the other road that forked away from the house toward the river. Once more he heard Ivan Romanych's rusty voice: *Put on your cap, old boy. Take up your stick and decamp. And the farther, the better.* . . . For an instant he saw himself running freely along that other road, holding Nelly's hand, and he looked with longing at the route of escape that disappeared into the twilight. Two figures appeared in the nursery window, pulling his gaze away from the silent road. Nurse Galina was holding his young son, and Andrei held his breath. She pulled a garment over Bobik's head, and then their heads became one as the boy clung to her neck. There was never another choice, was there? Not for a Prozorov. He glanced once more at the window, but the silhouettes had retreated. With a sigh he pointed the stick toward the homeward path, walked heavily through the treeless garden, and up the veranda steps.

Our Side of the Lake

(*The Seagull*)

Provincial Russia. Early fall 1897.

Paulina arrived on foot, swept up the veranda and into my front hall without knocking. Loose hair swirled around her face, and for the first time I noticed how much she'd grayed. She tore off her shawl, struggling for breath, and announced, "Do something, Genya! They've torn it down!"

I had no idea what she was talking about.

It was midday, and I was having a conversation with my housekeeper over the condition of the wall sconces—was it time to clean or could it wait? Zoya glanced at the flustered Paulina and left the room, murmuring, "I'll bring tea." I could scarcely get her to sit until Zoya returned with the tea tray, at which time she dropped onto the settee. I told her to breathe deeply, lifted her wrist, and took her pulse, pocket watch in hand. I knew her well enough to guess that her husband had laughed off whatever had upset her.

Nowadays Paulina blesses me with surprise visits. She believes all bachelors need cheering up—even if this bachelor does not recall an unhappy year in his life. In truth, it is Paulina who needs regular infusions of good cheer. It took me several months to realize Paulina's first visit coincided with Sorin's death. With the passing of my dear friend and neighbor, and Paulina's employer, she is at a loss for what to do. No household to manage, no old man to scold. So she has shifted her attention to this not-quite-old man who was once her lover.

Paulina consumed her tea in silence, sighed, and finally let her tale unfold: the new owners of Sorin's estate have dismantled the little stage that his nephew built. I confess I was taken aback. For three years, that sad and wind-battered structure stood on the path to the lake, reminding us of better days when Sorin's nephew Kostya was still alive. It had been the Summer of Little Theatricals, glorious and balmy, much like the summers of old when we year-round residents had fallen in and out of love with one another. Kostya had a literary bent and organized readings and events for our evening entertainment. He and the other young people and whoever else Kostya could recruit, including his thespian mother, read Lermontov and Pushkin or acted out scenes from Shakespeare, Molière, or the classics. As Paulina spoke, those evenings came back to me, more precious than ever.

Frankly, I don't know why the boy's mother, or Sorin for that matter, didn't have the stage removed after Kostya took his life. Evidently no one could bring himself to touch it. There the stage remained, like a ghost living in Sorin's garden.

Paulina finished her story and gave me a baleful look. "Put that in your memoir, Genya. I beg of you."

I don't know what to call this document that Paulina has urged me to write. An autobiography has a womb-to-tomb feel I find laughable. I've kept a doctor's journal over the years, an account of patients and epidemics and weather. It's nothing Paulina would consider a memoir, although I'm impressed by the number of medical anecdotes I've recorded. Besides, why rummage through the past when the present remains so engaging? Only age slows me down. When I turned fifty-eight, both Paulina and Zoya made note of my girth and formed an alliance, urging me to exercise. They're right, of course. My weight stands in shameful testament to my laziness, and I'm reminded that I once took exercise without anyone's urging. Nowadays, vests strain across my torso, and the chain on my pocket watch had to be extended.

I'd recently decided to cut back on my practice, since an obstetrician should have steadier and younger hands than mine. Fortunately, a young physician recently opened a practice on the other side of the lake, and with any luck he'll take up the slack. As soon as I made my announcement, Paulina took up the notion of a memoir, assuming that a semi-retired doctor would have time on his hands when, in fact, I've never been at a loss for things to do.

"Why don't you record our history?" she asked. "You've had such an interesting life, and you know everyone in the district!"

She delivered this final remark as though knowing every-one in the district was somehow suspicious. Any doctor will eventually meet most everyone in his district, whether he wants to or not. Nor did I like the finality of the word *had*, as if my life were over: *Poor Dr. Dorn, ready to drop in the harness.* In any event, I will not be showing Paulina these pages. I'm sure she's expecting to read them, since she was the progenitor. Instead, I will write in memory of my great friendship with Sorin, to the memory of his nephew Kostya, and last, as a tribute to the two dear girls who remain. In Sorin's house we watched not only the passing of a generation but the maturation, and loss, of our three darling children, the offspring of my friends: one to death, one to despair, and one who ran away.

But first Kostya.

Kostya had the little stage built in order to mount his own play. He was excited, and nervous. He was presenting his own drama before his famous mother. Sorin's workman Yakov had been pressed into service, sawing and hammering throughout the day. One of our other dear youths, Nina, would act. Indeed she was the only actor and would recite the play's extended monologue from the new stage, with the darkening sky and the rising moon as backdrop. Kostya's actress mother, our Irina Arkadina, had arrived earlier in the week with her lover, the writer Boris Trigorin. Still something of a celebrity and younger than Irina, Boris followed obediently in Irina's wake. For the most part, it was a mutually advantageous affair. She met his writer friends and enjoyed their bibulous parties; he consorted with theater people, fobbing off his own dramatic efforts onto this impresario or that director. Two creative and utterly self-engrossed people, feeding off one another. To whose benefit, I will never know. Certainly not Kostya's.

As for Kostya's play: the sky darkened and the moon rose. Perched on her stage "rock," Nina recited her strange hallucinatory monologue. Irina whispered. Irina coughed. Irina leaned into Boris and giggled. Then Irina made a disparaging remark, loud enough for all to hear. The humiliated Kostya dashed onto the stage and stopped the play, chiding his mother for her behavior. Never one to turn down an argument, Irina scoffed at Kostya's experimental little play. Was it satire, she asked in a huffy tone, knowing it was not? She then swelled into the role of offended diva. Was he trying to insult his own mother? If Irina had had a lick of sense, she would have gleaned that her son was only trying to earn her love. But that would have required a level of humility the great Arkadina did not possess. Instead she lavished attention on the impressionable young actress, Nina, and ignored the playwright.

And then our beloved diva unwittingly erred: She introduced Nina to Boris.

The unfortunate family drama was reenacted a year later. The impoverished Kostya, living in the country with his uncle, had taken up fiction and was having some success. At least he was selling his stories. A future seemed possible. And then Irina came to visit, dragging Boris along. Here she was, an actress in well-disguised middle age, requiring her beloved to cleave to her side since he was fond of casting eyes at younger women. Should I feel sorry for Irina, too? Something happened, unfortunately. Some catalyst that I have never parsed ignited Kostya's final despair. (I can only conclude that Boris' presence had something to do with it.) Curiously, minutes before his death, he tossed whatever manuscript he was working on into the waste can and burned it, left the study, found his hunting gun, and shot himself in the pantry. All this while elsewhere in the house, our party was enjoying after-dinner drinks and a game of cards.

We heard the *pop*, I went to investigate and found our boy. I importuned Trigorin to get Irina out of the house while I did something to clean Kostya up. The plan: he would tell her he was meeting a publisher at the hotel restaurant and urge her to come. (As if he needed to ask, since she never let him out of her sight.) After the fictitious publisher did not appear, he was to tell her Kostya shot himself. Being a coward, he did not. So that task fell to Paulina since I was still with Kostya. Meanwhile, Sorin was also kept in the dark by our third darling, Paulina's melancholy daughter. According to plan, Masha insisted Sorin stay with her and continue the card game. A kind listener, Sorin was forced, no doubt, to endure Masha's most recent lament against her dull husband and the dullness of motherhood. But that is only speculation. At the time, I was grateful that Masha provided Sorin this distraction. I do not believe Masha fully realized the person she yearned for most in this world was dead by his own hand.

We laid Kostya out on the large kitchen table while the maids tended to the unsightly mess in the pantry. Once he was cleaned, we transferred him to a hastily set up table in the back parlor. Paulina's husband Shamrayev and I changed his clothing. After that, I covered the wound with bandages, so the extent of the damage might be concealed from his mother and uncle. I then shrouded him with a sheet. When Boris and Irina returned, he escorted her as far as the parlor door and no farther. Irina walked into the room and froze. Paulina had failed to explain that Kostya was dead. He had attempted to shoot himself the summer before after his mother scorned his little drama. But in that incident, he only succeeded in scarring his forehead. Now he lay on a table in an unused parlor, growing cold.

Irina walked hesitantly toward the table and paused when she reached the edge. I stepped to the end nearest Kostya's feet. She turned to me and whispered, "What is the meaning of this sheet, Genya?" Slowly she lifted the shroud, gazed under, and in one pull, yanked it off Kostya's body and dropped it to the floor. A moment of unbearable silence followed. Then she shrieked. Irina threw herself on her son, grabbed his head, which dislodged the bandage, adding fuel to her hysteria. She fell to the floor. Boris and I leaped forward and brought her to her feet. As soon as we released our grip, she slumped back down as though her legs had turned to water. She pounded the carpet with her fists, imploring God, rolling onto her side, and grabbing the table legs to pull herself up. Since Irina's behavior was always histrionic and her moods volatile, I could not decide whether I was witnessing her finest performance or a sincere outburst of grief. Suddenly, she choked on tears and abused herself with words of astonishing self-reproach, and I realized she was dangerously shocked. I again brought her to her feet and half-carried her to a chair, pointed to my bag, which Boris quickly brought over. I pulled out a vial of laudanum and insisted she drink it then and there. (Another vial awaited Sorin.) In due course we got her to lie down. When she arose she was subdued but composed. I did not see her lose her composure again, except a few brief spells of weeping.

We buried Kostya in the churchyard. His uncle was never the same. Kostya had been his companion, his link with youth and forward-looking life. His ailments, once so imaginary, became real. After the original shock, Irina cloaked herself in the dignity one might expect of a renowned actress. She had the good sense to send Boris away, keeping the ceremony small— family, old friends, servants. Three days after the funeral, she was forced to leave for her next engagement. She sent for me in the morning since Sorin was clearly unwell. I detected a worrisome heart irregularity and promised her I'd stay. I was with him in the small parlor Kostya had turned into his study and where Sorin preferred to spend his time, as if to be in his nephew's room kept the boy close. It had rained overnight, and the day was cold and gray. A few straggling geese flew far overhead. The honking calls only added to the sorrowful mood of the house. Sorin refused to lie down in the daybed until Irina had departed. The train left at six. Shamrayev planned to drive her to the station. At four she came into the room, attired in a subdued outfit of gray, apologizing to her brother that she had nothing black in her travel wardrobe except her hat and veil. Sorin had not once removed his black armband. I offered to leave and they both looked at me with alarm. I must stay; I was needed. After all, I was like family.

Irina approached her brother's wheelchair and went down on her knees. I moved away and stood near the French doors that led onto a small terrace. She took his hands and murmured something I couldn't hear at first. Then the dear man began to cry. He assured her she was the best mother a woman could be who had no supporting husband and was required to support herself. Kostya loved her. He loved her. She kissed his cheeks, and he clung to her.

"Petya," she implored. "You must promise to take care of yourself. You must do everything Genya tells you to do. You are all I have, and I adore you. I might seem to you like an arrogant woman swirling through this insane world. But you are now all there is, and my rock. . . . "

By the time she was finished I was deeply moved and missed the boy more than ever. She rose finally and turned to me. "Genya, promise me you will come at the drop of a hat. I will return just as soon as I possibly can."

But with Kostya gone, Sorin lost heart for the great enterprise of living. We watched him fade, then rally, then lose heart again. Paulina reported that he roamed the house in his wheel-chair, lingering in Kostya's room—sleeping there, in fact—rummaging through Kostya's papers, rereading his stories, pestering Paulina with questions she could not possibly answer: do you suppose this story is finished? . . . Should I send it to Boris to be published? (Oh, the irony!) I confess I marveled he'd lasted until Epiphany, but since he had, we were cheered and assumed he'd be good through Easter at least. But that was not to be. . . .

Heaven knows how long Sorin lay suffering in his bed before his estate manager took it upon himself to drive over and fetch me. Sorin was a bit of a hypochondriac, so I should not be so quick to blame Shamrayev, but it's hard not to blame a man famous for denying his employer the use of his own horses! *Sorry, Sir. Can't. We're bringing in the hay.* Evidently, Paulina importuned her husband to send for me, accompanying him, in fact. They arrived with a great clatter, Shamrayev calling out my name before he'd stopped the horses. They insisted I come in their carriage, which gave me pause. It was a mild enough April day. I would have happily driven myself. Before I stepped into the wagon, I remember asking if he would bring me home afterward. It was ill advised to go anywhere with Shamrayev unless such matters were settled. The man had left me stranded more than once. He said to consider the matter settled, but Shamrayev is a man with a convenient memory.

When we arrived at the house, Sorin's cook was boiling a hen for broth. His maid looked pinched and worried and said, "I haven't seen 'im this bad, sir."

The bedroom was cold, and I asked her to build up a fire in the grate. When I bent over the bed, Sorin was barely conscious.

"What has happened to you, Petya? Why didn't you send for me sooner?"

He opened his eyes, glassy with fever, and whispered, "Hello, Genya."

I asked the maid for hot water bottles and more pillows to prop him up and examined him, which offered no good news. The fever and congestion I heard in his lungs were all I needed to confirm what I feared. "I stay away for a fortnight, and look what happens," I said, but he couldn't even smile at my little joke.

I'd already decided to spend the night and queried Paulina and everyone in the house: when exactly did Sorin take this turn for the worse? It wasn't like Paulina to neglect anyone's health. She tends to flutter over the simplest head cold. Throughout the night I stayed in his room, turning two chairs into a bed. Shortly after midnight, he rallied, and I heard him whisper my name. His head was strangely cool, his pulse sluggish.

"You'll see to Irina, will you?" he asked. "You'll call her?"

I told him Paulina had sent a telegram. What I did not tell him was that his sister's theater company was on tour, and we were still tracking her down.

"Will she come?" he asked, his voice beginning to fail.

"Of course, Irina will come! She's probably dashing here as we speak."

I saw the endearing Sorin smile at last. Was there ever a kinder man? Ineffective with his servants, to be sure, but controlling staff was never a skill he aspired to. For thirty years a contented government worker, he'd retired to the country, unwillingly. He missed the city, he said. But it was cheaper to live here by the lake, even if his estate manager, Shamrayev, annoyed him and left him cash-strapped. Now the household grew tense, awaiting Irina's arrival. Paulina observed, with unusual compassion, "This death may shatter her as much as Kostya's." To lose a son is an unnatural event, and brutal in its unnaturalness. But to lose a brother reminds us we are that much closer to the end. Age was always Irina's great enemy. She had perfected the art of disguise as an actress, but grief is hard to disguise and ages us.

I stayed at Sorin's bedside. By noon of the following day, before Irina could reach him, he was gone. His cook let out a heart-rending wail the likes of which I had never in my life heard from a house servant. His man Yakov fled to the barn, unwilling to say a word to anyone while he painstakingly cut and planed and hammered Sorin's coffin.

When the estate went on sale in July, I felt as if bandages had been ripped prematurely off a wound. We'd hoped Irina might keep the house for a summer dacha, but Sorin hadn't kept the property up. Irina made it clear that she wasn't willing to interrupt her acting career to oversee improvements. (Always the derelict mother, she hadn't interrupted her acting career for Kostya either.) "Not even for a week!" she told Paulina. "I can't afford it." Truth be told, Irina was unwilling to drop a single kopek to improve the house but was more than willing to take what little savings her brother left her, plus the income from the sale.

"Was there ever a woman as cheap as the great Arkadina?" Paulina's words, not mine, but true nevertheless. With Sorin's passing and Irina's abandonment of the property, Paulina has turned against the woman she once fawned over. How does one reconcile the grief-struck sister with the uncharitable actress?

One final note: Paulina's husband has importuned the new owners of Sorin's property. So he'll stay on as manager of the estate he ran for more than eighteen years. In my view, Sorin should have sacked Shamrayev years ago—not only for bullying his own employer but for being such a colossal bore. My god, the tired jokes! The clumsy puns. The deadly, unending stories of his youthful military exploits.

The new family has not yet moved in. I assume that has something to do with the remodeling that needs to take place. Shamrayev took the income and poured it back into the farm so that little was left to keep up the house.

⌒══✦══⌒

I haven't told Paulina that one of our two remaining darlings wrote me. Nina, our child of the lake, will again join the theater in Yelets for the winter season and is currently staying at the hotel in town. Nina didn't come to Kostya's funeral. When she finally learned what had happened, Nina wrote, blaming herself. I made the mistake of mentioning this to Paulina, who indeed blamed her for Kostya's death. What she really blamed Nina for was being the focus of Kostya's adoration, eclipsing her own Masha, our third darling.

Poor Masha. She was besotted with Kostya, who found her increasingly annoying. If Masha walked into a room, Kostya hurried out. Who would be attracted to a hard-drinking, snuff-using girl who dressed only in black, aspired to nothing while mooning over you, and then grew depressed as a result? She married the schoolmaster because he pestered her and because she needed an avenue of escape. But our Masha has made a career of ennui. Even though she now has a beautiful little boy, the child seems to bore her as well. Fortunately, her husband took a more prosperous teaching position elsewhere, away from his cloying mother and sisters, and from Masha's impossible father. Paulina misses her terribly.

A month or so before Sorin died, I had a talk with her. She and her husband would be moving the following week. We were all at Sorin's for dinner and cards, organized by Paulina to cheer him up, forcing a conviviality we did not feel. Masha's husband was hurrying her toward the door. They still lived with his mother and unmarried sisters. Not a good arrangement for a woman of Masha's temperament or for any young wife, in my view. Masha wanted to linger and helped herself to another glass of vodka.

"Not now," he cried in his nasal voice. "The baby, dear. We must get back."

She turned on him in fury, hissing, "Semyon, why are you always instructing me in my duties. As if I were one of your students. I wish to speak to Dr. Dorn. In private. Be so kind as to wait!"

Semyon slunk out of the parlor and my heart sailed out to her to have married a milquetoast. She turned to me tearfully, glass in hand. She brought the vodka to her lips and threw it back like a laborer. I cautioned her to slow down.

"It's the only pleasure I have," she said.

"No, you have your son. When he grows and becomes a little person, you will enjoy him more. And he will need your sober love and guidance."

She put the glass down on the sideboard and wept silently. I folded her into my arms and patted her back.

"It's no good, Dr. Dorn. No good. But we are moving Monday and perhaps that will help. At least I won't have to deal with his family."

I knew they were a trial to her. Not that they were unkind or mean-spirited, but because her husband deferred to them so much.

"Not enough Semyon to go around, eh?"

She raised her face and smiled.

"You must train him, my dear. Tell him what you want. All husbands need training."

"That's just it. I don't know what I want. Now that Kostya's dead, I don't know anything anymore."

She turned back to the buffet and helped herself to yet another drink. For a moment, I saw her as a little girl: dark curly hair, dark searching eyes that looked deep into you. She was such a serious child I remember thinking she would have been happier as a boy.

If Masha continues to drink at her current pace, she'll be dead before she's forty, but that seems to be the goal. So much for unrequited love. . . .

So I'll not be telling Paulina that I arranged dinner with Nina.

I met the girl at the hotel in town. There is a small, inadequate restaurant on the premises, and I took her there since she was reluctant to come to the house. I didn't know what to expect, and when she entered the lobby, she appeared remarkably well turned out in a fitted dove-gray suit, a pert new hat, new dress boots, a cameo brooch at the throat of a laced and pleated white blouse. I didn't recognize the cameo and commented. Her late mother's brooch, she said, one of the few heirlooms she was able to secret away with her when she fled her father's home. I'm proud of her for having made her way in the world under such painful circumstances. Of our three dear children, she is the only one who's carried on.

After the Summer of Little Theatricals and Kostya's interrupted play, a year of tumult followed. Nina ran away to Moscow to become an actress. A bad one, Kostya reported since he'd seen her perform. The sort of actress who waved her arms and shrieked. I can only assume she has made some progress in her career.

I ordered a bottle of unfamiliar red wine that turned out to be tasteless, grateful at least that the menu offered fresh local trout and bream. She struck me as underweight, but I suppose all actresses aspire to an unhealthy thinness. Certainly Irina did. Nina dropped her head slightly and smiled. A practiced gesture, I thought. Something Irina was good at, one of many contrived gestures an actress, no doubt, has to learn in order to make her way through the wolf-infested forest of the theater. But Nina's face had lost its softness, and her eyes loomed out at me. For a man who admires a certain roundness in his women, I thought her eyes looked owlish and off-putting. A consumptive's eyes.

I asked about her career. Again the practiced, head-angling, La Giaconda smile, the eyes gazing up from the slightly down-turned face, which made the eyes appear even larger. If I had not known her since infancy, I might have thought a child I'd delivered from the womb was flirting with me. I looked away, chuckled, and draped my napkin over my lap. Nina was our success story, and I told her so.

"I'm not quite a success, doctor, but I persevere. I told Kostya this when I last saw him, but I don't believe he understood."

"Perhaps you're made of sterner stuff." I did not think to ask when she'd last seen Kostya. He'd told me she did not accept visitors to her dressing room.

"Do you really think so?" She gave me a small smile. "I only know that as long as I keep working, I'm not afraid of life."

I gazed at her proudly, reached over, and squeezed her hand, saying I would like to see her act. She looked somewhat distressed and murmured, "Not yet." When, then? In a year or two, she thought. When she'd had more experience. Then she'd have better parts and would like her friends to see her.

The waiter presented the soup—spoiled by too much salt. Nina did not even pick up her spoon. I remonstrated: she must keep up her strength.

"I'm not poor anymore," she said.

From her wardrobe, I'd assumed she'd lifted herself out of poverty but wondered whether it was her theater work or an admirer that allowed her to leave an offered meal untouched. She gave me another tiny smile, as if she had to ration them.

"Ah, the look of Venus... the svelte Diana. It's hard work, isn't it? Being an actress."

The smile vanished. I had offended her, and I realized how insecure she remained in her new profession. To cover up my transgression, I quickly asked about her schedule. What parts would she be performing? She mentioned one or two supporting roles scheduled for the Yelets Theater, and one starring role, but I had almost stopped listening while the voice in my head ruminated over the wealthy patron I'd invented.

"Tell me, my dear," I said when she finally paused. "You were close to Kostya. Did you love him?"

She glanced at me, but her eyes wandered somewhere beyond my shoulder. "I did at first, and then as a friend. I knew he loved me, but Kostya was still a boy, stumbling through life."

"He may have done better to run away from home, as you did."

"I was pushed, if you'll remember."

Her face remained expressionless, as if the event were nothing more than a fact and not a source of pain. Her father had disowned her when she became an actress. Before that, he'd been simply a garden-variety tyrant. I separated the bream from its skeleton and offered to do the same for her, but she demurred, letting the fish grow cold on her plate.

"Forgive me for bringing this up," I said finally, "but Trigorin —Boris—. I didn't quite understand his appeal."

From the start, Kostya had perceived his mother's lover to be his great rival. Totally irrational, of course, but understandable. Trigorin was actually a passive sort. I came to like him, and he posed no real harm to Kostya. And then, *l'amour. L'attraction.* Vanity. Lust. Trigorin noticed our sweet Nina, because she threw herself at him. Like Kostya, she was starved.

Nina lowered her gaze to her lap. It was not a "nice" question, but twenty minutes in her company told me she was strong enough to answer almost anything. I had been curious for so long about her ill-fated *affaire* with the writer who'd been such a frequent visitor at Sorin's. Trigorin had used Nina badly and then walked away after giving her a child. A weak little creature, apparently. Kostya told me the baby had died before it could walk.

"Trigorin was a success," she said, and raised her eyes to mine. "And I wanted to be a success. Besides I admired his books."

"Funny, I never did," I mused. "But then I don't enjoy reading novels. I suppose I don't understand them."

Trigorin always seemed uninterested in everyone when he accompanied Irina to Sorin's. Not a snob, by any means, but aloof. I liked him personally. I liked the fact he enjoyed fishing. Although it wasn't his fault, his presence stirred things up.

"He's still with Irina, I gather?" I watched her closely.

"Yes. . . . Boris is like many men, isn't he, Doctor? He takes what he wants and discards the rest, without conscience. Kostya had a conscience, and it harmed him. I wanted to learn how to be strong—stronger than mere conscience."

"And Boris taught you how?"

"No... Boris was not as strong as I thought. . . ."

She shook her head. I wondered if she still loved him but dismissed the thought. I didn't want any further unpleasantness on my conscience, assuming I still had one. She poked through the fish, taking a few bites, then nibbled on a cabbage leaf, ignoring the potatoes altogether and taking a sip or two of the wine. When I suggested a tart for dessert, she declined, accepting the coffee instead.

It was then I realized there were no bracelets or rings or ostentatious earrings to indicate an admirer. There was no such wealthy patron, except in my head. I wondered if she'd encouraged me to assume this phantom existed, and my heart went out to her. How brave she was, the bravest of our three young people and certainly the most determined.

I ordered two apple tarts and had the waiter put one in front of her. "Make an old man happy," I said.

She threw herself back in her chair and laughed. "Shame on you, Doctor Dorn. And another thing—you're not old! You'll never be old!"

She picked up the fork and took small sampling bites of the tart, then larger bites. I shouldn't have been surprised, considering how little of the meal she'd eaten. Perhaps there was still something of the child in her, longing for sweets. When she'd finished hers, I offered her the rest of mine as well.

"You were always so good to us," she said suddenly. "Masha adores you, you know? And you were the only one who believed in Kostya. He told me so."

At that moment I thought of Kostya's strange play and her performance on that little stage, the moon rising over the lake and everyone in the audience watching it through the stage. His words were beautiful, moving. I wanted to tell her that he was beginning to sell his stories, but she interrupted.

"—He didn't believe in himself. And she didn't believe in him either."

"She?"

"His mother. Irina Arkadina."

"Ah… well. And did your father believe in you?"

She looked down at the dessert plate and mashed the remaining crumbs with her fork. "That's different. My parents weren't artists, and there was never any hope of impressing Father. But Kostya had hope."

. . . Kostya had hope. Her words followed me home. I couldn't sort out why the young man with hope had shot himself while the young woman without hope had tenaciously pursued an acting career and succeeded. It seemed to me Nina had it exactly backwards. The two women Kostya most adored both loved someone else. Never mind that the countryside was full of people who cared for Kostya: Sorin, Masha, Paulina, the servants. I loved the boy, too. But it always seems the case that we shun those who love us while yearning for the fruit hanging out of reach.

Nevertheless, one of the few things worth remembering in our collective past was Kostya's talent. I was happy that he was at last publishing his stories, but he thought little of them. We had no idea why he should have despaired just as a career was opening up. The problem was he did not understand his talent, nor did he have the clarity to see where he should take it. One story might feel abstract to the point of dryness while in the next he'd release so much emotion I was reminded of frightened horses fleeing a torched barn. Sorin thought having Irina Arkadina for a mother was a factor, and perhaps he was right. Still, I believed in the boy, even if he did not yet believe in himself. But why his mother could not have provided for him better—she with her actress's updated and lavish wardrobe—why she couldn't have bought him at least a new overcoat, I'll never understand. I will say it here because I don't wish to think of it again: she was stingy with her son, stingy with her love and maternal attention, stingy with her money. He looked so shabby at the end. It is one of the shameful episodes in our lives on the lake, something I would prefer to leave out.

But are not memoirs about truth telling? So in the interest of truth, I'll lay out all our parental sins: Kostya's mother behaved with undiluted self-interest; by all accounts Nina's father was equally, even monstrously, selfish. Although Paulina is devoted to her daughter, Masha's boorish father still causes her great pain. And I had an *affaire* with Masha's mother and never felt an ounce of regret. All this makes me glad I never married.

I returned from my midday meal with Nina to find a different horse and carriage standing in the yard. I felt my old heart leap. It took a second leap when I recognized Sorin's former servant, Yakov, sitting atop the trap. I gave my own horse to the boy and went over to greet Yakov, who grabbed his cap and greeted me with smiles and needlessly downcast eyes. I was pleased to see him but needed to inquire whether he was satisfied with his new position. After a brief chat I went up to the house. Zoya met me at the door.

"She's in your office," Zoya said, wearing her stern expression. Zoya has several stock expressions that she rotates as though they were party masks. I was never fond of the stern one, as though my private affairs fell under the category of housecleaning, and thus, her business. I gave her a questioning look—my feeble attempt at innocence. Zoya sighed in exasperation.

"The young widow," she went on. "She is your patient, is she not?"

Zoya took my coat, hat and gloves and left me alone in the entry. I paused in front of the antique pier mirror to assess myself. The mirror once belonged to Sorin. It was the only offered memento from his estate that I willingly took. How many young swains and virginal women had straightened their ties and coiffures, their lapels and ribbons in front of this full-length glass? My mind's eye could see it in its original location, in Sorin's entry hall, the cherry wood polished to a shine, the mirror spotless.

Now what I saw was a rather stout man on the cusp of old age, grateful that he was still ambulatory and with a full head of hair. I pulled down my waistcoat, which had ridden up slightly. Finally, I walked down the hall to my office, knocked, paused, entered, and unobtrusively locked the door. In a moment of overzealous housekeeping, Zoya has been known to intrude.

My "patient" was seated on the edge of the visitor's chair, still in her dark widow's weeds, the veil of her hat pulled fully over her face.

"Ah, my dear," I said. I don't know when I acquired this avuncular tone. I cannot say I much admire this quality of voice and wonder how it came about. At the moment, it didn't seem appropriate for the woman in whom I had recently taken a romantic interest.

She rose, a plump and tiny wren, murmuring *oh, my dear doctor,* and rushed into my arms. I raised her veil myself. A score of years fell away as I embraced her, kissed her hands, her trembling lips. It is not in vanity I write that I have always been a lucky man.

Nina was allowing herself a few days to rest in town before moving on to Yelets. At dinner I'd suggested I pick her up for a ride around the lake this next day. She used to come around from her father's to join us at Sorin's. In those days we always gathered at Sorin's, and we all walked. Taking the air, we called it, decked out in walking boots and walking sticks, suitable mufflers and wide-brimmed hats.

When I arrived at the hotel the following afternoon, she was wearing the same dove-gray suit and hat. I thought of Irina Arkadina—that clotheshorse—a gown for morning, another for afternoon, a third for the evening meal. Nina had added gloves and a shawl since the weather was turning cool. I was willing to take her anywhere she wished and suggested we pass by her old home. Since the carriage was mine, no one would cause a fuss. It was common knowledge her father had trained his servants and dogs to keep her out, but she shook her head. "I'd like to visit Sorin's old place," she said quietly.

In spite of the chill, the day was bright. I tried to remember if it wasn't an August evening that Nina performed Kostya's strange Symbolist play. There'd been a huge harvest moon, adding to the effect. I asked if she remembered any of Kostya's little drama. She turned away and gazed out over the back of the horse. "How could I forget? I was the only character. It wasn't even a character, was it?" She laughed lightly. "More of a disembodied Voice of the Future. I can still recite the lines. Shall I?"

I was delighted.

"'Humans, lions, eagles, and partridges . . . you antlered deer, and wild geese. . . .'" Her voice took on an incantatory tone as she listed all the creatures of sea and earth and air that Kostya had invoked in her monologue, ending with the passage about the inevitable death of all things. Finally her

voice faded. Then something about the universal soul, I remember. Not a traditional play. More of a metaphysical position paper.

I clucked to the horse, and we turned down the lane that
traveled to the lake. I considered asking if she wanted to visit
Kostya and Sorin's graves but thought better of it. She would
have visited already if she wanted to, and it was not for her
childhood doctor to force it on her. I tried to reconstruct in
my mind the feeling, the chill in fact, of hearing Kostya's play
for the first time. Perhaps it was one of those fleeting emotions
that can never be fully recalled, like trying to remember the
scent of honeysuckle or lilacs—impossible until you smell
them again the next spring. I asked if she remembered the entire speech from the play, and she nodded. "The words are so
odd, they're hard to forget."

Perhaps she could recite it all for me before she left. She
turned her head and looked at me intently with that odd half-
smile on her lips. "If you like," she said at last.

As I made small talk—who remained by the lake, who was
new, and who had moved away—the horse pulled us on toward Sorin's old home. I rattled on about the sale and the new,
yet-to-appear householders. I did not share with her news of
my new friendship with the young widow. I realized later that
Nina was probably the one person I could have shared this
news with. At the time I could only think, how can an older
man's private affairs be of any interest to such a young woman?

So, for the sake of the record—my so-called memoir—
here are the facts: Shortly after Sorin's funeral, a young matron
summoned me to one of the ostentatious new homes at the far
end of the lake. I didn't know the couple, an older landowner
in a new marriage, grown sons from the first wife who'd died
of cholera years ago. The new wife was beside herself: her husband, the landowner, had had a massive stroke. I did what little
I could but the damage was extensive, and he lay unconscious
for six days. Fortunately for the young woman, he didn't linger

but died with merciful speed. The young widow inherited the house and a comfortable stipend. Her stepsons inherited the farm, which seemed fair enough except the boys wanted to push her out. Such an old tale: a family divided by envy and greed. I offered my services and arranged for a lawyer who kept the stepsons at bay. As a gift, I had two purebred pups delivered, and they grew quickly into enormous wolfhounds that patrolled the premises, giving the widow a small measure of security. I advised her to clear her house of servants loyal to her husband and stepsons, and so at my suggestion she hired Sorin's former workman, the imposing Yakov. I was also pleased to learn that Sorin's old cook is happy there as well. All this news I could have easily shared with Nina but did not.

"Shamrayev has inveigled himself into his old post as farm manager," I said with deliberate irony, since no one was fond of Paulina's husband. From his first day in Sorin's employ, Shamrayev played the petty tyrant, a man unable to free himself from the worst of his military training. Other than the good health of her young son, I did not discuss Masha, even though the girls were once friends. Nor did I go on at any length about Paulina, out of respect, perhaps, for our shared history. If Nina had asked after either, I would have provided some suitable news, but she did not ask.

I turned right, onto the familiar dirt road lined with poplars. Even from a distance the large cream-colored house appeared empty, the outbuildings too quiet and unused: no arguing poultry in the side yard, no croquet wickets in the back garden, no horses nickering impatiently in the barn or milk cow tethered in the pasture beyond. I drove up into the yard, not planning to get out but only to sit, since there would be no one to hold the reins. As soon as I stopped, Nina climbed down nimbly and walked toward the lake path and stopped. She was only a few meters from the carriage.

"Oh, look!" She ran back, looked up at me and pointed. "The stage is gone."

"… I'm surprised it stayed up as long as it did."

Her eyes looked troubled, and the tears welled up. "When?" she asked in a whisper.

"Recently," I said. "When I heard, I dropped by to see for myself. Shamrayev said the mysterious new owner sent over a workman. He claims he wasn't there at the time."

We didn't speak for a time, both of us gazing down the path to where the stage once stood. I was remembering Yakov, sawing and hammering throughout the day, remembering the soft light and shadows of that midsummer evening.

"It's very blue today, isn't it?" Nina said, looking out at the water. "I'm going to have a look." She took off briskly for the lake. She did not want me to see her cry.

I debated whether to join her, to climb down and tie the horse to the post—but the post seemed to have vanished as well. As I mused, an ancient woman tottered out of the house and stood on the veranda, her hands deep in the pockets of a clean white apron. I half rose in the seat and doffed my hat and greeted her, identifying my connection to this place, explaining I'd come to pay my respects.

The old woman grabbed the edge of the veranda, then the railing and slowly, ponderously, first one leg and then the other, made her arthritic way down the three steps, approached the carriage and stopped. She introduced herself as the family nurse who had come ahead to watch after the workmen and painters. But they were not here today, *it being God's day*, were her words.

Nina had evidently reached the lake. At least I could no longer see her. I explained this to the elderly woman who nodded. "I seen her." Her voice croaked so hoarsely I wondered how it could have ever comforted children. I explained that Nina used to come here, too, since she once lived across the lake. I felt no need to explain that her father and stepmother still lived there.

I didn't wish to chase after Nina but was beginning to wonder when she'd make her way back. I was running out of things to say to the old nurse and did not want to impose on her any longer, or keep her out-of-doors. I thanked her for letting us stop by and inquired when the family might be arriving.

"God knows," she shrugged. "They're still in the city."

By which I assumed she meant Moscow since we are sixty kilometers south with only the town and a few villages close by. I asked if she would not mind giving me their names so I might greet them properly when they arrived. She gave it and the master's pedigree: a retired colonel and his wife, as well as an almost-grown son, a married daughter who would join them on holidays, and an old mother.

"Ah, so there will be children playing on the lawn again," I said, hoping to infuse a cheerful prospect into this recitation. She shrugged once and grunted.

"With any luck," she said dryly and wished me a good day, making her slow way back to the house.

I do not relish the thought of more military people in the neighborhood, but I suppose there is a qualitative difference between a retired lieutenant (Shamrayev) and a colonel. Nor should I judge all military people by Paulina's husband. I always wondered if it was Shamrayev's relatively low military status that made him such an insufferable popinjay.

I glanced up. Nina was making her way along the path, head down as though charting the progress of her feet. She frowned when she saw me watching her. There were too many reeds along the shore, she said, and someone would need to clear them out. I reminded her no one had lived here for over six months. This wasn't quite true since Sorin's employees stayed on after his death until the property was sold, hoping until the end that Irina would change her mind. I suddenly felt weary, as though I'd just lifted an enormous sack of grain and carried it down the road. Could there be anything sadder than the dismantling of a household? What were the servants to do? I suggested we continue on and moved to get out of the carriage, in order to help her in. She laughed and sprang up without assistance.

"I've learned to do everything for myself, Doctor." She said this with an amazing smile, still flushed and slightly breathless from her walk. Strands of dark-blond hair had sprung loose from her chignon and floated around her face.

"And is that a good thing?"

"Yes. It means I'm free."

I laughed out loud and snapped the reins. As the carriage turned, I glanced once at the house and saw the old woman watching us through the front window. We passed the church-yard on our way back. Once again she did not ask to stop but looked the other way. Tomorrow she would leave for Yelets, and I would miss her bracing stamina, her remarkable determination, so unlike Kostya and Masha.

"How do you manage?" I blurted out, which wasn't quite the question I'd intended.

"What do you mean?"

"You're alone," I said. "I'd be concerned for any young woman alone, especially one I'm fond of."

She laughed—an artificial titter. She'd resumed the rehearsed gestures of an actress. At the lake she'd been herself, the spontaneous Nina I remembered. Yet that younger Nina from the summer of '95 had been stagestruck and blinded by stardust, ridiculously impressed with Boris Trigorin. For his part, Trigorin had noticed Nina's infatuation, devoured it, and then shook himself off like the leech he was, in order to return to the more reliable meal. It was Kostya who told me that Trigorin never stopped being his mother's lover throughout his affair with Nina. During that strange summer, I suspect I was the only contented person on the lake.

"I don't know how I manage," she said. "I manage because I have to. Do you think about how you manage?"

Taken aback, I laughed out loud. She would let me know, wouldn't she, when she passed this way again?

"Of course. I'll never forget you."

"And if you need anything... at any time."

"Not to worry."

We were approaching the hotel, but I didn't want to lose her company and slowed the horse. I told her I once advised Kostya that if he didn't come to grips with his talent, if he was not aware of what he was writing, he would lose his way.

"He never understood, did he?"

He did not.

A valet from the hotel ran up to hold the reins. Nina moved to disembark, and I touched her arm to stop her. I felt there was so much more to say.

"I also told Kostya that I'd always longed to experience, just once, the excitement an artist must feel, creating something. . . "

Her expression was full of pity. "It's everything you think it is not... hard work and practice and drudgery. But when you are able to strike the one true note. . . . yes, then it's wonderful."

I took her gloved hands and kissed them.

"You used to sing from Faust, do you remember?" She smiled but her eyes looked sad.

"I still sing Faust," I said.

"Something else. Kostya used to call me *the seagull*, do you remember?"

If I knew, I'd forgotten.

"I'm not that girl anymore. . . . I don't believe I ever was, do you?"

I gazed at her fondly but said nothing. If only she knew how like a shorebird she'd once been, how vulnerable. For all I knew, she still was, even though it was Kostya who'd met a gull's fate. Since it was affirmation Nina wanted, I shook my head. "No, you're not."

"I saw him that night," she said, looking away.

I sat straight up, as though icy fingers had touched my neck. "Kostya?"

"Yes. I was on my way to Yelets for the first time. I stopped here to spend the night." She pointed to the small hotel. "I wanted to see Kostya, but I wasn't quite myself."

"Did you know his mother was there? And Boris?"

"I heard their voices, and he confirmed it."

I stared at her. Had she come to catch a glimpse of Boris as well? "Surely Kostya was glad to see you," I said.

"He was. I was so afraid he hated me—for everything. I wanted him to forgive me. But he was also afraid that his mother might catch sight of me. Funny, isn't it? I'd come in through the French doors off the terrace. Do you remember them?"

I nodded, but my heart felt suddenly weighted, my limbs sodden.

"I had come to implore Kostya not to despise me. I'd come to talk—to my best friend—to tell him that to survive he must believe. Above all, believe. To keep working and believing, and only then did one stop being afraid... I knew he was afraid... of so much."

She paused and looked at her hands, pulling at the fingers of one glove. "He declared his love again. He said, 'I kiss the ground you walk on.' I didn't want to hear this. I still loved Boris even though he'd spurned my life and ruined me, our *affaire* over forever. And then I foolishly told Kostya that I loved Boris more than before. . . . I was not myself that night, Dr. Dorn. . . . I was so feverish and tired."

I could scarcely breathe and forced myself to take her small, gloved hands and kiss them. So here was the element I had missed in Kostya's final despair. Oh, how our youths had suffered, and no one was to blame.

Another man from the hotel had come up to the carriage to help Nina down. I kept seeing her as a child, this young woman who did not expect help. Suddenly, she threw her arms around my neck, and for an instant, I was afraid I might weep. Then she pushed away and held me at arm's length and said if she wrote me, would I promise to write back? Unlike my own, her eyes were dry. "Of course!" I said with mock indignation. When had I ever turned one of our darlings away?

"Maybe this is the season I'd like my friends to see me act." She spoke in a playful tone I hadn't heard all afternoon.

"You only need to send word. Why, I could arrange an entire party to come and see you!"

She laughed, and I heard myself laughing with her. What kind of foolish father would toss her away! I wished I'd had a child just like her. I held her elbow as she navigated the hanging step of the carriage.

"Don't forget us," I called. Again, I felt the salt in my eyes. She turned and smiled.

I used to think being a doctor had taught me to accept farewells as part of the great human pageant, a cycle of loss and gain that was neither cruel nor kind. *C'est la vie*, I used to tell Paulina when we were younger and there was still some possibility that I might whisk her away from her officious spouse. Now I saw it for what it was: a doctor's vanity. For so long I'd prided myself on my control, believing I was immune to unwanted emotion; but as Nina walked away from the carriage, there it was, springing up like a housecat to a windowsill.

At the hotel entrance she turned and threw me a theatrical kiss before disappearing indoors. I rebuked myself for not seeing her into the lobby. Yet had I stayed with her an instant longer, I'd have released these elderly tears and embarrassed us both.

Nina's revelation shook me more deeply than I realized, and I returned home in an uncharacteristically pensive mood. I left the horse and trap with the boy, only to find Paulina in my living room, indulging a fit of pique before the stalwart Zoya. When I entered, she whirled around, in full throat.

"Genya, this is the second time in as many days that I've come to call and found you gone!"

"I am a doctor."

"Retired, I thought."

I shrugged. Her cheeks were flushed, and her dark eyes pierced me. I thought for sure she knew where I had been and was about to call me out. And it was only a miracle that she had not discovered the widow's carriage in my yard. Meanwhile, my housekeeper struggled not to smile, for she'd become used to these flamboyant appearances. Truth be told, she was fond of Paulina, for her spirit if nothing else. When flushed and excited, Paulina was, indeed, a bracing sight. For a moment I felt the thrill of our old passion. Then the heat left her face and body, and she sighed deeply.

As close as I am to Paulina, her unhappiness puts me off. Even if she were to leave Shamrayev, she'll never be satisfied. Having formed the habit of dissatisfaction, she'll be dogged by it forever. It's been well over a decade since our *affaire*, and still she clings to the memory, ever hopeful.

"The new people are tearing up Sorin's back garden," Paulina said finally, bringing us all back to the present. "Ilya tells me they're planning to remove the apple orchard as well."

I had no intention of saying I'd just been to Sorin's house, but at least I knew nothing had been dismantled—except Kostya's stage. "The orchard is a disaster, my dear," I said. "Even Sorin wanted the orchard gone."

"Oh, I don't know what to make of it!"

Paulina flung herself on the settee while I took the armchair. And so she lingered for another hour while Zoya and I consoled her over tea. There'd been no word yet from the new owners as to whether she would remain as house manager, and it was this uncertainty that surely lay at the heart of her outburst. Then she looked at me again, her eyes dark and sad. "You saw her, didn't you?"

I must have given her a puzzled look.

"You know who. Nina."

I shrugged. "Of course I saw her. She wrote. She's on to Yelets, you know."

"Why the secrecy?"

"What secrecy? By your tone, you'd think there was some inappropriate interest on our parts. And that, my dear, makes as much sense as an affair between Masha and me."

Paulina gasped and recoiled slightly. I raised my eyebrows to emphasize my point: it was a ridiculous suggestion.

"I am the old—" I emphasized the word, "—*old* family friend, the good father she never had. I was always the good father, Paulina: to Nina, to Kostya, even to your Masha." I held her gaze until she dropped hers.

Masha planned to visit soon with the little boy, she said. Would I speak with her?

"Gladly. When have I ever turned her away?"

What I did not tell her was that it was utterly useless to advise an alcoholic. Masha and I will speak of other things. Masha will trot out her boredom and her hopelessness as if they were pieces of art I must admire. Paulina stood up, walking to the windows where a wedge of lake was visible in the middle distance. My home was not situated directly on the lakeshore as Sorin's was. When she finally left, Zoya raised her eyebrows, and I raised mine in reply, saying, "Does the poor woman think I have nothing to do? I could have been visiting a patient."

"Indeed," Zoya replied with a bob of her head, hands clasped in front of her apron, and left the room, returning momentarily with a tray to clear the tea things.

Why my visit with Nina should bedevil her still, I don't know. The girl has made her way against all odds, even suffered the loss of a child. If our third darling, Masha, is still pining for the dead Kostya, then Masha has truly lost touch with the world. Masha said to me once, *I'm in mourning for my life, Doctor.* I am still dumbfounded by her remark.

Can we not love the ones who remain? Heaven knows Masha needs our love as much as Nina does. Are they not both equally dear to us? Does Paulina actually think I would favor one of our darlings over the other or that Nina would feel anything for me except what one might for a favorite old uncle? I would think being a mother would put a woman in touch with all the world's children. This urge to classify children into *yours,* not *mine* makes my head spin. Then, of course, there's Irina—the great Arkadina—who could not cherish her own son for fear he was constantly subtracting from her pocketbook or her fame.

I called out to let Zoya know I was leaving again, grabbed my walking stick, and headed for the lake. I followed the tangled path through birches and evergreens, oaks and alders, feeling briefly consoled. Then the unwanted nostalgia rose up again. How I missed Sorin and our musical evenings, the card playing, the dinners and saint's-day parties, the young people swimming in the lake, the tournaments of croquet in Sorin's back garden. Who remained of the old group?

Yet oughtn't life's journey move one forward, not back? I have always believed that for every loss there is a gain. My chance meeting with the widow has offered a glimmer of light. Her appreciation has taken a pleasant turn, and she'll accompany me this fall to Baden-Baden. Of course, this presents a logistical problem in my friendship with Paulina. I've found myself musing how best to introduce the widow to her neighbors without upsetting Paulina. The young physician across the lake is still single, and perhaps he can be drawn in at the same time. I only hope the Colonel and his family will welcome our company, should they ever arrive. . . .

In spite of the cold, I felt my temperature rise as I chuffed along, and I chided myself, yet again, for my excess weight. By the time I reached the lake, sweat had moistened my underarms. I gazed out over the water and realized I even missed our diva, Irina Arkadina. Here was a woman who knew how to enjoy herself! For all her shortcomings, she was the one who gathered us into Sorin's gardens and parlors and dining room. I can only assume Irina's twin losses influenced her decision not to return. I suspect I might have done the same.

A slight breeze was stirring, and small waves lapped the bank. I looked across to the opposite shoreline where a few gulls landed and then took off. At the south end of the lake, a fishing boat bobbed in a strand of late-afternoon light. The grass along the lakefront has already browned and withered even though we have not yet had a killing frost. I bent down slowly, cursing the stiffness in my joints, and finally sat with a thump. I once kept this stretch of shorefront mowed, with two wooden chairs and a small table positioned where I sat. When a storm swept them away, never to be found, I didn't bother to replace them. We spent our free time at Sorin's anyway, with an occasional uproarious party that traveled from house to house.

I lost track of time until I noticed the wind had picked up, pushing scrolls of gray clouds down from the north. To the south, the fishing boat remained anchored under blue skies, and all around it sunshine glinted off the lake. Each new gust shushed through the evergreens in that toneless whisper that reminded me of a voice from Kostya's play. A rich pine scent perfumed the air, and I breathed it in with pleasure, gazing out across the lake, until my worries drained away.

Catherine Browder is the author of three previous books of short fiction: *The Clay That Breathes* (Milkweed), *Secret Lives* (SMU Press), and *The Heart* (Helicon Nine Editions) . A playwright and actress who grew up in the Midwest, she has lived in England, Japan, and Taiwan. She has taught ESL here and abroad and creative writing at University of Missouri-Kansas City. She has held fiction fellowships from the NEA and the Missouri Arts Council, and her work has appeared in *Ploughshares, Prairie Schooner, Shenandoah*, and elsewhere. She lives in Kansas City, Missouri, with her husband.

Acknowledgments

Anton Chekhov's plays have had numerous translators of note. The ones I relied on were Constance Garnett, Ann Dunnigan, and especially Paul Schmidt, whose rendering of the plays into an accessible "American English" I found especially reassuring. Various biographies and Chekov criticism offered useful insights and inspiration into the man himself as well as his creations. These include the work of Ronald Hingley, Richard Gilman and Robert Brustein; also Simon Karlinsky's selection and annotation of Michael Henry Heim's translation of Chekhov's letters. All of these writers grounded me as I "lived" with the characters of Chekhov's plays for several years.

I was blessed with kind readers from the beginning, fellow writers who offered their time and criticism, from early in the evolution of the manuscript until the end. To these good friends I give my heart-felt thanks: R.M. Kinder, John Mort, Margot Patterson, Trish Reeves, Marly Swick and Chris Quinn.

Many thanks to Ben Furnish, managing editor of BkMk Press, who shares a love of Chekhov, as well as the staff of the press for their steadfast attention to the manuscript: Susan Schurman, Zach Folken, Elizabeth Uppman, Marie Mayhugh. And to Robert Stewart, the guiding spirit at University House.